In the pit, the combatants battled furiously. They were after each other's life's blood and would accept nothing less. The Gundermen attacked Conan simultaneously, and he was hard put to parry their whistling strokes with his own blade. He held the long grip of his blade in both hands, but even this added leverage barely gave him the speed and sureness to deflect the furious rain of steel.

He saw his opening when one of the brothers collided with the frantic Axandrias. In the instant that Wolf was off balance, Conan's sword sheared through his waist, ripping through armor and scattering blood and entrails the width of the pit. Gunter cried out in rage and redoubled his attack.

Now not so hard-pressed, Conan parried his opponent's sword without difficulty. As he stepped forward for the killing blow, the Cimmerian's foot came down in a pool of blood and offal and slid from beneath him. With his superb balance, Conan kept himself from falling, but he was bent over and, for an instant, vulnerable. Grinning ferociously, Gunter darted in, blade raised to shear down through the Cimmerian's spine . . .

The adventures of Conan
published by Tor Books

CONAN THE CHAMPION by John Maddox Roberts
CONAN THE DEFENDER by Robert Jordan
CONAN THE DEFIANT by Steve Perry
CONAN THE DESTROYER by Robert Jordan
CONAN THE FEARLESS by Steve Perry
CONAN THE INVINCIBLE by Robert Jordan
CONAN THE MAGNIFICENT by Robert Jordan
CONAN THE MARAUDER by John Maddox Roberts
CONAN THE RAIDER by Leonard Carpenter
CONAN THE RENEGADE by Leonard Carpenter
CONAN THE TRIUMPHANT by Robert Jordan
CONAN THE UNCONQUERED by Robert Jordan
CONAN THE VALIANT by Roland Green
CONAN THE VALOROUS by John Maddox Roberts
CONAN THE VICTORIOUS by Robert Jordan
CONAN THE WARLORD by Leonard Carpenter

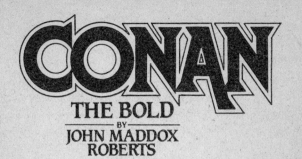

CONAN
THE BOLD
BY
JOHN MADDOX ROBERTS

A TOM DOHERTY ASSOCIATES BOOK
NEW YORK

CONAN THE BOLD

A TOR Book
Published by Tom Doherty Associates, Inc.
49 West 24 Street
New York, N.Y. 10010

Cover art by Ken Kelly

ISBN: 0-812-55210-5   Can. ISBN: 0-812-55211-3

First edition: April 1989

Printed in the United States of America

0 9 8 7 6 5 4 3 2 1

One

The steading was set in a small clearing, surrounded by low hills dense with a cover of hardwood forest. The householder, a graying man named Halga, leaned on his spear as he watched his three sons driving his cattle to pasture. He felt a deep satisfaction, for the winter had been mild and the herd had increased significantly. Now the trees were in full leaf, the streams were full of fish, and the rigors of past months had given way to a time of plenty. Then his gaze was drawn from his cattle to a youth who had emerged from the stone house.

The young man came toward Halga in long strides, showing no effects from the wounds he had borne when he had staggered in from the Pictish Wilderness a few weeks before. For days he had lain in a near-coma while Halga's womenfolk had nursed him. Cimmerian nursing was primitive, consisting mainly of keeping the wounds clean and stitching the greater ones with long hairs from a horse's tail. They believed it best to let the body heal itself. Since the lad was Cimmerian, he survived. When he was well enough to speak, they had found that his name was Conan, and he was a high-lander from the northeast. He was younger than Halga's sons, seventeen at most, if that, but taller than any of them. In the mild weather he wore only his weapon belt and loincloth and sandals. Over his brawny shoulder he carried a short hunting-spear.

"So, you feel up to a day of hunting, Conan?" Halga said.

"I am near mad with lying abed and being cared for," said the youth. "Your sons tell me there are stag and red deer in the hills, and wild bull in the lower marshes."

"Seek the deer and the stag," Halga cautioned. "Wild bull is no quarry for a lone man, especially one regaining his full strength. And good hunting. Venison will be a welcome change from beef and mutton."

Without further words, the youth turned and headed for the gate of the stockade. Halga watched him with calculation. His daughter, Naefa, had appropriated most of the nursing tasks to herself, much to the amusement of her parents and brothers. Not that they disapproved. The girl was of marriageable years, and Cimmerian women were forbidden to marry within their own clans.

The lad was a likely prospect for a son-in-law. His recovery from his terrible wounds was swift even among Cimmerians, a race that would never nurture weaklings. Even before full recovery, Conan could best Halga and his sons in practice-bouts with swords. Never had the older man seen such swiftness with the blade. True, the youth seemed to be unruly, and of a mind to go wandering. That would fade with age and attachment to a wife, and his healthy battle-lust could be sated in raids against the neighboring Picts and Bossonians. Halga and his neighbors would soon be making a raid against one land or the other, unless the enemy struck first. It mattered little. Fighting was nearly the sole recreation of Cimmerians, and the honor was the same, whether one attacked or defended.

The object of Halga's thoughts was confused in his own mind as he left the steading, passing through the gate in the timber wall that still seemed alien to him. The highlanders did not use such fortifications. The southwestern Cimmerians, living so near enemy peoples, needed more protection than those who faced little but neighborly feuding. Each isolated steading was surrounded by a timber palisade, and several such family holdings would maintain a central fort where all could hasten in time of war. Never defensive fighters, the Cimmerians used the forts to protect the women, children and livestock while the men sallied out in sanguinary attacks.

Spear on shoulder, Conan marched toward the densely wooded hillside. He felt fully recovered, and he had spoken frequently of leaving, yet he had made no move to hasten his leavetaking. He longed to travel widely among foreign lands, to seek his fortune among alien people and see wonders denied to those who lived amid the barren mountains and forested lowlands of his native land. Already, he had fared farther than most Cimmerians his age, and his adventures had whetted his appetite for more.

But now there was another urge pulling at his heart, causing him to doubt the wisdom of the wandering life. The source of that urge was Halga's daughter, Naefa, who was making no secret of the fact that she wanted Conan for her husband. Working in her favor was his whole Cimmerian heritage. Men of his nation were encouraged to marry young and raise many children.

Life was savage in Cimmeria, the most primitive of the Hyborian lands. Men were slain by droves in the constant feuding and warfare. Women and children were lost in slave-raids, although most grown women managed to kill themselves rather than be slaves. All were faced with starvation in the hard winters, which far outnumbered the mild ones. The only answer to extinction was a high birth rate.

True, the Cimmerians had wrung some hard-won advantages from their harsh history and environment. The process of ruthless selection had made them stronger and more enduring than most other peoples. Disease was all but unknown among them, and their powers of recuperation were legendary. It was for this reason that Conan was going hunting on a morning which would have seen a man of any other nation several weeks in his grave. The strength and endurance of Cimmerians made their children especially desirable to slavers, increasing the need for fighting-skill on the part of the adults.

None of this passed through Conan's mind as he stalked his prey. Instead, he thought of Naefa. He could marry her and settle here. It was not unusual for a man to join his wife's clan, especially if he were at odds with his own. Conan's relations with the Chieftains of his clan had been little short of openly hostile for years and he had had few qualms when he had left his people to seek his fortune elsewhere. Since his arrival here, Halga and his sons had been as father and brothers to him, and Naefa . . .

With his thoughts still in turmoil, Conan cut the trail of a buck. Overjoyed to have something basic and uncomplicated to occupy his mind, he gave chase. The size and depth of the cloven hoofprints told him that the animal was large. A tuft of hair clinging to a twig told him that it was young and in perfect health. His mouth watered at the thought of roast venison. He pictured himself coming into Halga's steading with the dead beast over his shoulders, accepting the praises of Naefa and her mother. It was an attractive thought, entirely too attractive for a youth who had set his heart upon seeing the wide world and making something of himself, perhaps something great.

As Conan tracked the buck, alternating between fierce concentration upon the task at hand and romantic reverie, he was watched. Dark eyes followed his progress, and a stocky but lithe form silently dogged his every step. The man who followed him was a Pict, a man of a race so ancient that it had become an integral part of the land. Silently as a shadow, he followed the tall young Cimmerian, a feral gleam in his dark eyes. The younger man took no notice.

Just before noon, Conan spotted the buck. It stood browsing in a little clearing; a fine, fat creature putting on weight early after the easy winter. Conan stalked it as he had been schooled, taking a few silent steps when the beast had its head down, nibbling the grass, freezing like a statue when it raised its head to scan its surroundings. The primitive eyes and brain of the animal could register little but movement, and a hunter might escape notice if he could stand still enough, though he was in plain view.

As he stalked, Conan admired the glossy hide, the bright eye, the fine young antlers that still bore the drying shreds of their velvet. He stopped when he judged the range short enough. The next time the head went down, his arm went back and his spear flashed, quick as thought. He cast with a straight arm, releasing at the proper moment and giving the spear a tiny twist of the palm as it left his hand that imparted a rapid spin, ensuring a straight flight. Spear-throwing was the most difficult of battle-arts, and young Conan accounted himself a master.

Most men would have cast for the body behind the shoulder, trying for the heart but sure of a kill in any case. A hit in the lungs or belly would bring death as surely, but it might be lingering. Conan was different. He preferred a clean kill or a clean miss, and had chosen a spot just behind the buck's ear. It was a target that would have been judged difficult even by a fine Bossonian archer. Few would have essayed it with a spear.

The weapon struck precisely where Conan had aimed, passing between the vertebrae and dropping the buck dead as if it had been struck by a thunderbolt. Conan rushed forward with his knife out and slashed its throat, but the mercy was not needed. He began to dress the carcass, but finding that his weapons got in the way of his messy task, he removed his weapon belt and hung it on a nearby limb. He was halfway through skinning the beast when a sound from behind caused him to whirl, knife in hand.

The man who leaned casually against the tree behind Conan was a foot shorter, but equally broad through shoulders and chest. His hair was as black as Conan's own, but his eyes were dark brown and his skin was swarthy. Conan cursed himself for a fool as he noted his sword in the man's hand, his bloodied spear propped against the tree behind the man's shoulder. A Pict. Picts were the ancient blood-enemies of the Cimmerians.

"Death is the price of carelessness, Cimmerian," said the Pict.

Conan felt his ears burning with mortification. "I am not so easy to kill, Pict, even when it is knife against sword."

The Pict grinned, distorting his face-paint. "Brave talk, but you know better. Have you forgotten my lessons so soon?"

Conan turned back to his task. "I have not forgotten. The first lesson my father taught me was never to leave my weapons out of reach."

"It must be a woman on your mind. That is no excuse. Women have no use for dead men. Any other Pict would have slain you on sight."

Conan merely grumbled. Months before, he had been fleeing across the hills of the Pictish Wilderness, closely pursued by a war-band of the Black Mountain Picts. He had taken refuge in a cave, only to find it already inhabited. The occupant was Tahatch, a warrior of the Great Valley Picts. Tahatch had hidden in the cave the night before, pursued by another war-band of the Black Mountain people. Forced into uneasy proximity, the two had spent three days and nights in the cave, trading stories in low voices.

When they had emerged at length, the two ranged the hills for several weeks, hunting and occasionally making midnight forays into Black Mountain villages. Tahatch was out seeking adventures and honors to gain admission to the Gray Wolf fraternity, the most prestigious of the warrior brotherhoods. Conan had accounted himself an excellent woodsman, but he had found that he was a beginner compared to the Pict, and he had learned much.

Weeks before, they had been separated during a running fight with a band that had been scouring the hills in search of the two nighttime marauders. Conan had

barely escaped with his life, and had assumed that
Tahatch was dead. Now here was the Pict, unwounded
and sleek with a coating of fresh bear grease.

"A fine buck," said Tahatch.

Taking the hint, Conan gestured toward a pile of
offal. "Help yourself. I can't carry it all."

The Pict squatted and picked up the buck's liver,
holding the slippery organ in both hands. He proceeded
to eat it raw. Conan looked away. He had been anxious
to learn Pictish fighting skills and woodcraft, but he had
no admiration for their dietary habits.

"How did you escape?" Conan asked as he quartered
the carcass with his hatchet.

"I hid all day in a marsh, breathing through a reed. It
is an old trick in the valley, but the hill people must not
have heard of it." He took another bite of liver and
blood dripped onto the necklace that covered much of
his rippling chest. The necklace consisted of multiple
rows of bear claws. Boar's-tusk armlets circled both his
arms above the biceps, and he wore a mantle of wolf-
hide, a magnificent pelt complete with a snarling mask
that covered the top of his head. Tahatch was a splendid
hunter and it was Pictish custom to leave no one in
doubt about such things.

When Conan was finished quartering the carcass he
wrapped as much as he could carry in the hide and
hoisted the load to his shoulders. He found that it was
an awkward burden for a man who was already harnessed
with weapons and carrying a spear.

The Pict rose, belching with satisfaction. "I will help
you carry it," he said, then amended, "if it is not too
far." He lifted half a hundredweight of venison to one
shoulder without visible effort and paid no attention to

the broad smears of blood it left on his skin. "Where do you bide?" he asked as they trudged downhill.

"At a Cimmerian steading not far from here. We will be there before the sun is down."

"You may be there," grunted the Pict, "but not I. Your kinsmen would slay me. My own people would never understand how I could have befriended a Cimmerian. No, as soon as we are within sight of this steading, you and I must part ways again."

Halga knew something was amiss when he saw his sons running back toward the steading. The cattle were nowhere in sight and only great danger could have induced the younger men to abandon their kine. He met them at the gate. The last one through quickly shut and barred the portal.

"Raiders," said the eldest, speaking briskly. "Perhaps thirty."

"Picts?" Halga asked.

"No," said the young man, whose name was Dermat. "A mixed band. I saw two or three Bossonians, some Gundermen, and many whose nation I cannot guess."

"Slavers," said Halga, grimly. He wished that Conan were there. Another sword would be of use at such a time. Four men against thirty made poor odds, even when the four were Cimmerians. There was no use in wishing.

"Slavers will have no stomach for a death-fight," said the youngest of his sons. "When we kill a few, the others will run, you'll see."

"That may be," Halga said. "We can always hope. But be prepared for the worst. Should that happen—" he turned a stark gaze upon the two older sons, "—you must be ready to tend to your women. I will see to your mother and sister." He was glad that the younger children were fostering with another family this year.

"Aye," said Dermat, thumbing the razor edge of his sword. "They will not have my woman for their plaything." The Cimmerians were a fierce and proud people, contemptuous of death but horrified of slavery.

While his youngest son went to gather their javelins, Halga and his two older sons informed their women of what they might expect. They accepted his tidings with the stoicism of their race. Death was an everyday reality. Only shame was unacceptable.

"If we are to die," said dark-eyed Naefa, "Conan will avenge us."

Halga nodded. "Aye. I'd not want to be the slaver who has that young man on his trail." He said this to comfort her. He knew that Conan would round up some of his kinsmen to hunt the slavers down, but the raiding-party would quickly cross the nearest border. Cimmerians were loath to leave their homeland, even upon a mission of vengeance.

When he returned to the stockaded yard, the raiders were in sight. He counted thirty, just as his son had said. The light of afternoon glinted on helm and spearpoint. From the wooden walk atop the palisade he saw their leader come forward, a tall man in gold-chased armor. He was the darkest man Halga had ever seen, and was flanked by a pair of flint-eyed Gundermen.

"Greeting, Cimmerian," said the leader, teeth flashing in his mahogany face. "I am Taharka, late an officer of the army of Keshan. My companions and I are on a hunting expedition. We seek two-legged game."

"I know what you seek, foreigner," Halga called. "You'll find nothing here save death and a wolf's belly. We do not bury slavers in our land."

"You would do well to reconsider," said the dark man, still wearing his false smile. "The life of a slave is still a life."

Halga spat over the low parapet. "Some things are more important than life."

"Some of my men warned me that you Cimmerians are a stubborn, unreasonable people." His smile was gone now, replaced by a fierce scowl.

"They did not warn you sufficiently," said Halga, "else you would have given this place a wide berth."

One of the Gundermen turned to Taharka and said in a low voice, "It is no use talking with this one, chieftain. Slay him and the other warriors and we'll have good profit out of the women and the cubs. But we must do it swiftly. Cimmerians are known to slay their own families, rather than let them be taken."

"Savages," said Taharka contemptuously. "They have no idea of how civilization is ordered. A decent society must have slaves, it stands to reason. Some are born slaves, some are taken in war, some are sold by starving parents. There is nothing wrong with that. Many slaves have risen to high rank and honors. A slave merely has farther to rise than others."

"So you say, master," said a Gunderman. "But such reasoning shall avail you nothing with these stiff-necked barbarians. Let us kill them."

"Very well," Taharka said. "Send in the scum to do away with the grown warriors. Do not involve yourselves unless it is necessary. We are on business here after all, none of us is in search of a reputation. There are no poets here to sing your deeds."

The two yellow-haired men ran off to do his bidding. Taharka smiled to himself. This was a wretched land of barbarians and their poor farmsteads and scrawny herds, but it had possibilities. A twisted path had led him here, and on that path he had narrowly escaped the dungeon and the noose many times. A flight from the authorities of Tauran had led him to a bandit's hideout in the hills near Tanasul. There he had gathered his band of cut-throats and vagabonds, dominating them by his superior force of will, his powerful personality and excellent education. Their first slaving raid into northwestern Nemedia had netted a handsome profit. He had decided on his border area of southwestern Cimmeria for their second foray because he had learned that the unbelievably tough and hardy children of this land fetched the highest prices in any slave market. Starvation, disease, and overwork simply would not kill them.

Taharka was a tall man, and strikingly handsome, and he knew it. He was not quite as dark as a Kushite, and had the high-bridged nose and aquiline features of the riverine tribes that dwelled along the Styx south of Stygia. He liked to affect the airs of an aristocrat, although he had no noble blood. His father, a humble shopkeeper, had hoarded every copper coin to procure the best education available for the youth, and then had bullied him into excelling at his studies. The education and his very evident talents had secured him a cavalry commission in the service of the king of his land.

Unfortunately, neither education nor talent could for long conceal the fact that Taharka totally lacked honesty, honor, or any other redeeming quality of any sort. An especially blatant piece of treachery sent him running for his life with his erstwhile colleagues of the king's cavalry in hot pursuit. Once across the borders of Keshan, he took up his true vocation. He became a thoroughly accomplished criminal in many lands.

To Halga, the man was just another foreign raider,

although an uncommonly dark one. When he saw the two Gundermen rush from their leader's side, he knew that the attack would soon commence. He had few hopes for the coming battle, but he was prepared to sell his life as dearly as possible. To an observer who knew nothing of Cimmerians he and his sons would have looked relaxed, almost bored. The impassive demeanor of Cimmerians when at rest gave no hint of the near-insane ferocity that overcame them the moment battle was joined.

The raiders made no attempt to surround the stockade, for which Halga was duly grateful. Four warriors were insufficient to defend even so small a fort. For a moment it occurred to him that he should have built a strong blockhouse such as the Gundermen and Bossonians dwelt in, but such depressing lodgings, however strong, were alien to the Cimmerian way of life.

The first rogues who reached the wall crouched with their shields over their backs and others sprang onto the improvised platform. The instant the first of them came within reach, the four Cimmerians exploded into furious action. The first face to appear above the parapet was that of a Zingaran pirate, and it was instantly sheared away above the eyes by Halga's sword.

A Nemedian with a broad, curved blade appeared before Halga's youngest son. The youth bore a spear in each hand. Even as the curved sword swung, the boy's left-hand spear pierced the man's lower jaw just behind the tie-strings of his helmet, plunging upward through tongue and palate and deep into the brain. Even as the Nemedian toppled back, his killer leaned over the parapet and cast his righthand spear down, piercing the shield and back of the man upon whom the Nemedian had been standing. This proved to be a miscalculation, for as he cast the spear, he received a severe slash on the left arm from a billhook wielded by a Bossonian who stood below. The youth made no outcry, but drew his sword and prepared to fight one-handed henceforth.

Halga's sword flashed down in perfect unison with those of his two older sons, as if this were a movement in a dance all three had rehearsed, and three raiders fell to the ground, not one of them with all the limbs with which he had ascended.

"Archers!" shouted a Gunderman, his face twisted between the cheek-plates of his black helmet, "Shoot them now!"

Halga had seen the bowmen among the enemy, and they disturbed him. Arrows were easy to dodge most of the time, but a man occupied with enemies before him could not watch for missiles while defending himself from swords. Soon the long Bossonian arrows were hissing like hungry serpents.

Halga slew two more, then the first arrow struck him in the side. He grasped the shaft in both hands and snapped it off. He could still fight, but he knew that they would be finished in a few minutes. He turned to his youngest son.

"My son," Halga said, his voice was steady as if he had been discussing that day's pasturing, "your brothers and I have duties to perform. You must tarry here and hold them for a while."

"Go, Father," said the youth as he sheared the hand from an Aquilonian bandit. "Even a one-handed Cimmerian can delay this rabble a bit."

Halga leapt to the ground, holding a hand against the arrow-stub. It was not the pain, for pain was nothing, but he did not want the arrowhead to induce further bleeding and cause him to fail in this final task. He

sheathed his sword and grasped a broad-bladed spear.
For this duty, he would not use a sword fouled with the
blood of slavers. For the last time, he entered his house,
as his two older sons entered theirs.

When Halga emerged from the house, the spear was
covered with blood. With careful deliberation, he drove
the head into the doorpost of the house. Now he had
done all that he could do to ensure that his honor, and
the honor of his family, tribe, sept, clan and nation
were unsullied. It was with a calm heart that he drew
for the last time the sword given to him by his father.
When he reached the palisade the raiders were inside. A
knot of them stood thrusting spears into something that
lay on the ground. With an almost joyous shout, Halga
waded amongst them, closely followed by the two older
sons. Each slew many before being slain himself.

Some time later, Taharka stood surveying the carnage
within the enclosure. "Four men did this? A greybeard,
a youth, and two warriors in their prime. How many did
we lose?"

"Twenty-two, Chieftain," said a Gunderman.

"And how many slaves did we capture?" He asked
quietly.

"None!" shouted an Argossian whose face bore the
marks of the executioner's hot irons. "And there were
no children for us to take to begin with! Just four
women, all of them slain by their men ere we had
breached the walls!"

'It would appear," said Taharka, "that this is not
good slave-hunting territory after all."

"And who led us on this fool's errand!" demanded
the Argossian. "It was you, Taharka! You, with your
fine talk of easy prey and quick riches!"

"You were happy enough about the first raid which I

planned for you," said Taharka. His voice was dangerously quiet, but the Argossian was too enraged to notice.

"One profitable raid does not make up for this disaster!" He strode forward and stood almost chest-to-chest
with Taharka. "I question your fitness to lead. I—" At
that moment, Taharka's large, brown hand shot forth
and his fingers knotted in the curly hair of the Argossian.
With a powerful flexion of the wrist, he turned the man
to face the others as a short, curved dagger appeared in
his other hand. The point plunged in beneath the
Argossian's right ear, sinking in until it reemerged,
bloodied, beneath the left. With a powerful forward
slash, he cut entirely through the neck, leaving the head
attached to the body only by the spinal cord. A huge
gout of blood and stomach contents jetted through the
severed neck, whipped into a ghastly foam by a wheezing blast of air convulsively expelled by the dead lungs.

"Now," said Taharka as he dropped the still-twisting
body, "there are still seven of us. That is enough to
form the nucleus of a new band. After all," he gazed
around upon the remaining men as if they were his
brothers, "it was the weaklings who perished. It is just
as well that they are gone. Men such as we should not
be burdened with trash like that. Better that they should
perish." He saw the faces of the remaining men lose
their downcast expression and brighten. This was a
lesson he had learned during his military days: men
would endure almost anything, so long as one merely
assured them that by so enduring they were part of an
elite. Gods of the Styx! he thought, but these barbarians
are simple!

"Let us take what we can from this place and be
away," Taharka said briskly. "This was a mistake, but
there are plenty of rich places to raid. We are not far

from the Aquilonian border. Let us go there and see what pickings we may find."

The sun was almost down when Conan saw the smoke. For a moment he thought it might be the evening cook-fires being built up, but a second's thought dismissed that notion. The smoke was too thick and too black and it meant trouble. The Pict, trudging behind him with his burden of venison, saw the smoke at the same time, but his nose gave him a far more accurate assessment of the situation.

"Thatch and hazel twigs, and some wool. Someone's house is afire, my friend."

Conan dropped the venison he had been carrying and broke into a run. The Pict followed at a more cautious pace. He was not going to run headlong into a situation of unknown peril. The two descended the long slope to the valley in which the steading of Halga lay. Conan burst from the brush into the cleared land and then he stood rigid, his eyes widening with the horror of what he beheld. Slowly, he walked into the ruins of the steading. He knew that nothing lived within.

He found the bodies piled before the burning house. All had been hideously mutilated. It took some time for him to decide which of the four women's bodies had been Naefa's. Tahatch found him there, covering the bodies with smoldering blankets he had found in one of the burning houses.

"They did not die easy," said the Pict, surveying the corpses of raiders that littered the landscape. "This was a good score for just four warriors. Initiates of the Gray Wolf fraternity could scarcely have done better."

"I must bury them," Conan said, "and heap a cairn over their bodies." Then he saw the bloodied spear thrust into the doorpost. The heat had turned the blood on it black, and Conan studied it with a somber expression.

"What means the spear?" asked Tahatch.

"It is a reminder to me, an ancient custom of my people. It means 'Avenge us'. It must have been with this spear that Halga slew his women."

"And will you?" asked the Pict.

"If it takes the rest of my life," Conan vowed. "I swear it by Crom."

Never in his fierce life had the Pict seen so grim an expression upon a man's face. "Then you had best be after the raiders. This smoke must be visible for miles. Soon this family's neighbors and kin will be here to raise their cairn."

"You are right. Will you come with me?"

Tahatch shook his head. "Dead Cimmerians are no concern of mine. I have been away from my clan too long as it is."

"Then help me read these signs," Conan insisted. "Every bit of knowledge I can gain about these animals will help me to track them down and kill them."

"Gladly," said the Pict. He walked about the steading, head low, squatting here and there to examine footprints, broken weapons, bits of cloth and things even Conan's keen eyes could not descry. Satisfied with his search of the steading, Tahatch made a circuit of the stockade.

"They left that way," Tahatch said, pointing to the south.

"I'll wager that is where they left their horses," Conan said. "Come, let's see if there is anything to be learned there."

The two followed the trail of the raiders at a fast trot.

Occasional patches of blood on the grass told them that not all of the survivors were unwounded. After a few minutes, they came to a trampled area littered with fresh horse-dung. The raiders had chosen a spot near the steading but out of sight.

Once again, the Pict examined the site. After several minutes of this, he straightened. "There are seven still living, and one of those is wounded. There were two Bossonian archers among the raiders, and none of the dead are Bossonians."

"How do you know there were two of them?" Conan asked.

"At the steading I found a broken arrow with a nock of horn, and one with a nock of bone. A single archer would not use both types." Conan knew that this was true. The Bossonians were notoriously finicky about their shooting tackle.

"Some of these horses are shod in the Gunder fashion," the Pict continued, "and there were no Gundermen among the dead. The horses may have been stolen, but two of the Gunder-shod horses were carrying riders when they left this place."

"Even with so many spare horses," Conan mused, "they would have mounted the ones that already bore their saddles. It is likely that there are two Gundermen among the survivors. Can you read aught else from this ground?"

Tahatch shook his head. "They were not here long, they left little behind, and some belong to nations of which I know nothing." He held up a few threads of red-dyed cloth. "I have never seen fibers like this, and the dye is unfamiliar to me. Did I know, we might guess at the nation of another of them. And this," he held out his hand and Conan had to look closely to see a single hair across the palm. "This is a hair of a man's beard. He is of a breed I know not. His beard will be very black and very curly."

"It is sufficient," Conan said. "And now I must be away. It would make things simpler if I could catch up to them before they split up and go separate ways."

"I must go as well," said Tahatch. "It would not be wise to be near here when the other Cimmerians come to see what is burning. Perhaps you should speak to them. It would cost you time, but you would have a better chance if you were not alone."

Conan shook his head. "Nay, here we are too near the border. My countrymen are fierce and implacable when they seek vengeance, but they are damnable timid about leaving their own country. I must go alone. Farewell, friend, I am in your debt. You or your clan may ask what you will of me hereafter."

"Farewell and good hunting, Conan." Tahatch watched as Conan loped out of sight. He did not expect to see the Cimmerian alive again. He set off, making a wide circuit around the still-burning steading. With the practicality of his race, he went in search of the place where he had cached the venison.

Two

Conan ran all night and half the next day. The tireless Cimmerian's steady trot devoured the miles, taking him out of the hill country and into the gently-rolling country near the border of the Bossonian Marches. Even in the moonlight, he had no difficulty in keeping the trail. So many horses left abundant signs of their passage.

He had hoped that the raiders would stop for the night, but they had not. Apparently, their diminished numbers made them apprehensive of pursuit. He was sure that they would slow as soon as they crossed the border. He planned to make use of that overconfidence.

As the sun burned high in the thin-clouded sky, Conan began to regret that he had not returned to the steading to gather some food and a waterskin before setting out on this pursuit. Conan's strength and endurance were greater by far than those of most ordinary men, but he was human. He knew that he would soon begin to tire and to weaken. Seven hardened bandits could be a formidable foe should he come upon them in less than his best condition.

It was with these somber thoughts in his mind that he saw the man who lay abandoned upon the grass. As Conan neared the inert form, he saw that the man wore ragged clothing of Nemedian design, and that he was still breathing. He walked slowly to the man and squatted next to him. Dispassionately, he studied his clearly dying subject.

The man had received a deep sword-cut on his side that would kill him in no great time. Bloodied earlobes and bands of pale skin around fingers and wrists proclaimed that those who had abandoned him here had wasted nothing. One of his erstwhile companions, prompted by some vestigial compassionate urge, had left a skin of water and a satchel of dried meat and cheese for the dying bandit. Conan took a long drink of the water, then splashed some on the man's face.

The fellow blinked a few times, then his eyes focused on Conan. The Cimmerian noted that the bandit's beard, though black, was straight. This was not the curly-bearded man.

"A Cimmerian," said the bandit in a weak, croaking voice. "I am doomed."

"You have been for some time," Conan said, gesturing toward the great rent in the man's side. "That was a shrewd stroke. It must have been Murcha, Halga's second son, who did that. It was a favorite blow of his."

The bandit cursed for a while. "Those dogs left me here like spoiled meat! Mitra's curse upon them."

"I plan to find them before Mitra does. Tell me who they are."

"Why should I tell you anything? I am already dying." The man tried to put on an expression of defiance, but it was a poor showing.

"You have hours yet to live. Those hours can seem like days."

The ashen face went even paler. "I had heard that you Cimmerians did not torture."

"We take no pleasure in the torment of helpless people, it is true," Conan agreed. "On the other hand, this is not a matter of pleasure. You and your companions slew my friends. I intend to exact vengeance. Your silence delays me in my task. I will not scruple to break that silence." He let the threat sink in, then went on. "Come, man, speak! They were no friends of yours, to leave you to die like this."

"Set take them!" he spat, showing a broad tolerance in religious matters. "Very well. There are six left now. Two are Bossonian archers, Murtan and Ballan, just ordinary thieves. Two others are Gundermen, brothers named Gunter and Wolf. They are dangerous men, outlawed in their own land for some killing affair." The bandit grimaced and groaned as some new pain washed over him.

Conan waited for the spasm to pass, then: "And the other two?"

"One is an Aquilonian named Axandrias. He is a smooth, serpent-tongued swindler, a charlatan. He claims sorcerous power but I never saw him perform aught save cheap conjurers' tricks."

"And the last?" Conan asked.

"Ah, him. I would spit had I the strength. He is our leader, who took us into that wolf's-den. His name is Taharka, a man of Keshan. He has skin the color of cured leather, but he is not a Kushite. He swaggers like a general and talks like a king, but he is just an unhung rogue like the rest of us."

"Did he say where they are headed?"

"There was talk of Ophir. There is war there, and it would be a good place to gather another band and go a-raiding. There is always a good living to be made on the outskirts of a war."

"Good," Conan said, standing up. He picked up the satchel and the waterskin. "You'll not need these."

"Will you take my head now?" asked the bandit.

"Nay. I will leave you to the death you have so richly earned."

"But what of your vengeance? Slay me."

"It is not my vengeance I seek, but that of the family you slaughtered. One of them gave you your death-blow. I am content. You spoke and I did not torture you. I promised no further mercy. Think on your sins while the vultures draw nigh."

Conan heard the man cursing weakly as he walked away. He felt immensely better now that he had some provisions. The rations were austere, but they were all he needed. His perfectly developed system, trained by the hardships of mountain life, would extract the last possible vestige of strength to be wrung from the dried flesh and stony cheese. He had eaten far worse in his few years, and this would be adequate fuel for his mission of vengeance.

Taharka was in a good mood. The land around him was green and pleasant, the air was fresh, his horse was a fine one, and he himself was in the best of health. Such surroundings and conditions set a man's thoughts upon the good things of life; loot, beautiful women, sparkling wine and the flowing blood of enemies. The men who rode behind him were gloomy and downcast, and he was fully aware of the fact. It merely showed that they were inferior creatures, allowing the misfortunes of others to cloud their own enjoyment of life.

Axandrias the Aquilonian rode up until he was beside his chief, and Taharka smiled at him. The mountebank was the only follower he valued. In Axandrias he sensed a fellow spirit, a man as devoid of conscience and scruple as himself. Unlike the stern Gundermen and the fearful Bossonians, Axandrias did not allow silly irrelevancies of loyalty, fear, or honor to come between himself and his enjoyment of life.

"Our comrades, my chieftain," began Axandrias, "are unhappy. They feel it unworthy to return from the high country thus empty-handed."

"I sympathize with their grief for our flat purses," said the dark man. "However, such grief is quickly cured. It is not as if we toiled our lives away in drudgery to earn our living. Let others work, and with a moment's risk, what they have is ours. This is the glory of the outlaw's life, Axandrias."

"Just as you say, my lord." The Aquilonian ran a beringed hand through his wavy yellow hair, ashine with a scented ointment. Above his broad belt he wore only a sleeveless vest of green silk, which displayed his smooth-muscled shoulders and arms to advantage. Axandrias was a striking figure of a man, and was anxious that all who beheld him should share his delight in the fact. "However, they are simple men and feel that some baleful spirit dogs our expedition. They are not men of learning and culture such as you and I, master. They are superstitious and feel that bad luck has descended upon them."

Taharka smiled in the midst of his handsome beard. The insinuating familiarity of the man amused him. "This is the defective reasoning of stupid men. They think that it was ill fortune that their comrades died. They should realize that instead it was good luck that they were spared."

"I understand that of course, master," said Axandrias. "But these poor fellows, innocent in their old-fashioned and rustic way of thinking, are depressed by this radical reduction of our numbers. When we were thirty strong, we had little to fear save from the organized forces of kings and border lords. Now we are only six and far more vulnerable in consequence." He continued to smile, showing that he regarded all such cavils as idle. His breeches of red velvet, slightly stained, shone bravely in the sunlight. The narrow Aquilonian sword and dagger at his belt glittered with jewels. Every line of his bearing declared his fitness for the position of second-in-command.

"Ah, but these fellows have the wrong attitude," said Taharka. "You see, we lost many men back there, but that is no matter. In all the world, nothing is so easily replaceable as men. Each likes to believe himself unique and irreplaceable, but this is sheer self-deception. If you would ever be a leader of men, my friend Axandrias, you must understand that men, whether they be slave or free, few in numbers or in the tens of thousands, are nothing. Their death, if it serve your purpose, is acceptable. Their life, if it is inconvenient to you, is intolerable."

"Wise words, my lord," said the Aquilonian.

"We shall cast about here. Perhaps there is surplus wealth to be appropriated. This land has the reputation for being rich."

"Well-policed, too, master," said Axandrias. "As a native, I speak with some authority. I have scratched my name on the walls of some of this nation's finest dungeons."

"Ah, but that was when you were young and foolish. Worse, you lacked proper leadership. All that has been remedied. Now," his mien grew more serious, "are you quite sure that we have escaped pursuit by the kinsmen of those savages we slew?" He leaned from his saddle and plucked a wildflower that grew below his stirrup. He raised it to his nostrils and inhaled its aroma, closing his eyes in appreciation.

"Assuredly. Once raiders have escaped across their borders, the Cimmerians give up the chase. This has always been their custom."

"Then we may rest somewhat," said Taharka. "After all, one does not take up the profession of thief in order to toil and endure hardship."

"The district in which we find ourselves," said Axandrias, "is a border region populated by Bossonians, Gundermen and Aquilonians. Should we fall in among any of them, some of us should surely be hung. We are unwelcome among our own people, I fear. Perhaps a swift passage through this land would be advisable. We can relax and make merry in Nemedia, thence in leisurely fashion to Ophir."

"Nonsense. Men who cannot outsmart, outfight, or outrun such frontier bumpkins as inhabit these parts have no business being in my band. I tolerate many bad qualities in my men, nay, I encourage them. But not cowardice. We must take such risks as come our way in following our chosen calling."

Axandrais smiled and nodded, thinking in his heart that these windy sentiments were easily spoken by a man who had no king's men seeking him in these parts. Nevertheless, Taharka was a cunning leader, and

Axandrias had not forgotten how he had dealt with the insubordinate Argossian.

Taharka turned in his saddle. "Murtan, Ballan, ride you ahead of us and range about. If you find any easy prey, ride back immediately. We look for travelers few in number and bearing goods. Remember, we will strike nobody near any town. In the meantime," he leaned back contentedly, "we are honest horse-merchants."

He turned to Axandrias once more, as the two Bossonians rode off. "You see, it is best to keep men occupied when their spirits are low, lest they grow rebellious. A little theft and throat-cutting will restore their good humor. As soon as we reach a market town," he gestured at the horse-herd tended by the two Gundermen, "we shall sell these off and have a fine carouse."

"I look forward to it, master," said the Aquilonian.

Conan had been on the trail for six days when he came upon the first of their depradations. The road he followed showed only the marks of many horses, but his nose told him that death had visited this area.

He examined the road and saw a great confusion of hoofprints, and among them were blackened specks of drying blood. In several places he found where a booted foot had kicked dirt over large pools of blood, but the fluid had soaked through and flies were humming busily over the spots.

His sense of smell and a great buzzing of insects led him to a clump of dense brush by the side of the road. As he had expected, the bodies of the victims had been dragged there and abandoned. Fortunately, there was no need for him to approach them closely.

There were four of them, three men and a woman.

Their clothing had been too bloodied to be worth stealing, and from their dress Conan took them to be a merchant and his wife and two servants. All jewelery and other valuables had been stripped from the bodies. Conan hurried away. It would not be well to be found near the scene of slaughter. King's men often took the nearest available stranger after such an act. Besides, the ghosts of the slain might be lurking about, ready to work mischief on any passerby.

It should be easy to keep on their trail, Conan decided, if they were to indulge in such murders at every convenient opportunity. Conan was himself lawless by nature, but such indiscriminate murder was far beyond his understanding. The slaying of such men would be among the worthiest of his accomplishments.

As he trotted at his mile-eating pace, he reflected that he must soon find a mount, or risk losing his prey. He might have lost them ere now, save that they were ambling along at an easy pace, confident in their numbers and safety from pursuit. Should they take fright at any time, he might not be able to keep up with them.

That evening, he arrived at a town. Built at the confluence of two sizable streams, its low stone wall enclosed a triangular huddle of houses and public buildings. The city gate was in the center of the wall forming the base of the triangle, and the grassy mead without the wall was fenced to form a common pasture.

Conan's limited experience of towns told him that the livestock of visitors and traveling merchants would be pastured upon the common. Although he yearned to find whether certain horses he sought were there, Conan studiously ignored the pastured beasts as he strode toward the gate.

A guard leaned upon his spear and eyed the youth

disdainfully. "What is your name, Cimmerian? And what is your business?"

Conan seethed and his first impulse was to draw his blade and split the skull of this insolent dog. He would gain nothing and might even be called to account for the act. City people had no true sense of honor. Worse, the bandits he sought might get away while he was trying to break out of the local dungeon.

"My name is Conan. I seek certain men who may have passed this way. Have you seen a dark man of the south, traveling with an Aquilonian, two Bossonians and two Gundermen? I believe that they would have sought to sell some horses."

The man's gaze narrowed. "Why do you ask such things?"

This seemed to be an odd reaction, and Conan decided he had better not mention the murders on the road. "I have business with them. It is nothing that you need concern yourself about."

"I know nothing of them," said the guard. He stepped aside. "You may enter the city, but stay out of trouble. I suggest you keep silent about these men you seek. It may be that someone may wish to speak to you about them."

Mystified, Conan passed beneath the arched gateway and through the vaulted tunnel in the city wall. It was clear that the guard knew more than he was willing to speak of. The young Cimmerian was suspicious of the devious ways of civilization. Perhaps he would come back after dark and wring some answers from the man.

First, though, he needed rest and refreshment. For many days he had been on the trail, running hard on short rations. He was thirsty, famished and bone-weary. When he had come to the bottom of the provision sack, he had found a scattering of small coins, forgotten by the bandit who left it with the dying man. Now he would put some of them to good use.

A few questions revealed that the town's sole inn was near the gate. It was a low, rambling structure of wood and stone pierced here and there with small windows. Smoke rose from a stone chimney at one end of the building. Conan ducked through the low doorway and went inside.

Within the inn, he stepped to one side so as not to be silhouetted against the sunlight. As his eyes adjusted to the interior dimness, he saw that he was in a cavernous room with two long tables down its center. At one end was a fireplace on which meats turned, skewered on long iron spits. At the other end was a curtained door. Beside the curtained door, a huddled form sat on the floor, wrapped in a blanketlike cloak.

The innkeeper came across the room, wiping his hands on the apron that covered his bulging paunch. He eyed the near-naked Cimmerian with suspicion. "What would you have, stranger?"

"Food and a place to sleep," Conan said. "I can pay for it."

The man gestured toward the turning spits. "We have just begun preparing the meats. The bread has not come from the baker's yet. If you would wait, you may take a seat and I will bring wine, which is always ready, at any hour."

Thirsty though he was, Conan knew better than to begin guzzling wine early in the day with an empty stomach. "Show me where I may sleep for a few hours. I will eat when I rise. I have a trail to follow, and little time to waste."

"Say you so? Follow me and I will show you our accommodations."

The man led Conan toward the curtained door. As he was about to pass through, the cloaked person raised a tan-haired head and looked at him. To his astonishment, it was a woman. Rather, it was a girl of about his own age. She had strong, regular features that would have been comely save that the left eye was covered by a patch of black leather. He paused for a moment, startled by her gaze. The look in her single eye was not quite sane.

In a straw-floored room divided by curtains into tiny chambers, Conan laid down his few possessions while the innkeeper lit a candle. "This will do," the Cimmerian said. "Who is the wench who sits without? That was no friendly look she gave me."

"That is just Mad Kalya. Pay her no heed. She is famous in these parts. She thinks well of no man."

"I know a hawk's eye when I see one," Conan commented. "What is she famous for?"

"For being dangerous. Have nothing to do with her. There are far more accommodating wenches to be had. Kalya ranges the frontier district, searching for some man upon whom she must wreak vengeance. If you ask me, he exists only in her own deranged mind. The king's men will not touch her, because she is mad and has some claim to noble blood. She comes to this town from time to time. She always has a little money to pay her way, and no man enquires too closely as to how she came by it. She came in late last night and has been sleeping as you saw her ever since. She always sleeps like that, sitting with her back against a wall." The fat man clucked and shook his head. "A shameful waste of what would have been a fine-looking wench."

"Wake me when dinner is prepared," Conan said, stretching out on the straw. He had no time for madwomen. He laid his hand upon his sword-hilt and drifted into sleep.

Conan jerked awake with his sword half-drawn when someone came into the tiny chamber. He resheathed the weapon when he saw that it was a ragged boy whose eyes had gone wide at the barbarian's reaction.

"We are serving, master," the boy stammered. "You wished to be awakened."

Grinning ruefully, Conan thanked the boy and strapped on his weapons. He found a basin of water by the door to the common room and he splashed his face and hands, then dried them upon a towel of no great cleanliness. He pushed through the curtain.

There were a score of people in the common room, most of them bearing the look of traveling men. The madwoman still sat beside the door. Apparently, she had not moved, but now her head was erect and she ceaselessly swept the room with her eagle's gaze.

Conan took a seat at one end of a table and helped himself from the platters lined at its center. He had no idea when he would next find a meal, so he settled down to some serious eating. The boy poured him a cup of raw red wine from a pitcher and the Cimmerian began to work on a rack of beef ribs.

He was halfway through the rack when a man in a greasy hide jerkin sat opposite him. He took a cup from the serving-boy and drank deep before turning his attention to Conan. He smiled, revealing a mouthful of stained teeth. Droplets of wine gleamed on his ill-trimmed mustache.

"Stranger, I have heard that you are asking questions concerning certain men who may have come through here with horses to sell. My name is Rario. I am a horse trader by profession, and I may be of some assistance to you.''

"The men I seek are bandits," Conan said. "A southerner called Taharka, an Aquilonian rogue called Axandrias, a pair of Gunder— ''

The horse-trader held out a palm for silence. "Please, keep your voice down. There are matters here best not brought to public attention.''

"I grow weary of these mysteries," Conan growled. "These men are under the protection of no god I know of. My business with them is my own.''

"And I am most anxious to help," said Rario. "But perhaps this is not the place. I keep my stock in the horse compound without the city wall. Perhaps we can meet there later.''

"Aye," said Conan, "If that is the only way I am to obtain any answers.''

"Excellent. Now, finish your dinner, have some wine and take your ease. I shall meet you at the compound. Give the gate guard my name and he will let you through with no questions. Until then, Cimmerian.'' The man bowed somewhat mockingly and left.

Conan cleaned the last rib-bone and was searching the platters for something more substantial when he noticed a cloaked form standing by his bench. He looked up to see that it was the madwoman. Her cloak was a voluminous, circular blanket of rough brown cloth, with a slit woven in its center for the head to pass through. It fell from shoulders to ankles and what she looked like under it was a complete mystery.

"I would speak with you," she said without preamble. The last thing Conan wanted was company, but it was the custom of his people to humor the mad. He gestured to the vacant seat opposite and signalled to the pot-boy to bring another cup.

"I am Kalya. Mad Kalya, men call me. You have probably been warned." Her voice was startling; a hoarse grating that might have been made by a raven rather than a young woman. Squinting in the dim light, Conan descried a pair of scars on each side of Kalya's neck. At some time in the past, someone had passed a dagger through the girl's larynx. That accounted for the voice. He also realized that she must have been a mere child when it happened. He took another swallow of wine. It was a hard world, and the matter was none of his concern.

"You have my name," she said, "what is yours? You are a Cimmerian by your look."

"So I am. My name is Conan." The boy placed a cup beside the woman and filled it with wine. There were vertical slits at the side of the cloak and her left hand emerged from one of them. Lurid light from the fire and candles glinted from the hand. Conan was astonished to see that she wore a close-fitting steel gauntlet.

"You seek some men. I heard you talking with that vile swine, Rario. I seek one man. It may be that he is among those you search for."

"What is that to me?" Conan asked. "Here, eat something." He waved toward the heaped platters.

"I am short of money," she said.

"I will pay. The men I look for provided this meal, although unwittingly." Indeed, his motives were not entirely generous. She had already emptied her cup and the boy rushed over to refill it. Bad enough to share a table with one who was mad. A drunken madwoman would be intolerable. He saw with some relief that she ate ravenously.

For a space they both ate in silence. None of the other diners seemed anxious to speak to them and that suited Conan well. It did not occur to him what an intimidating sight the two of them were. The wolfish barbarian youth and the fierce madwoman would have been daunting to a harder-bitten lot than inhabited the inn that evening.

At last Kalya leaned back with a sigh of repletion and blotted her mouth with the hem of her cloak. She used her left hand to do this. Conan had yet to see her right. "You have not said why you seek these men, Cimmerian."

"That is so." Conan answered. It was not his nature to prevaricate, but the puzzling attitudes he had met with here made him reluctant to confide in anyone.

"You spoke a name when Rario was here," she said. "Axandrias. It is he whom I seek." The set of her head, the glare in her good eye, made the hairs on the back of Conan's neck prickle. In this moment she looked truly demented.

"I know nothing abut the man save his name and nation, girl. There may be a thousand Aquilonians named Axandrias, for aught I know."

"It is he!" she hissed. "Is the one you seek a mountebank, a would-be wizard and swindler?"

"So I've heard," said Conan, uncomfortably. "I've not met the man. My business with him shall be brief, when we do meet. Besides, he is only one of six."

She slapped her gauntleted hand on the table, causing heads to turn. "I knew it! Mitra has answered my prayers at last and he shall soon be within my grasp!"

Conan waved a hand. "All this is none of my affair. I have some business to transact with these men and I

waste time here. I must go now." He rose, and the
woman rose with him.

"You go to see Rario. I shall go with you. I would
speak with him as well."

"This is none of your affair, woman!" Conan hissed.

"Oh, but it is," she said. "Now pay the innkeeper
and we shall be on our way."

Fuming, Conan paid their score and the two went out
into the torchlit street. He said nothing, but he noted
that Kalya walked not with the coquettish sway he had
seen most city women display, but rather with the
springy stride of the warrior. Her head barely reached
his shoulder, but he could understand why men would
give her wide berth.

"You seek vengeance upon these men, do you not,
Cimmerian?" she said abruptly.

"And what is that to you?" he demanded.

"Because my vengeance comes first!"

"Quiet!" he insisted. "The gate." In silence they
approached the portal. In the light of a torch, he could
see that the guard was the same man who had challenged him earlier that day.

"Ah, the barbarian," said the guard. "You go to
seek Rario? That is—but who is this?" He squinted
outside the circle of light cast by the torch. "Mad
Kalya! What do you—" His words were cut short when
Conan's hand, knotted into the front of his doublet,
lifted him from his feet and slammed him against the
wall of the gate behind him.

"Do you always pull such a long tour of duty?" the
Cimmerian asked.

"But," the man choked out, "how, what?" his eyes
bulged as he strangled. Then, desperate, "Hold! Rario
told me to keep watch this night. He gave money to my

relief that I might stand a double-shift.'' There was
terror in the man's sallow face. The savage before him
looked as pitiless as a stone, and the madwoman behind
the Cimmerian's shoulder looked thirsty for blood.

"Leave him, Conan,'' said Kalya. "This is a dog
who is in the purse of any who has a few coins. Rario is
the one who may have knowledge important to us. Let's
go find him.''

With a snort of disgust, Conan dropped the wretch to
the pave. "Stay there and remain quiet, '' Conan warned.

There was no sound behind them as the two walked
out through the gate. The common pasture was serene
in the moonlight, the only touch of color provided by a
large campfire kept by some herd-boys detailed for that
night's duty. It seemed to be a good enough point to
make for, so the two walked toward the firelight. The
herd-boys looked up as they arrived.

"I think it is a good time for you to check the
fences,'' intoned Kalya. The boys scrambled to do as
she suggested.

"Axandrias is mine!'' she said. "You may have the
others, but do not lay hands on the Aquilonian, do you
understand?''

"Girl,'' said Conan, nettled, "anyone can see that
you have been ill-used. I've no doubt that your vengeance is just. But I have sworn to track these men
down and slay them. I want no interference from an
addled wench.''

"Wench!'' Her eye glared feral hate. "From childhood I have devoted my life to the extermination of this
man! Do you think I would let some illiterate, un-
washed savage stand in my way? Let this 'wench' give
you some lessons in courtesy and swordplay, barbarian!'' She reached behind her neck and drew the cloak

over her head. Before the cloak struck the ground, her right hand flashed across her waist and a sword was in her hand.

For a moment Conan stood dumbfounded. Her shift from semi-friendliness to hostility was bewildering, and her garb was as bizarre as anything the Cimmerian had encountered.

The woman wore very little beneath the cloak, and most of what she wore was protective armor. An intricate sleeve of mail and small plates covered her right arm from shoulder to wrist. She wore light greaves on both shins, and her right thigh was further protected by a cuisse of studded leather. Her right breast was confined in a web of fine steel mail, the other was bare. Her left hand was encased in the articulated steel gauntlet Conan had noted earlier. It had a flared, fluted cuff that extended almost to the elbow. Aside from these protective accessories, she wore only a loincloth supported by her weapon-belt, and that, too, was made of fine mail.

"Have a care, woman," said Conan. "I have never drawn steel upon a woman ere now, but you try my patience!" Despite his scruples, his hand strayed toward his hilt. This creature had more the aspect of a wild beast than a natural woman.

Her sword was not large. It was narrow and slightly curved, and its hilt was an intricate basket of thin bars that completely enclosed the hand. Whatever school of swordplay the girl had studied, it was clear from the nature of her armor that it called for the swordsman to lead with the right arm and leg. Conan read this in a flash as the cloak came off, and he was moving into his defense even before the cloth finished collapsing.

As Kalya moved into her attack posture, extending

her sword-arm into a low advance guard, the Cimmerian's foot swept sideways. Before she could get her balance, Kalya felt her right foot jerked from beneath her and she toppled sideways, slapping the ground with her gauntleted left hand to take up the shock. Even as she fell, she turned her small saber edge-upwards and made a vertical cut. It would have gelded a lesser man, but Conan avoided the stroke by a margin so narrow that he felt the sweat spring out upon his scalp at the thought of what might have been.

"Crom!" Conan swore as he sprang back. "What is the meaning of this? We are not yet so at odds that it is a killing matter, girl!"

Kalya scrambled to her feet. "Stop calling me girl, you foul savage! Draw your sword if you'd not add murder to the crimes on my conscience."

Conan circled, trying to get the light into her eye. She circled with him, but always managed to shift back just as the fire came within her line of vision. She fought crouched, with knees well bent and the gauntleted hand held just beneath her chin, to cover the bare parts of her vitals. It was the oddest armor Conan had ever seen, but it seemed to cover well the vital areas with a minimum of weight.

"Draw!" she shouted, her face gone crimson.

"Yes, draw, Cimmerian," said a voice. The two whirled and faced outward from the fire. Several shadowy forms moved out in the dimness. Conan's sword hissed from its scabbard and his teeth shone brightly. At last, here was someone he could cut down cleanly.

One of the men stepped forward, and Conan was not at all surprised to see that it was Rario. "You have brought trouble with you, Cimmerian. A man should be cautious about his questions here on the frontier."

"I seek only the whereabouts of Taharka and his men," said Conan. "A few straight words and I will be on my way and trouble you no more. Straight words are hard to come by in this place."

"You are an innocent lad," said the horse-trader. "You have little more wit than this addled girl. You should have pretended to be some traveling peddler, and dropped a few veiled questions, and then we might have done some business."

"Stop speaking in riddles!" Conan demanded. "I stated my business openly. Do the same!"

The man shook his head and clucked at such callowness. "Boy, did you not reflect that these people you follow are bandits, and that the folk they do business with might have a similar antipathy to the forces of the law? You see, when an outlaw comes down out of the hills, he does not seek out an honest merchant who has all the proper licenses and the esteem of the authorities.

"No, lad, what he looks for is a shady trader who buys goods at a low price but without embarassing questions. In short, he comes to a dealer such as your humble servant." Rario smiled, and the firelight made circular glints upon the golden rings in his ears. "In fact, this man Taharka came to me some few days ago. He had some fine horses to sell, and I bought them at a good price."

"Then what stayed your tongue, man?" Conan asked, not taking his eyes from the forms that circled ominously beyond the firelight. "That was all I wanted: to know where they had been and whence they went."

"Ah, but those are embarrasing questions to such as I." There was a glint of steel in the man's hand now. "You see, horses are easily negotiable items. But, should someone bring up inconvenient questions as to their origin, or who legitimately owns them, or whether their riders were those who had recently met an untimely demise, then," he shrugged elaborately, "the royal authorities may step in. There will be questions, and court actions, and all manner of unseemly prying."

Conan was dumbfounded. "You mean that all this comes of your dealings for stolen horses? Mere greed and timidity have put us to this trouble?"

"Have a care, savage," Rario warned. "These are the precautions of my trade. Your insolence displeases me. I think it is time to punish such insolence. Boys!" The horse-trader made a handsign and three men stepped in from the gloom. They were large men, wearing hide and light mail armor.

Two of them attacked Conan. It was clear that they were well practiced in their craft. They closed in from opposite sides, one cutting at the Cimmerian's head while the other swept a slashing blow at his legs. Instead of engaging one attacker and leaving himself vulnerable to the other, Conan dealt with both at once.

The low-swung sword passed through empty air as Conan sprang upward, jerking his knees up almost to chin level. Simultaneously, he slashed toward the sword that was whistling at his head. He did not block the weapon, but instead cut for the wielder's wrist. The sword, with hand still gripping its handle, flew free, nicking the Cimmerian's shoulder in passing.

He whirled and landed facing his other opponent. The man was still recovering from his abortive blow when the Cimmerian's blade descended, crunching through mail to shear flesh and bone, hewing through ribs and deep into vitals. Conan jerked the sword free and spun once more. Blood flew from the blade in a great arc as Conan slashed the head from the man who stood staring at his handless wrist.

The action had taken but a moment. Conan now saw that Kalya was fencing with the third of Rario's cohorts while the horse-trader himself, wearing an expression of dismay, was hastening to attack the Cimmerian. Despite the distractions, Conan noted that the woman was using her sword to block or parry blows coming toward her right side, while using her gauntlet to stop attacks to her left.

Rario's blade licked out and Conan blocked with his own. His return cut almost gutted Rario, who avoided it only by springing back abruptly. Pressing his advantage, Conan rained a flurry of quick but half-strength blows at Rario, each blow drawing his opponent's parry farther to the right. Conan's last blow was full-strength, whizzing easily past Rario's overwide parry and cleaving his skull to the teeth.

The Cimmerian wrenched his blade free and turned in time to see Kalya finishing her opponent. As the man thrust for her bare belly, she swept the blade aside with the flaring cuff of her gauntlet and replied with a beautifully timed cut to his neck. Her point swept beneath his right ear, no more than an inch of the tip slicing beneath the skin. It was sufficient. The man collapsed to his knees, cursing dully as blood jetted several feet, to spray the fire, raising a cloud of foul-smelling steam.

"We'd best be away, Cimmerian," said Kalya. She wiped her blade and resheathed it. Casually, she examined the three men Conan had slain. "No elegance, but plenty of speed and strength. Who was your swordmaster?"

"I never had one. Cimmerians are born knowing how to fight. Some are better than others. What do you mean by 'we', woman? I am off after the bandits. I need no traveling companion. Go where you will.''

She resumed her enveloping cloak. ''We both seek the same men. Easier for us to join forces, don't you think?'' She turned and regarded him with her single eye. Her expression looked almost sane for a change. ''Barbarian, you may be a great warrior in your hills. I am sure you cut a fine figure in the Marches. Even here on the frontier you can pass inspection. But we have a long chase ahead of us, and in the great cities of the south you would be like some wild beast loose within the walls. You would grace a dungeon or a gallows long ere you found this Taharka and his men. I am at home in those warrens.''

It stung Conan's pride to be thus lectured, but he suspected that she was right. As a civilized man needed a guide in the wilderness, he was going to need one in civilization. He pondered the fact as he cleaned the last bits of blood and brain from his sword.

''Aye, you are right,'' he said, resheathing. ''We shall take the road together, at least until I can no longer tolerate you.''

''I am more likely to run out of patience first,'' she retorted. ''Come, let's see what kind of horseflesh this rogue had in stock. Any minute now, the watch is likely to work up enough courage to come and investigate this little affray. We must be mounted and away by then.''

Three

They rode down the eastern edge of Aquilonia, avoiding the larger cities with their garrisons, their king's watchdogs, and their prying ways. Taharka was well pleased with their progress. His five close followers were over their depression at the Cimmerian setback, and they had recruited several new rogues for the band. The land was fat, the merchants were wealthy and often traveled without guards, and the band was careful to leave none behind them alive to raise the alarm.

All of them now glittered in new armor, and their horses were the finest, colorful in bards of silk and dyed Shemitish leather. There was nothing, Taharka reflected, that gladdened men's hearts like a well-stuffed purse, good horseflesh between their knees and gaudy finery to wear.

"Master," called one of the Gundermen, "we grow weary of riding and sleeping beneath the stars. Let us tarry at the next town and spend a bit of our money."

Taharka considered the idea. Part of the art of leading was in knowing when to loosen the leash for a while.

They were many miles from the scene of their last crime, and so far there was no sign of pursuit.

"I like the idea," he said heartily. "Axandrias, is there a likely place within easy riding distance?"

The Aquilonian rode up even with his leader. "A quarter-league from here a road branches off to the east. If we take that road, before nightfall we will be in Croton. It is in territory claimed by both Aquilonia and Nemedia and garrisoned by neither. All the rogues of the border gather there, and it is as wicked a town as you could wish for."

"This sounds like the very place to take our ease for a few days," Taharka announced. "Let us ride to Croton!" The men raised a ferocious cheer behind him.

By sunset, they were passing through the ruinous gate of the town. Croton looked to be every bit as villainous as Axandrias had claimed. The wall was ruinous and animals were pastured all around the town. Not only horses and mules, but camels were cropping the grass contentedly. The Bossonians and Gundermen gaped at the awkward beasts, which were never seen in their part of the world.

"By Set," Taharka swore, "half the smugglers in the world must pass through this town."

"A fair estimate, master," said Axandrias. Nobody challenged them as they rode in. For a small town in a remote area, Croton was amazingly cosmopolitan. In the marketplace they heard the sound of many languages, and saw people in the dress of a half-score of nations. Aquilonian and Nemedian predominated, but there were Shemites and Ophirians as well, along with an occasional Hyperborean, Nordheimer or Brythunian.

The market was a riot of colors, sounds and odors, where the rogues of half a world hawked smuggled and stolen goods. In chaotic profusion, men displayed bolts of bright-colored cloth, racks of jewelry, glassware, weapons, and other goods. The nose endured no less assault than the eyes. Smells of rich spices, incense, perfumes, and drugs laced the air. As Taharka had expected, almost everything on display was of the sort favored by smugglers; items easily transportable, high in value, and much taxed in all nations.

Taharka leaned from his saddle and addressed a man who was examining a rack of ivory-hilted daggers. "Friend, could you tell me where weary men with money to spend might find rest, refreshment, and entertainment?"

The man pointed down a narrow street lined with stalls. "Make your way down the Street of All Possible Delights. At its end you will find the Traveler's Paradise. In that inn, only the dead can fail to find all they want, can they but pay. Mind your purse and keep your belongings secured, and you will not be disappointed."

Taharka thanked the man and the little band made its way down the crowded street. Stalls and awnings spilled into the throughway, making passage by mounted men barely possible. The wares in the street-level stalls were enticing, and those on display in the upper-floor windows and balconies even more so. From these, women clad in little or nothing gestured invitingly.

Here and there they passed small temples. The obscene sculptures and paintings on their porticoes made it plain that only the most disreputable of gods were worshipped within. A few minutes' traverse brought them to the courtyard of the Traveler's Paradise.

Since most of the town's population was transient, the inn was huge. They left their mounts with hostlers and passed through the wide timber doorway. The hos-

telry was built in the eastern fashion, three-storied with
a huge open area on the ground floor and two tiers of
galleried balconies rising above it. The center of the
roof was open to the sky, and there was a fountained
pool on one side of the flagstoned floor. On the other
side was a pit where slaves could be made to fight each
other or wild beasts. This was a sport strictly prohibited
in Aquilonia and frowned upon in Nemedia, but much
esteemed among the rougher element and practiced wherever enforcement was lax.

The polyglot company inside was numerous and up-
roarious. Taharka and his men found a table in the
center court next to the pit and slaves hurried over to
bring them refreshment. Taharka arranged for lodging
for his men and their animals, and called for a feast to
be laid before them. Soon they were gorging and guzzling while naked Nemedian girls danced lasciviously
on a platform erected over the fountain.

"This is the way men should live," the dark man
proclaimed. "Is this not a fine life we have chosen for
ourselves, my friends?" He knew that this sort of cama-
raderie was valuable in shaping his men's loyalties and
raising their morale. Thus they would be eager to please
him, and that much easier to sacrifice.

"The best, Chieftain," said Gunter, the Gunderman.
He eyed the pit. "I wonder whether there will be
fighting this evening. I am in a mood for some strong
entertainment."

Taharka watched as a crew of Argossian slavers came
into the inn: brutish men wearing belts and wristbands
of studded leather, and carrying the coiled whips that
were the adornment of their trade. The sight stimulated
the Keshanian's thoughts along a new path, and he

began to construct a scheme. He filed it among the many that continually occupied his mind.

"We shall see, Gunter. Perhaps we may prevail upon our hosts to provide us with such sport. My purse is open, and nothing is too good for my men." A ferocious cheer went up at these words. It pleased him that men could be so cheaply had.

The day wore on; the men ate and drank to repletion. From time to time, one or more would lurch from the table and stagger away with some of the amiable women who plied their profession among the roisterers. Eventually, the men would return to eat and drink some more. As the light grew dim, torches were set up around the courtyard and in sconces along the galleries. Servers provided the tables with candles in holders of curiously-wrought metal or fanciful bottles of foreign design. Soon the gibbous moon shone down through the open roof and the revelry continued unabated.

Taharka leaned back in his chair and surveyed the scene happily. He had eaten and drunk moderately, and he had not availed himself of the services offered by the working ladies. His pleasures were not the simple, uncomplicated ones favored by his men. By now the dice were out, and they were rearranging their loot according to the workings of chance. Taharka planned to join the game later. He would acquire most of the loot for himself by eliminating the element of chance.

He caught the innkeeper's eye and waved him to their table. "Join us, my host! Fill a cup with some of your excellent wine and grace our table with your presence. You look much in need of rest. Let your servants tend to the inn for a time."

"Gladly, southerner," said the man. He sat with a loud sigh and poured wine from a chased pitcher into a cup of fine glass. "This has been a busy time, and I toil day and night to keep my patrons happy. My feet were merely sore before. Now they are numb." He drank deep and sighed with satisfaction. The innkeeper had a broad, tawny beard that descended almost to his capacious paunch. Although he was not old, firelight gleamed from his bald head. He had the fat cheeks, twinkling eyes, and ready smile of the professional host. "Have you found all here to your liking, my friend? Should you require anything great or small, you have but to name it and it shall be my pleasure to provide it for you, should it be within my power."

"You are most hospitable. In fact, some of my followers have asked whether there is to be sport in the fighting-pit tonight."

"Aye, there is to be a match tonight. A merchant of this town keeps a famous fighting-slave, and a Zamoran caravan arrived this morning. Their whip-master is a plucky fellow who wishes to challenge him. They should provide excellent sport."

"Only a single match, then?" Taharka questioned.

"Alas, that is so. A few years ago, I could provide as many as ten matches in an evening at the height of the trading season. The kings were not so squeamish in those days, and there was more traffic from Zamora, Brythunia and Turan, where manly amusements are in high favor. The recent wars have been somewhat disruptive." The two men drank in commiseration over the decadence of the times.

"I have agents abroad," the innkeeper said, "who have promised to deliver a Zingaran fighting bull and a Hyrkanian tiger. These, unfortunately, will not arrive until much later in the season."

"Is that how the sport is conducted here?" Taharka

queried. "Just the occasional fighting-slave or free challenger? That would seem a haphazard and unreliable method of providing so important and edifying an entertainment. In lands to the east and south it is conducted in an orderly, businesslike fashion."

"Thus it was here in past years. There were many training farms in the towns of this district. In my father's time, Croton had three establishments that maintained each a score of skillful fighting-slaves. Now we must manage as best we may. Two or three bouts a week are the most we can exhibit, most of the year."

"To the death?" Taharka asked.

"Of course!" the innkeeper said, indignantly. "Times are not as they were, but we have not grown degenerate!"

"Suppose," Taharka hazarded, "someone were able to bring you a steady supply of doughty combatants. Say, enough to exhibit four or five good pairs each night? What would that be worth to a businessman such as yourself?" Taharka sipped at his wine and knew from the greedy gleam in the other's eye that his random-shot arrow had struck home.

The innkeeper twisted his fingers in his curly beard, turning the possibilities in his mind. "That would be worth much. There are four caravanserais in this town, although mine is far the largest. With nightly entertainment of this sort, no one with gold to spend would bother with the others. The busiest season of the year is just beginning. If you think you can bring me good fighting talent, you and I could put away a tidy fortune during the next three turnings of the moon."

"That is good hearing. I think we can do business."

"Mind you," the innkeeper held up an admonitory finger, "they must be good, willing fighters. No real man delights in seeing terrified slaves hack at each other's trembling bodies. A spirited, skillful fight is always a delight to behold. A man who spits defiance as his life's blood drains out is the most cheering of spectacles. I have seen places like mine torn apart by a crowd enraged by a sloppy kill.''

"Have no fear," Taharka assured him. "I am an expert in these matters. I shall bring you only the best stock. We may charge admission, increasing it as particular fighters gain a reputation, take a percentage of the bets, and so on. There is a fortune to be wrung from such events.''

They bargained for a while longer, establishing prices and rates. When all was in agreement, they gripped each other's wrists to seal the bargain. The innkeeper rose and left to tend his other patrons.

"Master," said Axandrias, who had been listening in respectful silence, "this sounds a fine scheme, but I detect certain impracticalities.''

"Name them," said his chief.

"For one thing, expense.''

"Have I not told you that nothing is so cheap as men?''

"That is so, but slaves of this sort can cost much to maintain. They must be men of high quality to begin with. High spirit and a fighting temperament are rare in slaves. Usually, you must go to where there has been a war and buy captive warriors. Then they must be guarded at all times, and fed upon a high-quality diet. You must have facilities to board and train them. I do not see how we shall find all these things in this thinly populated district. And then there are our own men to consider.''

"Why should they object?" Taharka asked.

"Why," Axandrias gestured widely, searching for

words, "it would be almost like making an honest living!"

Taharka grinned broadly, exposing jewels set in some of his lower front teeth. "Have no fear, my sagacious friend. There shall be no taint of honesty to the business. We shall expend little and reap huge rewards." The sound of cheering and a bustle of movement interrupted him. "Ah, here come the fighters. Observe, and then I shall explain to you how it is to be done."

The two combatants were led through the cheering throng by burly trainers who held chains attached to rings around the fighters' necks. At the edge of the pit the chains were taken off and the men descended into the shallow arena. Amid frenzied betting, an announcer called out the names of the two who were about to do battle for them. One was a man of the south, almost as dark as Taharka. The other was a northerner of some fair-skinned tribe. The men wore only close-fitting helmets of hardened leather and groin-protectors supported by studded belts.

Onto the men's hands were strapped heavy gloves with bands that wound around the forearm from hand to elbow. Each glove was plated with bronze and bore a row of three-inch spikes across the knuckles. Men whooped and clapped and some threw money into the pit.

"Twenty on the whiteskin!" bellowed Wolf, Gunter's brother.

"Done," Taharka shouted. He was only betting to be jovial, for he had little love for games which he had not fixed. It was no matter. Should he lose, he would win his money back afterward, when his men were too drunk to detect his artistry with the dice.

In the pit, the men faced each other squarely, fists

raised to chest level. The torchlight gleamed from the polished tips of the bronze spikes. At the pit-master's command, they advanced. The southerner fought more aggressively, throwing powerful, looping blows with great rapidity. The northerner was more cautious, fending off the flailing fists with his heavily wrapped forearms. Within minutes, his arms were bleeding. Still, no heavy blows had landed upon his head or vitals, and the dark fighter was tiring quickly.

When the southerner's arms began to sag with the weight of the bronze gloves, the northern slave began to attack. Blows to the dark man's chest tore great rents in his flesh, causing him to bleed and weaken. Soon his sagging arms left his head exposed, and his opponent closed in for the kill. A surprise blow to the pit of the stomach caused the dark man to jerk his arms down and double over. The next blow landed on his face, sinking the bronze spikes into cheek and jaw.

The northerner had to brace a knee against his opponent's chest in order to wrench the spikes from his face. The dark man was semi-comatose, unable to resist as the other man tore the leather helmet from his head. The victor gripped his victim's short hair and held him in a half-sitting posture, jaw sagging and eyes rolled up to expose only the whites. Wheezing breath bubbled in red froth from his nose and mouth. The winner looked up and around at his audience. His bronze-plated fist was cocked beside his right ear, the spikes dripping blood on his shoulder.

Amid clapping and cheering, the pit-master signaled to the winner to finish the battle. The spikes flashed down, there was a sickening crunch, and the vanquished collapsed on the floor of the pit, brains oozing from his crushed skull. Coins rained into the pit, cast there by happy winners.

Taharka counted out twenty gold coins and handed them over to Wolf. "You see?" he said to Axandrias, gesturing toward the pit. The torchlight now gleamed from a mixture of blood and gold. "Great wealth to be had, at the expenditure of a mere worthless slave. This is how we shall accomplish it. I shall speak with the slavers at yon table, perhaps hire some of them. We shall raid the farms and villages hereabout, on both sides of the border. What we need are vigorous young males of good physique.

"You have seen how the fights are conducted here; single combats with basic hand weapons. These are skills easily taught. Most of the viewers are not connoisseurs of artistic swordplay. All that matters is ferocity and courage. These things may be artificially induced."

Axandrias sipped his wine as the possibilities occurred to him. "You are thinking of drugs, master?"

"Exactly. With a combination of the correct drugs and certain simple spells, the dullest plowman may become a veritable tiger, at least for a few minutes. That will be sufficient, for these fights are not of great duration. It is not as if we were going to train them to shoot the bow, or wield a lance from horseback, or perform complicated troop evolutions on the battlefield."

The bandit chief beamed with satisfaction. "We shall stick to simple, close-quarter weapons: the spiked gloves, the short sword, the dagger, perhaps the club for those who are hopelessly inept. The basic skills can be imparted in a matter of days. When we bring them here, the drugs will take care of the rest."

"It is a good plan," Axandrias agreed, "but there

are still the authorities to consider. This is a lawless area, but slave-raiding on any scale will soon attract attention.''

"That is the beauty of a border region, my friend. When we raid in Aquilonia, we shall dress as Nemedian slavers. In Nemedia, we shall be Aquilonians. Any disputes will be between the two nations. Long before we are suspected, we shall be away from this place with our loot.''

"Excellent!'' crowed Axandrias.

"Now, my friend,'' Taharka instructed, ''you have some knowledge of magical and thaumaturgic arts. On the morrow, I want you to explore this town. Find a practitioner of those arts who has the requisite drugs and get him to teach you the proper spells. Be prepared to pay generously. The expense will be trifling against what we propose to make from this scheme, and we must have a good spell.''

"It shall be done,'' said Axandrias, with enthusiasm.

"Therefore I abjure you not to drink too much tonight and so incapacitate yourself for tomorrow.''

"I never drink that deep, master. I long ago learned that the outlaw's life is ten times more perilous to a man who deliberately renders himself helpless. Such fools grace gibbets throughout the civilized world.''

"Then you are of my own way of thinking.'' Taharka surveyed the befuddled faces of his other men. He seized the leather cup from the benumbed fingers of one of the Bossonians and rattled the bone cubes inside. ''Now, my friends, who is for some serious dicing?''

As men tossed their gold onto the table, Taharka turned to Axandrias. ''What a fortune we could have made in this place with a few of those Cimmerians, eh?''

* * *

The next morning, after rising late, Axandrias commenced his search. A few questions asked of drug-sellers in the marketplace led his steps to a small temple. It was not easy to find, and he made several false starts before he turned down the correct alley. On either side bulked two warehouses. The first thing that Axandrias noted was that, unlike the other streets of this town, the alley was paved, and that the paving stones were worn smooth. He deduced that this alley was far older than anything else he had seen in the town. It was a small mystery, but the world was full of mystery and there was no profit to be had from lingering over this one.

The face of the temple blocked the end of the alley, and the sides of it seemed to extend well beyond the structures built against it. Behind the temple bulked the city wall, at about twenty paces distance. The facade of the temple almost discouraged Axandrias from setting foot inside.

The carvings were so ancient and weathered that their details were obscured. What was conveyed was not a vivid picture but a haunting impression of vast, chaotic forms of great power, and of vaguely manlike but repellently ophidian shapes moving through corridors that led from nowhere to nowhere. Surely, Axandrias thought, such a temple attracted few worshipers. He took a deep breath and stepped upon the portico and thence across the threshold.

Despite the warmth of the morning outside, there was a distinct chill within the temple. High on the walls, narrow slots admitted a feeble light. Axandrias found himself in a modest hypostyle hall. On either side of him, tall columns carved in the likeness of serpent-headed men extended in a double row that receded in the gloom. Their bowed shoulders supported the roof and their unblinking gaze was directed downward toward any who passed beneath.

Axandrias saw a light in the dense darkness at the far end of the room. With some trepidation, he began to walk toward it. Several times he stopped and squinted upward at the serpent heads above. Always they were blank and enigmatic, but as he walked he had the uncanny sensation that they moved slightly, and from the corners of his eyes he kept half-seeing a flash of motion, as if long, forked tongues darted from scaly mouths.

He reached the source of the light, and found that it was a flame burning in a brazen bowl. The bowl stood on a tripod, and he could see no trace of fuel to feed the flame. This did not disturb him unduly. Since he was something of a conjurer, he assumed that most wizard's feats were the same sort of trumpery.

Something disturbed him, and he looked back the way he had come. The bright rectangle of the doorway was at least fifty paces away. Yet, when he had stood before the temple, he had estimated that the city wall was no more than twenty paces away. That meant that this structure must extend through and well past the wall. It was another mystery, but he had not come here to sort out puzzles.

"What brings you here?" The voice came from behind him and Axandrias whirled, his hand darting to his sword hilt. The speaker was a tall, gaunt man dressed in a featureless black robe. He was shaven-headed, his cadaverous face as immoble as those of the stone serpents.

With a relieved sigh, Axandrias relaxed. "Your pardon, good priest. You startled me. I did not hear your approach. Are you the sole priest of this temple?"

"I am. The gods I serve are ancient beyond the dreams of men, and are all but forgotten in this decadent age." The priest's accent was strange. Axandrias was widely traveled but he had never heard its like. There was something odd in the man's phrasing as well.

"Perhaps times shall improve. As it occurs, I sought you out because I am in search of certain drugs and perhaps a spell or two. In the market, I was told that the priest of this temple often has on hand magical substances not available locally, and that he is a wizard of repute."

"Did they tell you that I am a peddler as they are?"

Axandrias knew it was time to shift emphasis from a purely businesslike approach. He had known many wizards like this one; improverished but too proud to admit that they needed to sell their wares and services to live.

"Good sir, such a thing is far from my mind. I am a student of the thaumaturgical arts, although a small one. I am now at work on a book concerning the effects of certain ferocity-inducing drugs and spells. In order to write with authority, I must experiment, that I may observe these effects firsthand."

The priest nodded. "That is the only true way to gain knowledge. The substances you seek are quite rare in this remote district. They must be imported from afar and are costly."

Axandrias smiled inwardly. At last they were getting to the bargaining. Still, he knew that he had to stick to his false scholarship. "I expected as much. I am of a good family and have funds. And gold is mere trash when one's goal is the acquisition of knowledge."

"Come with me." The priest led him around the

flaming bowl and through a small portal. They entered another long chamber. Once again, slots high on the walls admitted sunlight, but there was something subtly wrong with its color. Axandrias decided that the light must be coming through colored glass.

The room was full of devices, books and instruments such as the Aquilonian had never seen before. The one quality shared by all of them was the impression that they were incalculably ancient. There were instruments of silver, gold, and age-blackened bronze. Crystal glinted, and stones and jewels the like of which Axandrias had never seen. He stopped at a pedestal which supported a massive book, its cover graced with the facial bones of a human skull. The eye sockets were set with two immense rubies.

"This appears to be a tome of great power," Axandrias said. In truth, he was interested only in the rubies.

"Great indeed," intoned the priest in his sepulchral voice. He opened the cover and exposed the first page. It was an oddly thick and creamy parchment, inscribed all over in tiny characters the color of rusty iron. Axandrias touched the page and found it strangely smooth. He commented upon the fact.

"This is a book of spells written by the wizard-king Angkar, of the pre-Atlantean Empire of Walkh. To one who can read these characters are revealed the secrets of communication with beings that ruled the universe ere the earth was created. He was a sorcerer of all-embracing evil, such as is not seen in these times. He compiled this book as the masterwork of his reign. He had his fifty subject kings send him their daughters, more than nine hundred in all. These pages are made from the flayed skins of those princesses. The characters were written with the blood of royal infants. When the book was complete, he had the bones of his own face set into its cover, cut from his skull while he yet breathed. The binding is his own skin.''

Axandrias jerked his hand away as if the page was red-hot. ''Truly,'' he said in a shaky voice, ''we live in decadent times. No mage alive would attempt such wizardry.''

''Aye, the great Arts have fallen to low estate,'' the priest intoned. ''And yet, the good times will return. These walls have seen much. As ancient as this book is, this temple was already old when it was written. Continents have risen and sunk since its building. Many cities have stood on this spot. The tawdry village of Croton is only the most recent.''

The deep-sunk eyes of the priest glittered with a strange light. ''Before the barbaric Hyborians overran this part of the world, the great city of Karutonia stood here, now remembered only in the degenerate corruption of its name. More than a million inhabitants dwelled in that city, and the remains of its greatest temples and tombs, covered with earth and vegetation, still stand nearby. So huge are they that for thousands of years men have thought them to be natural hills.''

''Truly,'' Axandrias said, convinced now that the priest was quite mad, ''this is an ancient place.''

''Ancient?'' The priest emitted a dry, humorless laugh. ''The city of Karutonia was a recent upstart. This temple stood here when there was naught here but sandy desert. There was a time when it lay at the floor of a great inland sea. Eons have passed over this temple, leaving it unchanged. The winds and rains which have diminished the carvings of the facade have worn mountains down to piles of sand.''

''I can see,'' Axandrias said, desperate to change the

subject, "that I have come to the right place. To one who is privy to such secrets, the trifling things I seek must be as naught." Idly, he raised the hinged lid of a plain, copper bowl. Inside, he saw a mind-shattering vista of the gulfs of deep space. He was looking as if from above into a monstrous whirlpool of stars. Abruptly he slammed the lid shut and tried to make his stomach return to its accustomed position. The wizard seemed not to have noticed.

"I have what you want," the priest said. He crossed the room and opened the carved wooden doors of a cabinet. To the bandit's great relief, there were exposed only drawers and cubbyholes. The fragrances of exotic herbs filled the room. The priest pulled open a drawer and from it took a wooden box. He slid back the lid and showed Axandrias the contents. There were hundreds of balls of a greenish, gummy substance, each about the size of a dried pea.

"The outer coating of each pill," said the priest, "is the hardened gum of the julak tree of the Barachan Islands. This confers strength and endurance. Once it was commonly used by the elite guards of kings before going into battle. It has been mixed with a secretion taken from certain Stygian scarab beetles, conferring extraordinary quickness of body and eye. In the center of each is the gum of the green poppy. Its virtues are twofold: while the dose is working, the taker feels no fear, but instead a great urge to attack, and he is all but insensible to pain."

The priest placed the box upon a writing-stand and took up a brush, which he dipped in ink. As he wrote upon the lid, he continued. "As they are, one who has need of this medication may take it without great risk of harm, as long as it is used with discretion, at infrequent intervals.''

The priest showed Axandrias the lettering on the lid. It was in contemporary Aquilonian letters, but the syllables were in some repellent language. "If you recite this spell when you administer each dose, the effect is both quicker to take hold and greater in its power. However, it is destructive. One who takes it daily will be used up within a very short time. I suggest such use only on expendable slaves, convicts or the like.''

''Such was exactly my plan," Axandrias said. "And the price?''

''Five hundred Aquilonian gold pieces.'' It was steep, but Taharka had told him to be prepared to pay double that. He took a well-stuffed purse from within his tunic and counted out the money.

As the priest escorted him to the entrance, he said, ''Should you have need of other sorcerous aid, you may come to me. In these worldly times, I am always ready to help a student of the Great Arts.''

''Rest assured, sir, that I shall not hesitate to seek you out,'' said Axandrias, vowing inwardly to do nothing of the sort. As he walked away, the priest watched him. Slowly, the beginnings of a ghastly smile tugged the corners of his mouth slightly upward.

When Axandrias reached the mouth of the alley, he looked back and saw the face of the temple once more. Consumed with curiosity, he hurried down a side street until he came to a stairway which mounted the city wall. With his prize tucked inside his tunic, he went up the stair and then made his way gingerly along the ruinous wall. When he saw the two warehouses which flanked the temple, he leaned over and surveyed the view. As he had estimated below, the flat, featureless roof of the temple extended about twenty paces from the paved alley until it disappeared into the wall.

He turned and crossed the thickness of the wall, a distance of less than four paces. He leaned over the parapet, expecting to see the greater bulk of the temple extending beyond. There was nothing. Just a featureless face of rough stone wall and beyond that, a grassy field where oxen placidly cropped the vegetation. His scalp crawled and his mind reeled. Where was the rest of the temple?

That night, he violated his self-imposed stricture and drank himself into a stupor.

Four

"How could we have lost them?" Kalya demanded. "Might they have taken the great road to Belverus?"

"They may have taken the short road to Hell, for all I know," said Conan.

He had grown short-tempered in recent days as the trail had grown first cold, then nonexistent. Soon they would reach war-torn Ophir and the chances of finding their prey would become far slimmer.

At first, the tracking had been easy. Scarcely a day had passed when the carrion-birds had not led them to some half-hidden pile of corpses, stripped of all valuables. On more than one occasion, they had met with bands of king's men or local militias looking for bandits. Most of these believed the depradations of Taharka's band to be the work of local outlaws. The Keshanian was too clever to stay in one locale too long and thus attract undue attention. Conan could now see that he and the woman had become overconfident, thinking that their task was always to be easy. They had been preparing for the eventual fight, rather than concentrating on the pursuit.

"This Taharka is more clever than we had believed," Kalya said. "He has changed his tactics again. In Cimmeria and the borderlands he went slave-raiding. On the road to Ophir he turned to highway robbery, leaving no witnesses alive. Now he has found something else."

Conan reined to a halt. They were at the edge of the hills, and a great vista of grassland stretched before them. Soon they would be on the Ophirian plain. "Think you they no longer expect to go to Ophir?"

She shrugged. "Such men as we pursue seldom stick to a course of action. They are like children, setting out upon some enterprise only to turn aside at the first distraction. Perhaps they shall resume their trek to Ophir, perhaps they shall turn to some other work entirely. Whichever it is, I fear that if we continue, we shall only draw farther away from them."

Conan brooded over the problem. The limitless grassland called to him. He longed to gallop over its breadth and see what wonders it held. But his duty was to his mission of vengeance. He could indulge himself with rambling at some later date. He wheeled his mount.

"Let us go back and find where we lost them," the Cimmerian said.

A week later, the two dismounted before a tiny, wayside inn. It was little more than a watering trough for horses, a hut for cooking food and storing wine, and a shed for horse fodder. Before the hut was stretched an awning which sheltered a few rough tables and equally rough benches.

There were a half-dozen locals eating and drinking in the shade of the awning, and when Conan and Kalya had rubbed their horses down and let them drink, they took seats at a table and called for cooled wine. A plump, graying woman brought their wine, and as she set the flask down she eyed Conan with a look of concern.

"You're a sturdy lad," she said. "Were I you, I'd not be traveling in these parts with no companion save a girl."

"What does that mean, grandmother?" the Cimmerian asked. "Is their some special hazard to being sturdy?"

"Aye, so it would seem," she said. "Why, these fellows here were just speaking of it. There is a band of slavers abroad, raiding hither and yon. They have struck farms and homesteads, and have even been bold enough to enter some towns. Strange to say, they ignore women and children, and take only men in their best years, only the strong and fit."

"She speaks the truth, stranger," said a man who wore a teamster's jerkin. "They have struck two freighting-wagons belonging to my master, and took off some stout young men."

"They are Nemedians, so I'm told," said a man whose peddler's pack rested beside him. "Some have said that there are Argossians among them."

"They do not just raid," said a fat man in the garb of a royal executioner. "A few days ago, I stopped in the town of Volsino, where I was to hang two rogues for cattle thieving. The king's reeve spun out a story of how they committed suicide while in custody. A little questioning around town revealed that he had sold them to these Nemedians, thus cheating me of my fee. I shall report him for corruption when I return to the capital." He drained his cup indignantly.

"This is strange," said Kalya. "Strong men are always in demand as slaves, but so are women and children. The weaker sort are easier to herd and eat less, as well. I never heard of slavers passing up the easy prey and taking only strong men unless some king had a great building project calling for much labor."

"Nothing of that sort here," said the executioner. "Not since the old king's tomb was finished many years ago. The Stygians are forever building temples, but with war raging in Ophir, captives must be cheap and that is where they would buy them"

"It is all very strange," said a herdsman who smelled much like his cattle. "But I am too old to interest them, and I've sent my sons into the hill pastures until this danger is past."

"You need not worry about me, grandmother," Conan said. "It would take a bold slaver to capture me, and this girl is not as harmless as she looks."

When the woman had returned to the hut and the others were engaged in their conversations, Conan leaned across the table. "What think you of this? Might it have aught to do with Taharka and the others?"

"I cannot say, but I feel that there is some connection. The man is full of plots and schemes, and this may well be one of them. What its nature is I cannot yet tell, but it must be something crafty and devious."

"Yet the slavers are said to be Nemedians," Conan said.

"Nemedian clothes are as easy to put on as any. Raiders of any kind know how to use false colors. I think this is a good area in which to concentrate our search. If there is any new villainy being done, we can be fairly sure that Taharka and Axandrias are at the center of it."

While their horses rested, Conan and Kalya engaged the local men in conversation. Conan wished to put his questions bluntly, but each time he did Kalya kicked him beneath the table. He lapsed into sulky silence, but he listened closely. He began to admire the artful, subtle way the woman learned many things of use to them without arousing any suspicion or reserve in the cautious, distrustful countrymen.

One thing soon became apparent: The nearest town where rogues, smugglers, rebels, and the like gathered was called Croton, and it was little more than a day's ride away, in the direction of the Nemedian border.

The sun had almost set when they rode within sight of the town. Conan gazed with wonder at the beasts grazing around the walls. "Are those things camels?" he asked.

"Aye," said Kalya. "We are at the beginning of the eastern lands. Beyond are Nemedia, Brythunia, Corinthia, Zamora, Turan, and the Vilayet Sea."

"And beyond those?" Conan asked, his mind enthralled at the recitation of far lands and strange peoples.

"Lands that are part legend: Hyrkania, Khitai, Vendhya. Beyond them there is said to be a great ocean that stretches to the edge of the world."

"I will see them all some day," Conan vowed. "When I have finished my business with these bandits."

"You are a strange one, my friend." For a moment, the armed truce between them softened somewhat. "I have met fewer than a score of Cimmerians in my life, and those had little yearning to see far places. They all spoke only of returning home."

"I am not like my countrymen," Conan agreed. "Before I was old enough to hold a man's sword I was always at odds with any who would rule me or order my life. My father, the village elders, the chieftain of my clan, they all had a go at thrashing me until I grew too large for such treatment. When I earned my warrior's standing at Vanarium, they gave up trying."

"You were at Vanarium?" she said. The news of that battle had been all over Aquilonia and the borders a few seasons before; The Aquilonians had pushed across their borders onto ancestral Cimmerian lands and had built the city of Vanarium, manning it with Gunder and Bossonian frontiersmen. The Cimmerians had annihilated the settlement in a day and night of screaming slaughter. All three races were warlike in the extreme and fought without mercy.

Conan's face twisted, as if this had turned his thoughts down paths he did not wish to follow. "That is past," he said shortly. "Let us see what is to be found in this town of rogues."

They rode within the walls and found the stalls in the market being closed down for the night. In the numerous places of entertainment, lamps were being lit and music was playing. The day was over, and the evening had begun.

Kalya asked a rug-seller where they might find lodging. The man eyed their dusty, rather ragged dress dubiously. "The best entertainment and lodging is to be had at the Traveler's Paradise, but their rates have tripled since new nightly revels began. My advice is that you try one of the stables built against the city wall, near the gate. You can board your horses and rent a room upstairs for a pittance. It is much quieter than an inn and the fleas are no worse."

"We'll take your advice," said Conan. "What is this entertainment that has tripled the rates of the place you mentioned?"

"You mean you have not heard? Go there tonight, and I can guarantee that you will have an experience worth the admission price and the high rates for indifferent wine."

They found a stable as the man had advised, and arranged for lodging for themselves and their animals. A few doors away was a public bath house, and there the two soaked away the grime of travel. At this late hour they were the only patrons, and as Conan leaned back in the wooden tub he pondered their next move. The men's section of the bath was separated from the women's by a wooden screen covered with cloth. Through it he asked Kalya's opinion.

"I think the Traveler's Paradise is the place to look," she said.

"We came here to find the bandits," he said, "not for revelry."

"Can you think of a better place to look for them?" Her scorn was plain even through the partition. "Men such as they, with money to spend, are going to spend it in dissipation. If that place has the best entertainment, that is where they will be."

"It may be the kind of place where women are not welcome," he cautioned.

"So was the place where I learned the art of the sword. I forced myself in and made them teach me anyway. If necessary, I will do the same here."

"You have the habit of getting your own way," he agreed.

"A woman alone who would make her own way in the world cannot be a weakling. We cannot all start out in life as hulking barbarians."

Conan winced. "You've a tongue like a swordmaker's file, woman, but I take your point. Very well, we shall go to this place of revelry, and if any object to your presence, we shall draw steel and lay them low!"

She gave one of her rare, musical laughs. "So we

shall, Cimmerian! That is the kind of talk I like to hear!''

In the event, there was no objection to Kalya's entering Traveler's Paradise. The steep admission price left them with little gold, but the crowds flocking to the place seemed to think the spectacle was worth it. As they pushed their way into the inn, the uproar was deafening. They took tankards of overpriced ale from a serving woman and tried to find out what was causing all the excitement.

At the serving woman's advice, they found a stairway and mounted to one of the galleries that ran around the courtyard. The press was considerably less on the balconies, and the noise fractionally less as well. A few men seemed to find Kalya's eyepatch to be no diminution of her desirability, and some whispered proposals in her ear. Conan buried a knotty fist in the belly of one, and they stepped over his gagging form. At another's proposal, Kalya's dagger flashed from beneath her cape to slice his belt in twain. His breeches fell to his ankles and he stumbled over the railing to fall onto a table below. This stimulated roars of laughter.

The two elbowed a space at the railing and found they were looking downward into a pit beside a fountained pool. In the pit, two armed men faced one another. They wore shiny iron skullcaps and studded wristbands, plated groinguards and nothing else. Each held a short, heavy sword with a slightly curved blade. Each had a small shield, no more than a foot in diameter, on his forearm.

''A fighting-pit,'' Kalya murmured. ''Have you ever seen such?''

''Aye,'' Conan said. ''In Vanaheim and Hyperborea.''

"Are there none in Cimmeria?" she asked. Her face was a bit pale despite her offhand words.

"Nay. My people do not keep slaves, nor do the Gundermen. The Picts only rarely. I fear we are too primitive."

"It is a civilized taste, to be sure," she said. Then, with puzzlement, "Something does not look right about those men."

The word to begin had not yet been called. Bets were still being placed. The men glared at one another with bulging eyes, their fingers worked restlessly on the hafts of their weapons. One trembled all over like a high-strung horse before a race. In his few years, Conan had fought men of many nations, and he knew that few of them had the relaxed Cimmerian approach to mortal combat.

"They are slaves made to fight," he said. "Not warriors."

"It is unnatural," she insisted. "I have only one good eye, but I can see when men are afraid. Those two have no fear, only hate and the desire to close with one another, to cut and kill. Men forced to fight strangers should not be that way."

"What do you mean to imply?" Conan asked uncomfortably.

"I do not know. I—" She was interrupted by the bellowed order to commence. A great shout went up as the two rushed together.

Despite his revulsion at the vicarious blood-lust of the crowd, Conan found himself to be fascinated by the combat. As Kalya had said, the men had no fear of one another. Both were well-muscled young men, well-matched in height and weight. They fought aggressively, their blows licking out with great rapidity.

Although the swords had clipped, upturned points, they were better designed for cutting than for the thrust. Thus were they used.

The little shields blocked most of the blows but, inevitably, a few got through. Neither man seemed to notice his wounds. They struck viciously, heedless of danger.

"Brave but stupid," Conan muttered. "I have always preferred attack to defense, but what good does it to wound an enemy if you are wounded yourself?"

"That was a shrewd cut!" Kalya said, clenching her gauntleted fist tightly as blood flowed below. "But look, he makes no sign he has felt it!"

"One often does not feel the pain of wounds in the midst of combat," Conan said. "That comes afterward."

"Not where he was wounded," she asserted. "See, they are slowing. But I swear it is from loss of blood and naught else."

They leaned far over the railing, and to hear one another above the uproar they had to place their heads close together. So close that, around her eyepatch, Conan could see a line of puckered scar tissue.

Below, a sword flashed and a man howled with rage and hate. The loser doubled over, his arms folded across his belly as he tried to keep his guts from pouring forth. It was futile, and he died making incoherent sounds. The victor raised his arms in triumph as coins showered around him. He staggered off and attendants tidied up the pit as the next pair were brought on.

Conan and Kayla watched three more pairs fight. Each time they saw the same thing: mindless ferocity, moderate skill, absolute absence of fear, and no reaction to pain. Blood loss, severed muscles or nerves, cut and spilled organs decided each combat.

As the last dead combatant was dragged away, Conan and Kalya surveyed the galleries and the courtyard below. The uproar quieted and many began to leave. The more sedate pastimes of drinking, wenching and gambling resumed their hold on the patrons' attention.

"Do you see anyone who deserves a closer look?" Kalya asked.

"No, but—" Conan's gaze caught something. On the far side of the courtyard, beneath the gallery, a row of shields were propped against the wall, along with spears and other staff weapons and a few walking-sticks too awkward to bear among the crowd. They were guarded by a dull-faced man with a club. Two familiar staves of yew leaned casually among the other weapons.

"There," he said, pointing, "against the far wall, between a Kordavan poleax and a silver-headed staff. Two Bossonian longbows. We are far from the Marches to see two such weapons."

Kalya smiled, and the demented gleam returned to her eye. "There are two men nearby with whom we should have some words."

Conan leaned on his elbow, chin cupped in a hard palm. He did not take his eyes from the bows, lest the weapons should be retrieved while he and his companion were not looking. "How should we go about this? Should we slay them, or take them aside and question them, or follow them to where the others are?"

"I recommend we take them to some private spot and find out what they know. If you slay them out of hand, part of your vengeance will be done, but I will be no closer to mine." She sipped at her ale meditatively. "It may be that the others have ridden on and these two have stayed behind. If so, we must know of it. As for following them," she thought for a moment, "it is tempting but dangerous. If they have separated, we might trail them for days accomplishing naught while the others draw farther away. Even should they lead us to the band this very evening, we might find ourselves facing six hard men. And it is likely that the band has grown. Your business is only with the six you were tracking. Mine is only with Axandrias. We do not want to take on perhaps ten or twenty at once.''

"That is excellent reasoning,'' Conan said. He drained his tankard and set it on a vacant table. ''When the Bossonians come to fetch their bows, we shall follow them to some deserted spot and ask them a few questions. When they have answered to our satisfaction, they are dead men.''

For the next hour, the two idled near the entrance of the inn, pretending an interest in the many games of chance that absorbed the others. They scanned the crowd carefully, but saw none who answered the descriptions of the bandits. The Bossonians were nowhere to be seen. Conan could see no Gunderman, and there was no dark southerner present. Aquilonians were numerous, but Kalya insisted that none was Axandrias. ''I would know that snake at the bottom of a well on a moonless night.''

Kalya had lapsed into the wordless, staring trance that had earned her the name of madwoman when Conan elbowed her side. ''The upper gallery, straight across from us,'' he said. She looked up and beheld two men emerging from a room opening onto the upper balcony. This was where the local trollops had been taking their customers all evening.

''It looks,'' she said, ''as if their tastes run to venery rather than pit combat.''

There was no mistaking their nationality. Both were

stocky men of medium height, strongly made. The hair of both was brown and square-cut. They closely resembled one another save the eyes of one were gray, those of the other, brown. They wore close-fitting steel caps and the padded, sleeveless leather jerkins favored by Bossonian archers, thickly covered with silver and bronze studs. They wore tight-fitting breeches of brown leather and soft, knee-length boots of the same material. The left forearm of each was encased in a bracer of stiff leather, fancifully decorated on its outer surface, but perfectly smooth inside to protect the arm from the snap of the bowstring. Short swords and daggers hung from chains at their belts.

The two descended the stair and crossed the noisy courtyard. They exchanged a few words with the man who guarded the weapons and shields, then they took their bows. With each weapon was an arrow-case of decorated leather, bristling with slender, bright-feathered shafts. They had not noticed that they were being watched by a Cimmerian and a one-eyed woman as they descended the stairs. By the time they picked up their weapons, there were no such persons in the inn.

Outside, the Bossonians began to make their way toward their lodgings. Bows held casually on their shoulders, they conversed in low voices. There was no public lighting in the city, but the moon was high in a clear sky, nearly three-quarters full. The light was plentiful for men raised in the dense woods of the Bossonian Marches, where men rarely lit fires at night lest they draw marauding Picts like a beacon.

They turned down an alley and went a few steps within. What happened next occurred so swiftly that the men were too bewildered to think or react. There was no warning sound as a pair of powerful hands swept

their skullcaps off from behind. The hands then closed
on the sides of their heads and cracked them together. A
dagger flashed twice and their sword-belts were jerked
away as the hands slammed into their backs, flattening
them against the wall of the alley. There was a hiss of
steel being drawn as they were jerked around to face
their assailants. The point of a sword dug beneath the
chin of each Bossonian. One blade was slender and
curved, its hilt in the hand of a one-eyed woman. The
other brand was broad and straight, and its wielder—

"Cimmerian!" hissed the gray-eyed man. "What black
fortune brings a dog of your race to this place?"

"Speak swiftly if you would enjoy breathing a while
longer," said the Cimmerian. "Are your names Murtan
and Ballan?"

"Why should we answer a swine of a blackhair and a
near-naked wench?" spat the one with brown eyes. He
winced as the point of the woman's sword lanced in and
a warm curtain of blood began to flow down his neck.

"Because we are the ones with swords at your necks,"
said Kalya. "Not you at ours. We will ask questions
and you will answer or die. It is that simple." She dug
her point in further for emphasis.

"I am Murtan," said Gray-Eyes. "And this is Ballan.
What of it?"

"I have sought you for a long while," Conan said
urgently. "You wiped out a Cimmerian family. They
were my friends and I have come to exact vengeance
for them!"

The man half-smiled despite the steel at his throat.
"So we did. What are a few less blackhair warriors and
their wenches? I wish their brats had been there too."

"These are a hard pair, Conan," said Kalya. Both
weapon-belts dangled from her hand and the Bossonians

eyed them the way starving men look at food. "Their manners might be improved." Her point flashed to the man's face and rested just beneath his eye. "There is no pain like that of losing an eye. I can vouch for it."

"Speak!" Conan barked. "You can die easy or die hard, but die you shall! Where are the rest of those who raided the Cimmerian steading? I want Taharka and the two Gundermen and the Aquilonian, Axandrias. Are they all still with you?"

Murtan shrugged, eyes still on his weapon-belt. "What are they to us? Aye, the wily Keshanian is still our leader. The Gunder brothers do this bidding as well."

"And Axandrias?" Kalya hissed. "What of him?"

The man eyed her with studied bravado. "You must be one of those wenches he always brags about, the ones he has used and left weeping behind him. Aye, the slimy city-man yet draws breath and grows closer with Taharka each passing day."

"Where are they?" Conan asked.

"On a slave-raid with the Argossians," said Ballan. "They should be back here tomorrow or the next day."

"It's true, then," said Conan. "They are the ones who have been taking slaves. And they put them in the pit to fight, is that not so?"

"Aye," said Murtan. "It is something Taharka and Axandrias cooked up between them. It is something involving a drug and magical spells. Axandrias fancies himself a great wizard. We merely get our orders to go slave-taking. It has been an easy life, but we were of a mind to leave the band and strike off on our own, now that the brown man and the Aquilonian have grown too good to let us in on their plots."

"We have learned what we needed from them,"

Conan said to the woman. "Have you any further use for them?"

"Nay." She dropped her point from Ballan's throat. "These two are nothing to me. It is Axandrias I want. Do as you will with them."

As she stepped back Conan snatched the weapon-belts from her hand and cast them at the feet of their owners. "There are your swords," Conan said. "Use them!"

Kalya stared at him incredulously. "Slay them now, fool! Is it vengeance you want, or glory?"

Ballan grinned wolfishly as he drew his sword, rubbing a hand over his punctured neck. "This is a Cimmerian, wench. I was more worried about you than this black-haired dog."

"Stand aside while we carve him," said Murtan. "We'll make use of you later. Your face is ill-favored but your body looks usable. Your little scraps of mail will be of no avail then."

Enraged, Kalya would have attacked them but Conan held up a restraining palm. "I'll not cut down unarmed men. But two armed Bossonians with swords and armor are not much more dangerous than one who is naked. Ask the ghosts who still haunt the ruins of Venarium, where my clan now pastures its cattle in winter."

At the mention of Venarium, the two snarled and began their attack. Their swords were short cut-and-thrust weapons, wasp-waisted and with long points apt for stabbing. They held the blades low, for a dagger-style upward thrust. Since their enemy wore no armor, they saw no need for a powerful chop or slash that would take more time to execute.

Conan stepped back and held his longer, heavier blade with a one-handed grip. Since he did not know which of the two would attack first, he did not bother with a guard position. Instead he stood casually, with his sword held loosely by his side. His pose was as relaxed as that of a great, predatory cat, and as deceptive.

Kalya held her breath, sure that the Cimmerian would be cut down in an instant, so unprepared did he appear. Her own school of the blade had emphasized many formalized poses and complicated, dance-like exercises. Her teachers had insisted that only by mastering all of these movements could one be safe from all possible attacks.

As Murtan darted in for a gutting stroke, the Cimmerian changed in an eyeblink from immobility to blinding speed. The long blade flicked across his body as he stepped forward, then flashed across again in an ascending backhand stroke. Simultaneously, Conan's left hand gripped Murtan's wrist behind the sword and jerked it aside. The rising blade caught Murtan just above the right hip, slashing upward through leather, flesh and bone. Conan continued his forward movement and as his sword broke free of Murtan's ribcage it continued its path to slash across Ballan's face.

The second Bossonian began to stagger back, and at that instant Conan's right foot came down and the sword reversed its direction and smashed down on Ballan's shoulder, shearing through collarbone and ribs, splitting the heart before the big Cimmerian twisted his blade free of clinging bone.

Kalya blinked, unable to believe the reality of what she had seen. She sorted it out in the few seconds that the Bossonians spent in jerking and spasming out their lives on the cobblestones. A fight that consisted of three blows, two of them mortal. All of them struck by one man before his foes could strike effectively. Her swordmasters had told her that the ascending backhand blow was the weakest possible stroke, as the descending oblique was the strongest. The latter had the full weight and most of the muscle power of the body behind it, while the former utilized only the muscles of one shoulder. They had taught her that certain very skilled fighters could use the muscles of the flank and the leading leg as well. She had seen that blow tear through leather, bone and flesh as through so much smoke. The man's art was minimal, but his speed, strength, timing, and coordination were little short of supernatural.

"That is two of them accounted for," Conan said as he cleaned his blade. With a single, sweeping movement, he returned it to its sheath. "Now we can wait for the other four. Check their purses. We can use more money."

She rifled the mens' pouches with the cold-blooded efficiency of the adventurer who lives ever upon the edge of existence. It was not theft to take valuables from a slain enemy.

"Men call me Mad Kalya," she said, "but I never saw anyone as mad as you! You set out willing to cross the world to avenge people who were not even your kin, yet when you catch two of the slayers, you are not willing to simply cut them down as they deserve." She looked up at him furiously. "These were not only murderers but slavers! Yet you let them fight man-to-man, as if they were honorable warriors!"

"Man-to-men," Conan corrected her. "To fight them one at a time would have been to give them too much honor. They were Bossonians. They knew Cimmerians. When I gave them back their weapons and challenged them to fight me together, it was the greatest insult I could have offered them and they were well aware of it. Rest assured, they died in the deepest shame.''

''Did you not think—'' she had been about to protest that, had Conan failed, the Bossonians might have sought to carry out their designs upon her. She felt an involuntary shudder at the thought of the two of them taking out their rage and humiliation on her. Then she stifled her protest, thinking that the Cimmerian might think it the cavil of a timid and unwarriorlike person. ''How could you be so sure you were not underestimating them?'' she amended hastily.

He thought for a moment as she scooped the dead mens' valuables into a purse. As they walked away from the alley, he answered her. ''The Bossonians are the enemy of my race, but they are for the most part an honorable people. These were scum, outcast from their people, and such men are rarely first-rank warriors.'' Unspoken but plain was his belief that he ranked high in that fraternity. ''Also, while the Bossonians are valiant fighters, stubborn and all but unbeatable when they are defending, they are not so skillful in the attack. Attacking and counterattacking are what we Cimmerians do best of all the world.''

His confidence was obviously unbendable. She decided to change the subject. ''This will keep us for a long time,'' she said, tossing up the well-stuffed purse. It was made of scarlet-dyed Kordavan leather and its embroidery of gold thread flashed in the moonlight. ''Those two were bearing more gold than I have seen in months. We may live high for many weeks, even months. Should Taharka and the rest somehow slip away from us, with care we can make this last for far longer. Buying only enough food to sustain us and our horses, this might carry us for the better part of a year. We can always sleep in the open in good weather.''

"That is excellent," Conan said abstractedly. "It could be a problem in this kind of pursuit should we be distracted from time to time by the need for more money. It is not surprising that they were well-supplied with gold. All the bodies we found on the road must have represented much loot. And this new slaving venture must be bringing them great profits.''

"Aye." She felt that she was speaking to fill the silence, and she had thought herself too sensible for that. She had been more comfortable when her relationship with the big Cimmerian youth was little more than suspended hostility. She had sworn before the altar of Mitra to have nothing to do with any man. Axandrias had been the cause of that, and every time she thought of him, her ruined eye burned as fiercely as when he had destroyed it with his red-hot iron.

Five

The priest cast some herbs into a brazier of glowing charcoal. The brazier was wrought into the form of three intertwining serpents, their heads on the floor and their tails holding a skull, its cranium removed to form the bowl holding the charcoal. All was wrought from the coffins of Valusian kings. Even the charcoal was of sorcerous significance. The wood of gallows had been employed in its manufacture. The smoke did not rise as natural smoke does. Instead, it writhed down the sides of the brazier in snakelike twists and made its way ropily to the floor.

The priest chanted long prayers and spells. He had been keeping up the chanting for many hours. The discipline of high sorcery required an endurance that would have felled all but the mightiest warriors. Each word was pronounced with perfect precision, and was pronounced with equal perfection no matter how many times it was repeated.

Long past midnight, a glowing ball formed above the brazier. For many minutes the ball wavered and pulsed, sometimes growing brighter, sometimes fading almost to obscurity. Gradually, it grew steadily stronger and a shadowy face began to take form within. The face was human, but its features were too perfect for true humanity. It was as if a sculptor had put together all the features men found closest to perfection and then animated it. Perfect though it was, it was not beautiful, for it lacked any trace of human feeling.

"It has been many years since you have contacted us," said the face above the brazier. The language was a very archaic form of pre-Stygian.

"This ancient temple has been far from the great paths of human events for generations," said the priest. "There has been naught for me to concern myself with save ceremonies, the working of wizardry, and the ineffable world of the supernatural. Now it seems that events of true significance are forming a nexus in this place."

"We had been aware for some time that shadowy forces have been making their way toward Karutonia, now called Croton. When all the forces reach the nexus-point, events of some interest may occur. What have you to report?"

"The things that have transpired so far have appeared trivial on the surface, but all the tests I have applied indicate that these are the precursors of great events. Some days ago, a man came to this temple, seeking certain drugs and spells. He was just a contemptible little bandit, posing as a student of the Great Arts. I would have had nothing to do with the scum, but just before his arrival I had warning of his significance. Therefore I pretended trust and interest, and let him have what he sought. I found that he and his cronies have used it to profit from a revival of slave-fighting."

The priest paused and inhaled deeply of the smoke coming from the brazier. "Yestereven, another event took place. Two strangers arrived. One was a great, swaggering bravo from the north; a mere boy, but he bears the look of the old Atlantean kings. His companion is a woman who has had all the softness burned out of her, to be replaced with warrior's steel. These two thirst for vengeance and little else. No sooner than they arrived they had sought out and slain two of the bandit's confederates. This I saw through the eyes which I have in place in every corner of this squalid little town.

"What these things portend I cannot as yet say. It is difficult to imagine such puny human matters attracting the interest of higher Powers."

"All the pieces are not yet in place," said the face. "You will keep us informed daily of new developments. Until this matter is resolved, we will devote much observation to events in that sector. Hold yourself in readiness for the return of the Masters."

"Until they return, lord, I wait," intoned the priest. He bowed deeply until his forehead touched the floor.

Conan awoke with steel half-drawn. The room was darkened, illumined only by a shaft of moonlight slanting through the latticed window. What had awakened him? As he rolled from the single bed, he thought he saw something at the window. It looked like a human face, but tinier than any human head could be. In two quick strides he crossed to the window and thrust open the intricately carved wooden screen.

There was nothing but a view of the town's rooftops, silver-lit by the moon's rays. He shook his head and rubbed a hand across his face. Perhaps an owl had perched upon the sill, and his half-sleeping imagination had given it human semblance. As he crossed back to his bed, he passed the sleeping, cloaked form of Kalya. In her usual fashion, she sat with head on knees while Conan occupied the room's sole bed. Their new affluence had permitted them the luxury of a room in a true inn, high beneath the eaves.

Something glinted on the carpet next to the woman and Conan poked at it curiously. It was the light steel plate and scraps of mail that served her as clothing. He grinned slightly at the sight. Apparently, even Mad Kalya was not hardy enough to wear steel all night. She stirred slightly. So silent had been his movements that he had not awakened her, although he knew the woman to be as alert as a cat.

Awake, he began to prowl restlessly. They had stayed near the Traveler's Paradise throughout the previous day, but the slavers had not put in an appearance. It did not seem likely that they would vacate the district while their business was flourishing, so the two had decided to remain in Croton until the men appeared or they had definite word that they had fled. Their greatest fear was that the whole pack might be apprehended and hanged by the authorities, cheating Conan and Kalya of their just vengeance.

Unable to return to sleep, Conan rose soundlessly and opened the door. Its oiled hinges did not squeak. He descended the stairs past three floors of chambers and to the common room. The inn was silent except for muffled snores. The common room was dimly lit by banked fires.

Outside, the streets were dark and still. The moon lay low in the west, its slanting light casting deep shadows among the buildings. The only signs of life were occasional unsteady torches borne by late revelers wending their way back to their quarters.

He paced about for a few minutes. There was nothing for him to do here. He turned to return to the inn when a voice stopped him.

"Young man, tarry a moment." The voice came from a dark alcove nearby.

Conan whirled, drawing his blade. "Who speaks? Show yourself quickly!"

A man stepped from the doorway. He was wrapped in a dark cloak, its hood shadowing his face. "Do I look so formidable? I bear no weapon, surely I am no threat to such a warrior as you."

Chagrined, Conan slammed his sword back into its sheath, the hilt making a solid clack as it struck the bronze throat. "Who are you, who lurk in dark doorways?"

"I am nobody, a mere humble priest of gods nearly forgotten. There are some questions I would ask you. Come with me to my temple where we may talk. I will make it worth your time. You are fond of gold, are you not?"

"Aye, but I've enough of that just now. What interest could you have in me? I do not know you or your gods." Conan was instantly suspicious.

"My questions concern a band of slavers, among whom is an Aquilonian mountebank."

"What do you know of them?" Conan said urgently.

"Let us retire to my temple," said the priest smoothly. "There, all shall be made plain."

"It had better be," Conan muttered. He felt that he was doing this against his better judgment, but if this man knew something of Taharka and the others he might be worth speaking to. As he followed the cloaked figure, his hand rested upon his sword-grip. Conan was young and inexperienced in the ways of civilized men, but he was not stupid. This might be a trap.

As he saw it, there was only one way a man of this town could know of a connection between himself and Taharka's band: Someone must have seen him kill the two Bossonians. If so, word might have been carried to the outlaw, and this man might have been sent to lure him into an ambush. The prospect did not vex him overmuch. Such was his youthful confidence that he thought he might cut his way free, perhaps slay the four remaining killers, and be free of his obligation in a few minutes of bloody work. Free to ride south, to ride east, to Zamora and Turan and those other lands he had heard Kalya and many others speak of.

This very day, as they had idled their time away, he had spoken to many traders and caravaners in the marketplace, his ears drinking in tales of foreign lands. Even this little town was an interesting place, filled as it was with people of many nations and the goods of those lands. The tales of huge cities with their tall, mysterious towers and their ancient buildings, tombs, and palaces filled him with the urge to go and view them with his own eyes.

As they turned down the paved alley, the young Cimmerian eyed the front of the temple. It was too dark to make out any detail. As for the man being a priest, he had no feelings one way or the other. Conan disliked wizardry intensely, but not all priests were wizards. He had met priests of Mitra, and of other gods, who were no worse than other men. His own god was Crom, who had no priesthood. Civilization was different, he knew. His kin would have laughed at the idea of one whose profession was to mediate between Crom and the Cimmerians.

As soon as he walked into the temple, Conan felt uncomfortable. He felt no presence of attackers, something indeed that he would have welcomed. Nor did he feel the presence of great, unclean sorcery. Rather it was the incredible age of the place, the certainty that it was far too old to have been built by truly human hands, that laid a chill coil around his spirit. He did not like this place, but a combination of pride and curiosity kept him from turning on his heel and walking away.

"What gods are worshipped here?" Conan said, feeling oppressed and subdued by the age of the place and its massive, uncanny architecture. Once again, up among the snake-heads, he thought he saw a tiny human face peering out at him. It was gone before he could be sure he had seen anything.

"The beings to whom this temple is dedicated," the priest said, "are not gods in the usual sense. They are beings unimaginably ancient and vast, but they are natural creatures of this universe, as are we. Their powers are truly godlike, as men reckon such things. We their priests do not truly worship them. We *contact* them. We do their bidding, and in return they grant us powers and other rewards."

None of this made much sense to Conan. He found most civilized religions ridiculous and this one sounded more nonsensical than most. "What are their names?" he asked idly. They were approaching a basin where a fuelless flame burned. The flames were greenish, and he felt no heat from them.

"Our gods have no name that humans could pronounce. We have titles for their kind: the Ancient Ones, the Great Powers. Most often we just call them the Masters. There are titles for individuals as well: the One Who Is Born From the Dead Star, the Suicidal God, and so forth. The Stygians set great store by their Set, whom they would have men think to be the most ancient of gods, yet Set the Old Serpent is an infant compared to the Ancient Ones, a mere reflection of their power and magnificence.''

''I want nothing to do with your gods, priest,'' Conan said. The uncanny flames would not release his attention. He put forth his hand and passed it through the fire. He felt nothing save a slight tingling. ''What manner of fire is this, that burns green and has no heat?''

The priest gave the faintest of smiles. ''This is one of the instruments whereby we contact our gods. Much of our communication is carried on via the flames. Fire is one of the elements, and the fire we know here on Earth is a gross and impure version of the true celestial flame.''

Conan nodded slowly, half-hypnotized by the blaze. ''Aye, my father was a blacksmith, and he taught me somewhat of the properties of fire.''

''This fire,'' said the priest, ''has already told me something of you. You are not as other men.''

''Eh? Of course not. I am a Cimmerian, and we are better than all lesser men.''

''That is not what I meant. Just now, for instance, you passed your hand through the pure flame. Had you been an ordinary man, your hand would have been instantly seared to the bone.''

''What!'' Conan snapped from his near-trance and turned on the man. ''And you did not warn me!'' He gripped his sword-hilt so tightly that his knuckles shone white.

The priest stepped back, appalled for a moment by

the unbridled savagery in the man's blue eyes. This was like dealing with a half-tamed tiger, one minute calm and courteous, the next blazing with primitive ferocity. He had met the like before, but it had been many years. Such barbarians were rare at any time. Savages there were in plenty, ferocious but unthinking, bound by custom and superstition. Civilized men were ruled by law and authority, although there were numerous outlaws among them who rejected those bonds. Rare indeed was the true barbarian, and rarest of all was such a man who was willing to leave tribe and clan behind to carve his own way in the world.

There had been men of this sort in the past, men who had become legends and centers of entire myth-cycles. They had become generals, kings, emperors, breathing a new and vital life into decrepit civilizations. They had overflowing, primitive life-force and a capacity for appalling violence.

The priest held forth a calming hand. "Hold! I knew you would suffer no harm, man. It is my art to know such things. Let us talk peaceably, and I shall explain. There are things I must know about you. In return, I can help you to deal with those you seek."

"Why do I need you?" Conan asked. "Soon they must return from their latest raid and at that time I will settle accounts with them."

"Your steel will not be sufficient," the priest warned him. "Taharka of Keshan is more than he seems, as are you. If you would defeat him, you must understand him."

"Why?" Conan demanded. "I will challenge him, fight him and cut him down. That is simple and the spirits of my friends will be satisfied."

The priest was patient. He spoke carefully, but not so

simply as to insult the volatile Cimmerian. "Were he an ordinary man, that would be sufficient. But, were the two of you men of ordinary stature, my attention would never have been drawn to you."

"Go on," said Conan, sullenly. He did not like the sound of this. Why should some priestly complication come between him and his vengeance? Still, he had to know if there was aught to what the man claimed.

"First, tell me something of your people and your ancestry."

"I am no poet," Conan muttered, "but I remember a bit of our people's history." He began to recite the tale of his family and clan. Like most barbarian peoples, to whom family lineage was everything, the Cimmerians kept careful genealogies. Although Conan was not one of those specially trained to store such things in his memory, any clansman could easily call to mind several centuries' worth of his own clan's history.

"That is sufficient," said the priest when the lengthy recitation was done. "I now have enough direction to guide me. Now I wish you to hold forth your hand over the flame. Cut yourself so that a few drops of blood fall within the bowl."

"I will do no such thing!" said the Cimmerian, scornfully. "I want no part of your spells."

The priest smiled slightly. "Afraid of a little bloodshed? Have no fear, I will cast no spell on you. The history of any race is in its flesh and blood. By a certain art which my order commands, I can conjure somewhat of your past from your blood. It could explain much."

Conan was nettled by the imputation that he was afraid to shed his own blood. An older man might have been more cautious, but he impetuously thrust his left hand over the heatless flame and made a shallow scratch with the point of his dagger. Drops of crimson fell into the bowl, but to his surprise they did not splash to the bottom, but instead vanished amid the green flames.

The priest chanted in a low voice, almost whispering. The Cimmerian youth stared into the flames once more, and again they exerted their hypnotic power upon his senses. The flames began to take on color, and in their depths vague, gorgeous shapes began to move. Pictures formed, and in a manner unclear to him he was drawn, dreamlike, into them.

He saw bands of dark-haired, white-skinned warriors locked in furious combat with rivals whose hair was golden or red, and with others who had tawny hair, or dark skins. These were his own people, the Cimmerians, and their enemies were the Aesir and Vanir, the Hyperboreans and Picts. They might have been his own close kinsmen, save their weapons were of bronze instead of steel. He knew that he was seeing his ancestors many centuries ago, before they had steel.

Soon he saw similar people, and their weapons and tools were of polished stone. They roamed up and down frozen valleys where the ice never melted, and they battled other men, and white snow-apes, and creatures for which he had no names. Somehow, he knew vaguely, the priest was taking him back through the history of his people. There were wanderings before the ice-times, when the Cimmerians clashed with a race of small men who rode across broad plains as one with their stocky, tough ponies. There were years in overgrown, jungle-clad mountains and valleys where giant serpents slithered and drums pounded a monotonous beat and tall, spear-bearing black men came forth to dispute passage, chanting savage war-songs from behind long hide shields.

Still further back did the flames take him. There was

a time of cataclysm, when mountains erupted into towers of fire and smoke, liquid rock forming glowing rivers down their slopes, a time when seas rose to cover continents and ocean-bottoms became dry land. Again he saw his people in an earlier age, and always they struggled and slew.

He saw men like himself, now not so primitive, but wearing barbaric finery of bright silk and feathered headdresses. He saw them knee-deep in water, repelling an invasion of people he knew to be Picts, but these Picts came in huge, double-hulled canoes such as no Picts now used. He saw a man seated upon a golden throne, chin on a great, knotted fist, his eyes haunted. Beside him was a two-handed sword and on his head was a crown. In face and form, he might have been Conan's twin.

Back and further back they went until his brain reeled with the span of time he was witnessing. Eventually, he saw a forest glade in which a family of hairy, almost-human creatures looked curiously at one of their children, whose skin was not so hairy and who could do things beyond the capabilities of its siblings. Then Conan was looking upon green flames once more.

He shook his head, deeply perplexed. "What was the meaning of that, priest? It seemed to me as if I beheld the whole history of my race, long ere they set foot in Cimmeria."

"That is exactly what you saw," the priest confirmed. "The history of each man's ancestors is written in his blood as on parchment. It may be read by one who knows how to release the tale."

"If this is true," Conan said, "then my people are far more ancient than any tale-teller has guessed."

"Most races are," said the priest. "Most cultures

remember only their recent history, a few centuries, a few thousand years at most. Yet men existed when the continents had different shapes than they bear now. Your people identify themselves with their mountainous, foggy Cimmeria, but they were the same people when the mountains of the North were islands in a great sea, peopled by pre-human creatures who no longer inhabit this world. And, as I had thought, yours is the blood of the conquering kings of Valusia, Thule and Commoria. In the ages since that time, they have degenerated into creatures little better than the apes they sprang from, to climb once more to barbaric culture, yet they have remained the same people.''

Conan did not like to think about such things. The very idea of the briefness and triviality of a single human existence compared to such a vista cut the ground from beneath a man's feet. ''What has all this to do with my mission?'' he growled.

''A great deal.'' The priest waved toward a doorway. ''Come, let us sit and discuss this.''

Feeling as if he had been riding for days without rest, Conan followed the priest. The room to which he was led was, to his relief, without exotic furnishings. There was a table of heavy carved wood, two chairs made in the same fashion, a sideboard set with flasks and goblets, and little else. The walls were covered with plain hangings and there was a single window, now tightly shuttered. At the priest's gesture, he sat in one thickly cushioned chair and was shocked at how exhausted he was.

The priest took a flask from the sideboard and poured two goblets full. He handed one to Conan, who was not too tired to wait until the other man had drunk before trying his own. The wine was rich and refreshing, a far finer vintage than the rough tavern-drink to which he was accustomed.

The priest sat. "We have had this night a glimpse of what lies in your past. Your ancestors have moved through some of the great ages of recent history." (*Recent* history? Conan thought.) "There have been few great men or great events of late. It is as if the gods and the Ancient Ones had lost interest in the petty affairs of mere men." He took a sip of his wine and pondered for a moment.

"In the past few years, something has changed. Certain ones have arisen among us; persons of destiny like those of elder times. These are persons marked out for great things, by the gods, or by other Powers. It may be that the great days are to come again." The man's eyes glowed with unhealthy anticipation, and Conan reminded himself that the priest was not acting out of pure benevolence, surely. "The priests of my order are trained to recognize the signs which identify such people and such events. It is my belief that you are such a man. Taharka of Keshan is another."

This was getting entirely too complicated. "Taharka is a mortal man," Conan insisted, "as am I. So are the two Gundermen and the Aquilonian mountebank. When we meet, we shall draw steel and learn which of us is the better. I have yet to find the man who is my match with any weapon."

"There is more to this matter than two men carving each other with steel blades. You and your foe are two such men as the fate of empires can turn upon!" For the first time, the priest showed genuine animation. "You must let me guide your actions."

Conan had to restrain himself to keep from laughing aloud. "A northern barbarian and a southern bandit and slaver? We have naught in common save this: Men of the civilized world would laugh at us if they dared. They do not do so because they know it would cost them their lives. Surely the gods would choose others for their great purposes." He drained his cup.

"You are truly a barbarian," said the priest, "and a boy. You have all the confidence in the world in your skill and in the strength of your body, but none at all in your other powers, the ones that set you apart from the common run of men. Until you come to understand your true nature, there is little I can do for you. Remember this: Taharka of Keshan is a man much like you. He comes of a somewhat higher culture, and he is well educated as that culture understands such things. But he is a barbarian nonetheless, and, unlike you, he suffers from no trace of conscience, nor of scruples. Civilized men find you savage and untamed, yet you have a rigid code instilled by your people. Taharka has no such thing. He has completely rejected whatever code his people have and now acts in any fashion that seems convenient to him.

"He would not have fought the two Bossonians, and he will not fight you if he thinks he might lose. He is as likely to send others or to use poison."

Conan rose from his chair. "Then I will not allow him the opportunity. I must confront him and kill him before he knows I am on his trail. My thanks for your advice, priest, but I will handle this in my own fashion."

"Good fortune, young barbarian." The priest favored him with another of his frosty smiles. "But I do not think it shall be so easy for you."

Conan stepped into the open air, glad to be free of the oppressive atmosphere of the temple. To his surprise, dawn was breaking over the town. The morning sounds of birds and beasts filled the air and he could smell bread baking. He made his way back to the inn and ascended the stair. As he entered the room beneath the eaves, he found Kalya glaring at him furiously.

"Where have you been all night? I'll wager you were out carousing and wenching!"

"What is it to you if I was?" Conan demanded, goaded by her proprietary manner. Had she asked him simply he would have told her of all that had transpired.

"We need what gold we have to pay our way as we pursue our vengeance. It is not for you to fritter away on wine and trollops!"

"When did you become my owner, woman?" Conan shouted. "I was tracking these men to kill them before we two met, and I can accomplish my task just as well without you! Do not get above yourself." He stripped off his weapon belt and threw himself onto his pallet. "I need some sleep. Do not disturb me." Then, as an afterthought: "Before you leave, count the money. If there is aught missing, you may carve me with your pretty little sword."

"So I shall." There was a clinking sound as she went through the gold. Then there was a louder smack as she threw the full purse against a wall.

"It is all there! Where were you?"

"If you would ask me less insolently, woman, I might tell you." He pulled a protruding straw from the pallet that had been troubling him.

She snarled something in a language Conan did not understand and stormed out, slamming the door behind her. Conan gave a half-amused grunt and turned over. Before he slept, he thought that he had not handled the situation well. The woman might get into trouble, out in the town without him, her unstable mind full of fury.

For a moment he thought of going after her, but a great weariness overcame him. The priest's delving into his ancestral memory had taken more out of him than he had realized. Crom take it, the woman had cared for herself well enough before now, she could do so for another day. He fell back on his pallet and was asleep.

Six

"This must be the last raid for this district, my chief," said Axandrias. He scanned the nearby high ground for sign of pursuit. The slaves they had rounded up were tied on horses for the sake of speed.

"Aye," said Taharka. "It seems we have overstayed our welcome."

One of their raiding-parties had been caught at their work by a squad of Nemedian cavalry sent to investigate the rash of slave-taking. Poor timing had led to the patrol and the slavers being on the same stretch of road at the same time. The felons had been hard-put to explain the presence of bound and gagged local farm lads in their possession. Taharka and his own party had been spotted, but distance had given them enough of a head start to lose their pursuit.

"Still, the gods of thieves and slavers yet look upon us with favor," said the Keshanian. "It was the Argossian crew and the scum we recruited in Croton who were so unfortunate. It is they who shall grace Nemedian gibbets while we drink away our earnings in comfort."

"They might still be in pursuit," said the Aquilonian, throwing another of his nervous glances over his shoulder.

"We crossed the border some time ago," said Taharka. "They'll not cross it. They will send word to the nearest center of Aquilonian authority and keep close watch on their own side of the border. By the time anyone comes seeking us in Croton, we shall be far away, riding for the profitable fields of Ophir. Is it not a fair prospect?"

"As you say, master."

Axandrias was beginning to doubt his own wisdom in choosing to follow Taharka. The man was ruthless and clever and his schemes were profitable, but he seemed to think himself completely invulnerable to the forces of authority. He took pleasure in playing his dangerous games close to the edge of disaster. The Aquilonian's own instinct was to cut and run at the first sign of danger. Had he been in charge, he would have abandoned their prisoners at first sign of pursuit and ridden at top speed from the scene of their depradations.

The Gundermen seemed downcast as well. Their looks were dark as they chivvied along the pack horses upon which the prisoners were bound. Axandrias knew they distrusted him, and were envious of his closeness to their chief. Their dislike he could live with easily enough, but he felt that it was only a matter of time before they buried one of their great, single-edged dirks in his back. It was not too soon to begin plotting actions to prevent that eventuality, and he occupied the rest of the ride in conjuring up schemes to rid himself of the two brothers.

It was yet early afternoon when they rode into Croton, their charges now in a drugged stupor so as to cause no trouble. Noisy greetings were called to them as they progressed through the crowded streets. They had become celebrated men, among those who enjoyed the entertainment they provided.

While the others rode on, Axandrias paused at a fountain which poured water from a carved demon's mouth into a stone trough. Parched from the lengthy ride, he leaned over and caught water from the stream as his mount drank from the trough. As he raised his cupped palm to his mouth, he saw someone watching him from a shadowed doorway. As he drank, he studied the figure surreptitiously. There seemed something damnably familiar in the man, or was it a woman?

Whoever it was stood swathed in a cloak, despite the heat. There was a glint of steel from the hand that clutched the cloak at its collar. One eye was deep-shadowed, and then he saw that it was covered by a patch.

There was little else to descry, but again there was that familiarity in something, perhaps the stance, the bearing, the falcon gaze of the remaining eye. He wiped his hand on a dusty trouser leg and rode on.

If the stranger had business with him, he would know soon enough. If there was danger, he preferred meeting it with the rest of the band to back him. After all, what was the point of running with a band if one had to meet danger alone?

He rejoined the rest at the great inn. The proprietor had given them the use of an abandoned stable that was wedged into a tiny lot between the back wall of the inn and the city wall. Workers had refurbished the ruinous stable into a pen for the slaves. The stableyard had been converted into a rough training ground where the slaves were taught the rudiments of weapon-play.

Since most of the slaves they brought in were herdsmen

or farmers who knew no weapon more sophisticated than the staff, it was here that the unfortunates were drilled in simple fighting-arts. As Axandrias rode up, he saw that a pair were being drilled in dagger-play, but the trainer was a stranger.

"Who is this?" he asked as he reined in beside Taharka. "Where are Murtan and Ballan?" The two had been left behind to train the slaves while the others went raiding for more.

"That is what I wish to find out," the Keshanian said, with a cloud of furrows forming above his eagle nose. "Am I always to be served by simpletons? I trust the rogues with the simplest of tasks, and they desert even this easy duty? They are great drunkards and no doubt they lie snoring in the straw somewhere. Their awakening shall be painful."

Taharka dismounted and tossed his reins to a horse-boy who ran tardily from the rear of the inn. He leaned upon the fence surrounding the old stableyard and called to the man who was drilling the slaves. "You! Trainer! Come you here at once!"

The man glanced over at him and cracked the whip he held in his right hand. The two slaves backed away from one another as he sheathed the short sword he had gripped in his left. The men were covered with sweat and trembled from exertion. They wore only padded loincloths and hard leather helmets. "You two rest in the shade while I speak with your master," the man ordered, then walked toward Taharka.

The Keshanian, as was his habit, sized up the approaching man. He was tall, gaunt but powerfully built. His hair and beard were the color of dark honey, almost brown. His features were straight but scarred, his eyes blue. He wore a vest of small plates connected by mail.

Splints of steel covered the high tops of his boots. He had the alert, springy stride of the born fighting-man, something never instilled by training. Taharka liked the look of him.

"A Hyperborean," muttered one of the Gundermen. "They are an evil breed." The Keshanian smiled. All men considered those of another tribe or nation to be evil.

"You must be Taharka," the man said as he coiled his whip. "I am Kuulvo. The innkeeper hired me to work with these dogs in return for room and board and all the wine I can hold. I have trained raw recruits before and these are no worse than most. They'll not disgrace you in the ring, when you have dosed them with whatever shaman's potion you use."

"You know my method, then?" Taharka said.

"I have eyes. For three nights I watched the fights. They are splendid entertainment but I know false courage when I see it. These local smugglers and caravaners may think they are seeing bloodthirsty fighters who have no fear, but I have been a soldier and swordsman too long to be fooled."

"What has happened to the two Bossonians I left behind when I rode out some days ago?" Taharka asked.

The Hyperborean shrugged. "You will have to ask the innkeeper who hired me. I heard that they had been killed, but I know not for certain."

"Killed!" Taharka exclaimed. "Without asking my permission! What insolence!" Then, calming, "Continue your work, my good man. You please me well. We shall speak at leisure this evening. Join me at table when I have rested and bathed. Come, Axandrias." As they went into the inn, Taharka turned to the Aquilonian.

"This man of Hyperborea looks to be a likely rogue, does he not? He is strong and skillful with his weapons, and seems to care little how he makes his living. Would he not make a good addition to our band?"

"Good fighters always come in handy, master," said Axandrias. "So long as they do not get too far above themselves."

"Aye, we cannot have that," Taharka agreed. "Now, where is that innkeeper?"

They found the man supervising the stowage of a great ale-cask in the taproom adjoining the common room. He turned from his work and saw the approaching men. "Ah, you have returned. Welcome! Had you a profitable journey?"

"Moderately," Taharka said. "Our Argossians and a few others grew homesick and have sought their native climes. We shall not be seeing them again. Tell me what has happened to my two Bossonians, whom I left in charge of the slaves. I returned to find them gone, and a hulking Hyperborean in their place."

"Ah, those two. A sad story, my friend. On the third morning ere this, they were found slain in an alley, their purses gone."

"They must have been drunk," Taharka said, disgustedly. "They were no great marvels as fighting men, but they were competent. How else would they have fallen to the daggers of a gang of cutpurses?"

"My wenches said that they left this place sober. Of course, they might have stopped at some tavern on their way, but why should they pay to drink when they have been drinking here for naught? Besides, it was not a gang of cutpurses with daggers. Each had been slain by a mighty sword-blow. Perhaps they encountered old enemies who wished to settle accounts then and there."

"It scarcely matters," said Taharka with a shrug. "They were of no great value to me, and I see you found a good replacement as a trainer."

"Aye, that was a stroke of luck. Kuulvo is a mercenary. He has tarried here numerous times in years past. The hired-band he was serving in was defeated in the wars down in Ophir, so he deserted and came here for a bit of rest. He had just come to the bottom of his purse and was about to go seek employment with another such fighting-band. I offered him room and food and wine to continue training our slaves until your return. I know him for a crafty fighter, well experienced in the art of training men."

"You did well, my friend," said Taharka. "I have spoken with the man and he has the look of a dangerous fellow. My limited experience of northerners tells me they are all a wild breed." He turned to go.

"Tell me, my host," said Axandrias, "have you noticed aught of a one-eyed man who goes muffled in a cloak despite the heat? I saw such a person in the marketplace and it seemed that he was watching me."

"One-eyed man?" said the innkeeper, baffled. "No, I—oho! The one you speak of is no man, but a wench! She has been in the town for some three or four days. She is not uncomely despite the eyepatch, and there are some who have wished to become more closely acquainted, but she is swift with a dagger, and with a steel gauntlet she wears upon her left hand. Where these are not sufficient discouragement, her traveling companion is."

The man laughed, causing his capacious belly to shake. "He is a great, strapping bravo. A man of Cimmeria, so I am told, and he looks fierce enough to stop a charging bull in its tracks."

Taharka stopped in the doorway and turned. "A Cimmerian, you say? Surely this is far from the misty hills to see a man of that nation."

"Aye, so I thought as well," said the innkeeper. "I myself was not certain of his people, so few of them have I seen, but a merchant who travels each year to Asgard confirmed it."

"An oddity," said Taharka. "But then, it is no business we need concern ourselves about. Come, Axandrias." His glare told the Aquilonian to ask no more questions.

After a bath and a change of clothing, the two sat at a table in the common room, sipping wine and awaiting dinner. When he had cut the dust of travel with a draught of golden wine, Taharka turned to his lieutenant. "Now, what means all this, my friend? Two of our band are slain, you find a one-eyed wench studying you, and she keeps company with a Cimmerian. What does this portend?"

"I know not, my chief. Something about the wench tugs at my thoughts, yet when I saw her I knew not whether the cloak covered a woman or a man." He drained his cup and refilled it. "As for the Cimmerian and the dead Bossonians, I cannot say. It is true that we were in that land, but that was many weeks ago. He could not have tracked us so far, and it is known that men of that foggy land rarely wander far from its confines."

"This one does," the Keshanian pointed out. "The two Bossonians were slain by the blows of mighty swordsmen, and we know from hard experience how the Cimmerians smite with their blades."

"The innkeeper mentioned only one Cimmerian," Axandrias protested.

"Perhaps one slew both. If so, this is a man to be reckoned with." He waved a dismissive hand. "No matter. If we have aught to fear from him, we shall know soon enough. Until then, we must stay on our guard, which is a good idea at any time."

Axandrias nodded, still uneasy, when he was startled by a man of giant frame who, without warning, was standing next to him. The Aquilonian almost jerked to his feet, snatching at the hilt of his ornate sword. A wide, scarred hand pressed on his shoulder and forced him back into his seat.

"You are nervous, my friend," said Kuulvo of Hyperborea. "I merely come to join you as your chief requested of me this afternoon."

"Do not sneak up on me like that," snarled the Aquilonian. "I am not to be trifled with in such fashion."

"Never would I trifle with so dangerous a man," said Kuulvo, not bothering to veil his sarcasm. He seated himself and took a cup from the platter next to the wine pitcher.

Taharka was amused by the friction. He intended to take the Hyperborean into his band, and it was always good to have rivalry between his men. They should be loyal to him, not to each other. Should one plot against him, there should always be a rival ready to betray the plot and gain favor with the chief. He raised the pitcher and poured the man's cup full to brimming.

"My host," the Keshanian began, "tells me you are lately come from the wars in Ophir."

"That is so," said Kuulvo, after a long drink that left the cup half-drained.

"I would hear of these wars, since I would take my little band there soon. Who is fighting, and over what?"

"It is a matter of wonderful confusion," said Kuulvo.

"There is an alliance of perhaps a dozen satraps in rebellion against the king. Another twenty or so support him. All of them are ready to change sides at the first hint of advantage. For instance, in the service of my last employer, Asnan of Khalkat, I fought in two battles against the king, and in three for him. In the last battle, none of us were certain on whose side we fought."

"Excellent!" Taharka said. "Just the place for men such as we. Kuulvo, I plan to take our band to Ophir."

"From what I have seen of your men," said the Hyperborean, "few are the mercenary captains who would wish to sign them on."

"That is not what I had in mind," Taharka said. "Having been a general myself, I would not wish to serve under a captain. The internal politics of Ophir are nothing to me, so I have no desire to choose sides there. Besides, such a course often ends not merely in defeat, but in annihilation. Rather, we would avoid all such conflicts, tour the country and, when we see our opportunities, take what profit we may from them." He spoke with many graceful gestures, his voice deep and mellifluous, his rings glittering in the light of the new-lit candles.

"Turn bandit, eh?" said Kuulvo. "There is wealth to be had in that, can you but avoid the many armies tramping about the countryside."

"A guide and advisor who is familiar with the land and the war would be of value. You seem to be a brave man, strong and a good swordsman. I know that you have reached the end of your finances and are in need of employment. I offer you a position in my band. Since the mysterious demise of my Bossonians, there are but four of us at present, yet our numbers shall swell as we make our way toward the slaughter-grounds."

The Hyperborean sat in thought for a moment. "You do not intend to stay here and fight your slaves? There is great profit in it."

"I grown weary of the amusement," Taharka said. "Soon, perhaps tomorrow or the day after, we ride from here."

"I see. The authorities have a way of making the best schemes go sour. Aye, another foray into Ophir would be agreeable to me. Most lands are at peace for the moment. That is a rare thing, and it is not agreeable to men of my sort." He grinned and for a moment Axandrias quailed before the feral gleam in the northerner's eye. "Like a shark in the great ocean, I am guided by the smell of blood, though it be faint and come from afar."

"A man after my own heart," said Taharka, raising his own cup in pledge. "I welcome you to our band. With me, you shall grow rich and never lack for excitement."

They were joined by the Gundermen and Taharka proclaimed Kuulvo's new status. The brothers accepted him with false heartiness and much back-slapping and pledging of eternal friendship. None of them took these ceremonies seriously. Bandits lived desperate lives, and had at all times to be willing to desert or betray each other to preserve their own lives or simply for profit.

Taharka looked up from these pleasant activities to see a man coming into the now-crowded room. He was a bald-headed creature, his age impossible to guess, dressed in odd robes. A serving wench greeted him and he spoke to her. She turned, scanned the room, and stretched forth an arm rattling with cheap bangles, pointing at the table around which sat the band of hard-bitten men. The robed man began to make his way, slowly, through the crowded room.

Taharka nudged Axandrias. "Do you know the bald man who approaches us?"

The Aquilonian's face registered surprise. "It's the priest who sold me the drugs. I wonder what he seeks now."

Something in the cut of the undecorated robe made Taharka uneasy. It looked much like vestments he had seen before, robes he had no wish ever to see again.

"Taharka of Keshan?" the priest said, with a deep bow.

"I am," said the chief, pointedly refraining from asking the priest to sit. "How may I be of service?"

"I wish to speak to you, sir. In private."

"I am well content with my situation and company at this moment. Wherefore should I take myself away from here and accompany you? I warn you, I have yet ample store of the medicine with which you provided me, and I have no need to buy more." His men smirked at what they thought to be the priest's discomfiture.

"It has nothing to do with that," said the priest. "It is a matter that will be of great profit to you, should you but hear me out. I crave but an hour of your time. You shall be back here before the evening's festivities have even begun."

The man's eyes were compelling, but Taharka could not have his men think him overawed by a mere prayer-chanter. "I am always willing to hear talk of profit," he said offhandedly. Rising from the table, he turned to his men. "Await me here. I shall dine when I return."

Axandrias was a bit uneasy when his chief left. He had not told Taharka of his own fears concerning the uncanny temple, because he had felt ashamed of his fears once he had recovered from them. He shrugged. Should Taharka not return, then he would lead the band himself. He was more concerned by the mysterious woman with the eyepatch and her Cimmerian companion.

Taharka followed the priest out into the twilit streets of Croton. They exchanged no words as they made their way no more than a hundred steps to an alleyway paved with worn stones. Taharka felt a cold hand grip his heart when he saw the facade of the ancient temple. Why had that fool Axandrias not told him of this? Then he realized that, to the Aquilonian, as to most others, it was merely an old, near-abandoned temple. Every land abounded with such structures.

The priest turned as he stepped upon the portico. "I am a priest of—"

"I know which gods you serve," Taharka said. He looked carefully down the alley. There was no one in sight, but he did not wish to take any chances. "Let us go inside to discuss this."

"I see," said the priest as they stepped into the gloom within. "You have been contacted before?"

"Yes," said Taharka, drawing his dagger. He buried it to the hilt in the priest's back, just to the left of the spine. As the man collapsed, Taharka plunged in his blade twice more. With a final, rattling breath, the priest expired.

Taharka gazed around uneasily as he wiped his blade on the priest's robe. He was a man seldom troubled by fear, and never by conscience. Yet, something in this accursed place made him apprehensive. He looked up and saw the leering serpent-faces of the supporting pillars. He had seen their like before.

He tried to shake off the unaccustomed mood as he disposed of the body. Grasping the ankles, he dragged the inert, robed form away from the doorway and behind one of the rows of pillars, where it would be well hidden in the gloom. He was in no mood to search the place for a more secure hiding place. Such a temple probably did not attract ten visitors in a year, so it could easily be days before the body was discovered. By that time he would be well away.

As he left, it occurred to him that carrion dogs might sniff out the corpse and attract attention, so he closed the door. As it was almost shut, he thought he saw a tiny human face staring down at him from atop a serpent-headed capital. Shivering, he shut the door and walked swiftly away. There was, he thought, no reason to be upset. Even should he be found, who in this town would question him about the demise of so unloved a man as that priest? Still, it disturbed him. The face that had looked down at him had worn an expression of *amusement*.

Axandrias looked up when his chief entered and was shocked to see the expression he wore. The man had never shown other than the highest good humor while inflicting hideous torture upon his victims and had always remained calm in the face of danger. Yet now he looked as if he had seen demons. By the time the Keshanian reached the table his face was bland once more, but Axandrias could see the effort it took.

"What did the priest want, master?" he asked. His concern was not altogether feigned. If Taharka had a weakness, he wished to know about it.

"A trifling matter," said the dark man. "The fellow had some more drugs and spells he thought I might want. I told him not to waste my time again. You know how these impoverished priests are, forever trying to cadge money from the gullible."

Axandrias thought of the treasures he had seen in the

ancient temple and he knew Taharka was lying. How interesting this was. "They are all alike, my lord."

Taharka picked up a roast fowl and tore into it with his recently-used dagger. "By all the gods, I am famished!" He poured a large goblet full of wine and drained it with what Axandrias thought to be uncharacteristic haste.

"My men," Taharka said when he felt a little restored, "I shall be glad to see the last of this place. From our new comrade's description, Ophir is the place for us."

The Gundermen nodded dutifully, but in truth they had enjoyed the easy life in Croton. Like most such men, they had little love for exertion. "As you say, Chieftain."

It was a great puzzle to Axandrias, but he felt that could he but find out what was behind his chief's strange behavior, he might well better his own position. This would bear thinking upon.

In the dark temple, something was stirring. In the shadows above the serpent-headed columns, tiny, manlike forms scurried, conferring in screeching voices like the cries of bats. One of them leapt from its perch beneath the roof and flapped on leathery wings to the inert form of the priest. It clicked and muttered as it examined the corpse, then it raised its head and screeched out a peremptory call. The air within the temple rustled as a dozen more of the little creatures fluttered to the body.

The things had bodies of human form, and their faces were caricatures of human faces, but they were covered with short, dark fur. Their fingers and toes ended in black talons and they had bare, lizardlike tails. When folded, the leathery wings towered above their heads.

After a few minutes of muttered conference, the creatures squatted upon various parts of the priest's body and began a demented chanting, punctuated with high-pitched shrieks. Their heads bobbed and their tails switched in time to their chant. From time to time, one or more of them would move to another spot, but never did they break the rhythm of their spell-casting. The demonic little ceremony continued with fearsome concentration for several hours. At last, the body of the priest began to move.

One moment the body was inert, then a series of long shudders shook the thin frame. The homunculi shrilled triumphantly, then resumed their chant. The priest began to breathe in long, wheezing, bubbling gasps. His lungs expelled bloody froth through nose and mouth, then the flow ceased and he began to breathe normally.

The eyelids quivered, fluttered, then flew open. The wide eyes stared sightlessly upward for many long minutes, then they focused and consciousness returned to them. Consciousness was quickly followed by comprehension. Expression returned to the gaunt face. First came shock, then fear, then a mad rage. Gradually, the face reassumed its accustomed mask of serenity.

Slowly, painfully, the priest raised himself until he was sitting with his back supported by a column. The diminutive demons flew about him in exuberant circles, tumbling through the air gleefully and singing of their victory.

The song, too hellish for human ears, brought a wan smile to the lips of the priest. "Well done, my tiny servants. You shall be rewarded well." Painfully, he levered himself to his feet. He leaned against the column for a space, gathering his strength. Returning from death was no light task, even for one such as he. A few faltering, unsteady steps took him to the next pillar. By the time he reached the bowl of the flame, he was walking almost normally. As he gazed into the green fire, strength seemed to flow back into his body at a redoubled rate.

He extended his hands until the flames washed over them. The fingertips described complex patterns amid the fire and as they did they left behind evanescent trails of brilliant colors.

"So, you have seen something of your destiny, Taharka of Keshan," said the priest, his eyes staring as if at something upon a far horizon. "And you are afraid of what you see. Very well. You shall yet meet your fate, however reluctantly." His fingers continued their dance, and gradually a face began to form amid the flames.

Seven

Kalya was furious. For most of her young life she had feared and distrusted all men. Then she had almost trusted this huge Cimmerian, whose code seemed so like hers, who was on his own mission of vengeance. Now he had proven to be as false as all the others. If for some devious reason he would not account for his whereabouts on the previous night, then she could no longer trust him. Very well, she would deal with Axandrias herself, as she had intended before ever she met Conan.

As she swept through the bazaar she brooded over the slight the Cimmerian had dealt her, and men avoided the demented gleam in her eye. For most of the morning she wandered aimlessly. There was little to do but she did not wish to return to the room she shared with Conan. Always before she had been able to speed the passing hours by simply sitting, wrapped in her cloak and her gloom, thinking of nothing. This habit had contributed greatly to her reputation for madness. She knew that, in her present frame of mind, that course would be impossible.

For a few hours she betook herself to the crest of the city wall. Its deserted expanse was a relief from the noisy crowds of the town. She cast aside her cloak, drew her weapons and went through a rigorous series of exercises with sword and dagger, cutting, thrusting, parrying phantom lunges, spinning to face unseen enemies approaching from the rear. Her weapons and armor made glittering patterns in the sunlight as she executed a dance of dazzling complexity. If any townsmen saw her, none approached. She had the demeanor of a feral cat playing with its prey.

At length, she ceased her exertions and stood gasping, her body sheened with sweat. The demanding discipline of steel had calmed her, although it did nothing to lessen her anger. Sheathing her weapons, she sat crosslegged on her cloak and did not move a muscle as the afternoon sun dried the sweat from her skin.

A sound from without the wall drew her from the near-trance into which she had fallen. She stared out over the rolling land to the east to determine what had distracted her. Then she saw that a file of horsemen made its way toward the city gate. Of their identities she could tell nothing at such a distance, but there was something in the way that several rode which suggested that their hands were bound.

Her heart began to pound as she stood to get a better view. Could these be the men they had sought? She shook her head and corrected herself. There was only one man she wanted to find. She was no longer interested in the rest. They could live a thousand more years as far as she was concerned.

The horsemen were nearing the gate. If they were truly Taharka and his band of slavers, they would have to pass through the main market square to take their prisoners to their slave pen. Swiftly, she resumed her cloak and ran lightly down the steps to street level. She forced herself to walk sedately through the streets and alleys, lest she attract unwanted attention.

In the market, she selected a doorway well-shaded from the sun and stood within its shadows. No sooner than she had taken up her position, the slavers entered the market amid much clamor and calling of greetings.

She stiffened when two yellow-haired men rode into view, then relaxed when she saw that neither was Axandrias. These must be the two Gundermen. They were a pair of northern wolves who looked as dangerous as any she had ever seen. These two led a string of horses bearing men with bound hands. The prisoners were silent and wore vacant expressions, indicating that drugs had already been administered.

The next horseman caused her to hold her breath in reluctant admiration. Towering and handsome, exotically dark, this could only be Taharka. He rode with the bearing of a king and his colorful, embroidered garments would have been absurdly gaudy on a lesser man. On him, they set off to perfection his splendid presence. So enthralling was the sight of him that she almost missed the smaller man who rode behind him. Then her blood cooled as she saw who that man was.

Fortuitously, the last rider tarried a little to drink at a fountain. She studied him and saw that he had changed but little. Still handsome, but with a slyness and furtiveness that made his aspect repellent. He rode well, and he stooped from the saddle to drink with insolent grace. Then he saw her.

She stood unmoving, too proud to try to hide herself. She saw him studying her, and she knew from his expression that he did not recognize her. That was hardly unexpected. It had been many years since he had seen her, and surely she resembled little the girl he had last seen. She saw the look of puzzlement on his face and then, feigning disinterest, he rode leisurely toward the inn.

When he was gone Kalya realized she was trembling all over. It was not from fear, for she felt none. It was the overpowering emotion that came from finally having run her prey to ground. All her life since girlhood had been consecrated to tracking and killing this man. In all that time she had never seen him, never been truly certain that he had not died and thus escaped her vengeance. Now she knew, and she knew as well that the climactic chapter of her life had arrived.

Had she been more philosophical and less single-minded, it might have occurred to her that a young woman of scarcely a score of years had much life to look forward to, and that it was an early age to be anticipating its final episode. So long had she been obsessed by revenge that the thought never occurred to her. Had anyone suggested to her that her concentration on hatred and retribution was a vain waste of her life, she would have scorned any such thought as unworthy.

In her world and Conan's the niggling day-to-day realities, the careful planning for a long and fulfilling life, were the concerns of insignificant people. Those whose hearts were set upon the heroic life and the road of kings had to discard all expectation of a peaceful old age. If a life was to have savor and intensity, one had to be willing to cast it away without a moment's thought.

None of this passed through her mind as she stalked through the ancient, winding streets of Croton. Her fist knotted and relaxed on her sword hilt beneath her swathing cloak as she exulted, in a state approaching ecstasy. Her enemy within her mailed grasp at last!

She knew that she was letting her emotions get the better of her, and that was certain death to one whose trade was mortal combat. Seeing the sign of a tavern, she ducked into the low doorway, took a seat near the single window and ordered wine. As she sipped the cool red vintage she considered her chances.

As her swordmasters had taught her, she tried to forget her anger and consider dispassionately the tactical problem facing her. Once this situation was perfectly clear, she would be able to devise a plan to accomplish her aim without being killed in the process. Her teachers had stressed that, in some situations, victory might be impossible and the enterprise abandoned. That was a possibility she did not want to face.

There was, they had said, a third path. Sometimes an aim could be accomplished, but only at the certain sacrifice of one's own life. This should only be considered in the highest of endeavors, as when one's liege demanded the death of a rival, and the only way of accomplishing this was to gain the enemy's side by stealth and stab him while in the midst of his bodyguard. So drastic a course was not to be undertaken lightly, but Kalya was willing to die in slaying rather than give up her vengeance.

She considered the odds. Now that the Bossonians were dead, Axandrias had three companions. Having seen them, she knew that the Bossonians had been the least deadly of the band. The two Gundermen would be formidable enemies, and she suspected that they had long experience in fighting in concert. A single opponent trapped between them would scarcely have a chance. The Keshanian was even more fearsome. She had seen many showmen whose martial display concealed a timid fraud, but her warrior's eye told her that this man was as every bit as indomitable as he looked. His slightest gesture of turning in his saddle betrayed the bodily control of a master swordsman. She wondered what trick of the gods had made this splendid creature into a squalid bandit.

She put the question aside as irrelevant. What counted was Axandrias. How could she slay him without being killed herself? The day before, the answer would have been simple: Talk it over with Conan and devise a way to kill all four, one at a time or in pairs. Perhaps even all at once. With the Cimmerian backing her it was just possible. Now her pride would not allow her to seek his aid.

It might be relatively simple to murder Axandrias, but it was unacceptable. It had to be from in front. He had to know who she was and exactly why he was dying. Nothing else would be satisfactory. It would do no good simply to challenge Axandrias to a duel. These were not men of honor. Axandrias would draw sword to engage her from in front and the others would laugh as they cut her down from behind.

She had one small advantage. He had not recognized her. She might be able to draw close without his realizing who she was and what she intended. There might be a way to approach him, perhaps gain his confidence to a small degree. As much as she disliked the thought, she knew better than most that he was vain about his ability to charm women. That, too, could be used against him.

The sun sank below the parapet of the house across the street, putting Kalya's table in shadow. It was time to go. She drained her cup and left the tavern.

She was not alone as she made her way toward the

Traveler's Paradise. The nightly entertainment made it the focus of all excitement-seekers in the hours after the markets closed. Both townsmen and newly arrived caravaners thronged to the huge inn, to cheer and lay bets and revel in the blood of the combatants. Kalya was looking forward to some bloodshed this night as well.

As usual, the inn rang with the accustomed nightly din. She dropped some coins in the doorman's hand and passed within. A serving-girl approached her with a tray of winecups, but Kalya waved her aside. As she passed, the girl made a face at her back. Kalya was not one of the more favored customers, for she bought little wine and confined herself to studying the combats.

Emerging into the common room, she stood upon an ornamental chest of exotic wood and bronze, inlaid with ivory in the Kushite fashion. As she had hoped, the slavers occupied a large table next to the pit. She was about to make her move when she saw that they had been joined by a fifth man. She bit off a curse as she saw who that man was. The Hyperborean!

In the long nights spent at the inn, she and Conan had passed the time in studying the various patrons and evaluating them in fighting man's terms. There were many tough men, clearly experienced with weapons. Most were caravan guards, bandits or paid-off mercenaries, but none of them had struck the Cimmerian or her as an especially difficult challenge in a fight. That distinction fell only to the tall Hyperborean. Conan had proclaimed a dislike of that nation and all its inhabitants, but Kalya knew that all northerners detested the inhabitants of all other northern lands. The Cimmerian had admitted, albeit grudgingly, that the Hyperborean might be able to give him a stout fight.

Could he have joined the bandits? She reminded

herself that it was no longer her problem. Conan would have to deal with the man when he confronted the surviving slavers. Her only concern was that Axandrias should not be one of their number. She took a deep breath, composed herself so that she should display nothing of her intent, and began to walk toward the table next to the pit.

At that table, Taharka was deep in conversation with his new follower.

"Tell me, my friend; what know you of a tall young Cimmerian who frequents this place of an evening?"

"The Cimmerian boy?" Kuulvo arched an eyebrow. "I have seen him. He speaks little, and is mainly in company with a one-eyed wench. One evening we had a few minutes' conversation on fine points of the combat below. He is probably a good swordsman, like all his nation, but he is an untried youth withal. Wish you to recruit him?"

"Think you he would be a valuable addition to our band?" said Taharka noncommittally.

"He is at least as good as the rest you have. But his nation and mine are enemies, and soon or late it would come to sword-blows between us. I would slay him and then you would have no—" He paused as the crowd parted near their table to reveal a cloaked figure who wore an eyepatch. "What is this?" Kuulvo muttered. "The very wench herself. She seems to be without her companion."

Kalya went to the table side and swept it insolently with her one-eyed gaze. It passed over Axandrias and stopped at Taharka. "Are you the foreigner who fights the slaves in the pit?" Her shockingly hoarse voice crackled with challenge.

"I am," said Taharka with a bemused expression.

"Have you a fighter you wish to pit against one of mine?"

"I hear that you offer a purse for any free challenger." The men around the table ceased their muttering and the silence spread. Whispered words rapidly passed the news that something interesting was happening at Taharka's table and soon all were straining their ears to hear what was being said.

"I have such an offer," said Taharka, "although ere now no man has had courage to accept it. One thousand golden Aquilonian crowns to go down into the pit with one of my fighting-slaves. Another thousand if he comes out alive. Should he fail to do so, the first thousand will be paid to whomever you wish. Who is your challenger? Is it this Cimmerian of whom I have heard somewhat?"

"Nay," she said. "It is I." She pulled her cloak over her head and let it drop to the floor. There was a moment of startled silence, quickly followed by whistles, stamping of feet, and scattered applause. Her bizarre combination of armor and near-nudity drew the appreciation of men accustomed to strange sights.

"*You* wish to fight in the pit?" Taharka stroked his scented beard and considered the possibilities.

"She hasn't a chance, Chief," grunted the Hyperborean.

"What of that?" asked Taharka with honest puzzlement. He turned back toward Kalya. "What are your weapons?"

"You see them," she said, crossing her arms before her body and drawing her sword and dagger. The polished blades flashed in the torchlight, bringing some bloodthirsty cheers from the audience.

Taharka glanced at the faces directed toward his table, all of them ashine with lust for blood or flesh. This

was developing well. True, he had not been training the
slaves with weapons of such length, but that was of
little importance. The drugged man might not even feel
the cuts of a blade so sharp and light. If, against all
odds, the woman should win and survive the experience, the sensation it caused would be well worth the
loss. Best of all would be a double kill.

"You are a free woman," said Taharka, "and your
life is yours to throw away as you wish. I accept your
challenge!" A ferocious roar went up at this announce-
ment. "The innkeeper will hold the purse." He nodded
and the man scurried off to fill the purse from his
strongbox, rubbing his hands together gleefully at the
thought of the profits to be gained from such a fight. A
warrior-woman dead on the sand! It would be the event
of the season and double his business.

"My man will fight with short sword and shield,"
said Taharka. "I have none trained to use that little
sticker of yours. Is that agreeable?" His eyes glittered
with amusement.

She shrugged, and the well-shaped muscles of her
neck and shoulders slid gracefully beneath her glossy
skin with the movement. "It is all one to me."

Taharka turned to the Hyperborean. "Go you to the
pen and select one of those who was to fight this eve.
One who is quick and skillful with his sword."

"As you command, Chief," said Kuulvo. He rose
and left.

"Now, brave woman," said Taharka, "you must
have an attendant to accompany you into the pit. He
will hold your weapon-sheaths so they do not encumber
you in the fight. Do you wish your body to be oiled? It
is customary."

"Ordinarily," she said, "I do not allow men to lay

hands upon my body, but, if it is the custom, I accept.''
Immediately there was a great clamor as men volun-
teered to perform this necessary duty.

"Excellent,'' said Taharka. He turned to the Gunder
brothers. "Wolf, fetch you the oil—''

"Nay!'' said the woman. She stepped to Axandrias
and resheathed her blades. The bare fingers of her right
hand stroked his fine-bearded jaw. "This one is the
prettiest of you. I'll wager his hands are the softest as
well. Let him be my attendant.'' Loud hoots and ribald
comments erupted throughout the common room and its
overlooking balconies.

Taharka roared with laughter. "As you will! This
pretty fellow shall do the honors. Axandrias, see to it.''

Axandrias had been staring at the woman open-mouthed
since the moment she abandoned her cloak. Never had
he seen so fair a body, its leonine muscularity beautifully offset by womanly curves of stunning lushness. So
what if she had but one eye? When she stroked beneath
his chin, his former suspicions melted like snowflakes
beneath a desert sun.

He stood and swept his arm wide as he made his best
courtly bow. "It shall be an honor to be at the service
of so fine a lady.'' Men made lewd comments and
gestures as he drew one of the serving-women aside and
sent her to the bathhouse for a flask of scented oil.

The oil was delivered and the two descended the
steps to the floor of the pit. Kalya went through a
minute of preliminary stretching, displaying herself to
best advantage, then turned to Axandrias. "What do
you tarry for? Oil me.''

With a broad grin and amid much raillery from the
spectators, he began to smooth the oil over her shoulders and back. Kalya smiled and posed for the crowd

while straining to keep her flesh from shrinking at the touch of the man she had come to kill. He spread the oil down her bare left thigh, his hand lingering far longer than necessary, then up over her hard-ridged belly. He stroked over her ribs beneath her mailed right breast, then slid his hand toward her bare left breast.

At that moment, her steel-gauntleted left fist smashed into his jaw, knocking him sprawling. There was much cheering at this, but it was cut off short when she whipped out her sword and leveled its point at the Aquilonian's throat.

"It is not some drugged slave I came here to fight, Axandrias," she hissed. "It is you! Stand and draw!"

He scrambled to his feet, rubbing his jaw. "What means this, slut? What have I—"

"Do you wish to see your handiwork, coward? Do you wish to see what your hot iron did to Kalya? Look, then!" She raised her eyepatch to display a ghastly pit of scar tissue, with no trace of an eye.

"Kalya!" he gasped, his face gone ashen and bewildered. "But Kalya died long ago!"

"You were not so lucky, murderer," she hissed, stalking toward him like a panther. "Your dagger through my neck ruined me for singing, but I did not die of it. I can understand why you thought me dead, though. Such a wound should have been enough to slay a nine-year-old girl! Now draw your sword, or I'll spit you like the maggot you are!"

She slid forward and her point darted out, but he leaped back dextrously and whipped out his own narrow blade. The two swords rang twice, then Axandrias pushed himself away from the wall of the pit and forced her back.

"You should have died with your mother, slut. Well,

I failed then, but there is yet time to set the matter aright!'' He attacked with a flurry of blows, but she managed to avoid them all with her two-handed defense. She smiled chillingly as she beat aside his attacks and began slowly to push him back.

Spectators cheered frantically at this rare sport. Taharka stared bemusedly at the action in the pit as Kuulvo came to him, leading a slave by a short chain leash.

"What is this?" asked the Hyperborean. "Could they not wait to start?"

"It seems the wench had a grudge against Axandrias and tricked him into the pit with her."

"She does not lack skill," said Kuulvo. "You may soon be minus one follower. Serves him right if he cannot best a wench."

"Oh, I'll not let it come to that," said Taharka. "After all, I have a reputation to maintain. How would I keep the loyalty of my men if they thought I might let them die over a matter of honor?"

The cheering redoubled as Kalya drove Axandrias against the wall of the pit. She threw her entire body forward in a lunge that would have pinned him to the painted banner at his back, but he avoided it by a sideways dodge and tumble that would have done credit to an acrobat. Some cheered this move, others booed its seeming timidity.

"Enough of this," Taharka said. "Wolf, Gunter, into the pit and slay the baggage."

A chorus of protests broke out when the grim, yellow-haired men descended into the pit. "No! Fair fight!" shouted many. The two paid no attention. Kalya cursed frantically when she saw them coming toward her. Another five or six passes would see Axandrias dead upon her sword, but the fight had taken too long. She had planned to kill him before his friends could render him aid, but he had proven too swift and skillful, like the oily adder that he was.

Kalya backed against a wall as the Gundermen drew near with broad blades in their hands. Axandrias ranged himself beside them, his terrified expression now replaced by a feral grin. There were shouts of rage from the crowd as the three closed in on the lone woman, who now looked frail and vulnerable when faced with such odds. All sound ceased for a split-second when a fifth form leapt from the parapet into the pit, landing catlike behind the advancing men. They whirled at his heart-stopping warcry.

"It is not to be so easy, dogs!" bellowed Conan. "Turn and face one who would rather drink Gunder blood than ale!"

"Cimmerian!" barked Gunter. "We'll carve your carcass, blackhair, before we play with your wench."

The two advanced on Conan while Kalya redoubled her attack upon Axandrias. She could have wept with relief, not that Conan had saved her life but because he had given her another chance to kill her prey.

The whole inn shook with the frantic cheering and betting. Only two men watched the action with cold-blooded calculation. "Shall I join them, Chief?" Kuulvo asked.

"Nay," said Taharka, stroking his beard with beringed fingers, "six would be too great a crowd for that pit. Too much chance of being struck by accident, and what profit is there in that? Nay, surely our three can handle these two."

"I'd not be so certain," said Kuulvo. "That Cimmerian could give even me a good fight."

In the pit, the combatants battled furiously. They

were after each other's life's blood and would accept
nothing less. The Gundermen attacked Conan simultaneously, and he was hard put to parry their whistling
strokes with his own blade. He held the long grip of his
brand in both hands, but even this added leverage barely
gave him the speed and sureness to deflect the furious
rain of steel.

He saw his opening when one of the brothers collided
with the frantic Axandrias. In the instant that Wolf was
off balance, Conan's sword sheared through his waist,
ripping through armor and scattering blood and entrails
the width of the pit. Gunter cried out in rage and
redoubled his attack.

Now not so hard-pressed, Conan parried his opponent's sword without great difficulty. As he stepped
forward for the killing blow, the Cimmerian's foot came
down in a pool of blood and offal and slid from beneath
him. With his superb balance, Conan kept himself from
falling, but he was bent over and, for an instant, vulnerable. Grinning ferociously, Gunter darted in, blade raised
to shear down through the Cimmerian's spine.

Axandrias had leaned too far forward in his attack,
and a clout from the basket-hilt of Kalya's sword sent
him sprawling. He was helpless and she hesitated in the
death-blow, savoring the moment. Then she saw the
Gunderman's sword raised over Conan. Without thinking, she turned from Axandrias and plunged her left-
hand dagger into the man's armpit above the rim of his
armor. The blade grated on bone, then slid in easily. He
froze, then began to cry out in agony. Her sword swept
swiftly across his throat, cutting off the cry.

As she turned to finish off Axandrias, she saw him
scrambling up the steps and out of the pit. She howled
in frustrated rage and gave chase, followed closely by

Conan. The inn rocked with frantic cheers as they burst
out of the pit. The innkeeper ran up to them, his face
crimson with excitement.

"Five thousand!" he shouted. "Five thousand every
night if you will fight in my pit. We will all grow
rich!" Conan knocked him sprawling with a backhand
buffet to the jaw.

"Better blood than yours stains your pit. Where are
the slavers? We want them!" He scanned the crowd,
but the yelling, bustling spectators made it difficult to
make out anything.

Across the room, Taharka, Kuulvo, and Axandrias
were conferring. "They are demons, master!" Axandrias
gasped. "Let us be away from here!"

"Your advice is better than your swordplay, my
friend," said Taharka. "More to the point, this crowd
may soon turn ugly over our unsporting tactics. Axandrias,
go fetch our best mounts. I shall gather as much of our
gold as I can. Kuulvo, come with me."

Conan thought he caught a glimpse of Taharka and
began to bull his way toward the bandit with Kalya
close on his heels. As he crossed the room, a commo-
tion broke out at the front entrance. People standing
there were shoved back as a pack of men trooped into
the room. "King's men! King's men!" shouted those
who were being thrown back.

The crowd fell silent as the men came in. First to
enter were two officers, one in Nemedian armor, the
other in the livery of the King of Aquilonia. Behind
them were armored men armed with swords and iron-
tipped staves bristling with hooks for catching fleeing
felons.

"Order in here!" shouted the Aquilonian captain.
"We seek a band of slavers who have been raiding in

our two nations, taking free men away in chains and cheating the royal executioner as well. All will remain here while we search for them.''

The eyes of the Nemedian officer grew wide with astonishment and delight as he scanned the crowd. "Mitra be praised! Half the unhung rogues of the borderland are in this room! Round them up, men, there is reward money in abundance in this place!''

As the king's men stormed forward, pandemonium broke out as men dove out windows, shinnied up support posts to reach the balconies, scurried for cellars, or tried to force their way out past the soldiers. Torches were snatched from sconces and tossed into the pool, plunging the room into darkness and even greater chaos.

Kalya grasped at Conan's arm. "Come, we must be away from here. They will round up everyone here, and we'll lie in a dungeon for months while they try to sort everyone out.''

"We'll lose the last two for good if that happens,'' said Conan. "Come.''

He took her hand and forced his way to the nearest stair. Forcefully, he cleared them a path upward, sometimes by the simple expedient of grasping the belt of the next man above and hurling him over the bannister to the floor below. In this way they reached the upper balcony. Behind them, soldiers were pounding up the stair. Below they could hear a clash of steel.

Conan grabbed a serving-girl by the arm. "Quick, is there a way to the roof?''

"No,'' said the terrified girl, "my master fears that some will seek to leave without paying.''

"Crom take them all! Kalya, abide here a moment.''

He sprang to the top of the balcony railing, sure-footed as a mountain goat despite the gloom. He stood

on his toes and reached for the edge of the roof above
him. He found that he could just grasp the timber
roofing, covered with its lead sheeting, with the tips of
his fingers. Kalya gasped as he kicked outward with his
feet and pulled himself up and over the edge, his sword
making a clatter as he sprawled on his belly upon the
roof.

Kalya heard the tramp of iron-shod boots behind her
and turned to see king's men approaching in the gloom.
One squinted in her direction and called out, "There's
one of the rogues, let's catch him!"

As they stamped toward her, Conan reached down a
hand. Desperate, she grasped the thick forearm above a
heavy bronze bracelet. With a surge of terrific muscle
power, he hauled her up. A hand behind her scrabbled
for purchase on her sword-belt, then slid away. Her
stomach lurched as she swung out over the courtyard,
then shot upward to sprawl next to Conan on the cold
lead of the roof. Even after his previous demonstrations,
she was amazed at the man's strength.

Below them, they heard a puzzled voice. "Where did he
go? By Set, but that rascal had the smoothest buttock I've
ever felt on a man!" The two above covered their mouths
to keep from laughing aloud and exposing their position.

"Come," whispered Conan, "we must get back to
our inn. Our horses and belongings are there."

She scrambled to her feet and followed him to the
outside edge of the roof. There was a narrow alley
between the inn and the next house. It was dark, but she
grew dizzy at the thought of the empty space below.

"Jump!" Conan commanded. "It is not far."

She shook her head. "No. Steel is one thing,
Cimmerian. I would rather go back down and fight my
way out."

"If you will not jump," he grasped her by two straps of her harness, "then you must fly, my little bird!"

She squalled in protest as he swung her far back, then out and up. There was a horrid, weightless sensation, then she crashed into the heavy thatch of the next house. She began to slide backward but managed to stop herself before she reached the edge. A sudden impact beside her announced Conan's arrival.

"Now, up over the ridge," he said.

She scrambled behind him over the ridge and down the opposite slope. Luckily, this building directly abutted another with a flat roof. They crossed this and found its far side built against the ruinous town wall. A quick trot along the wall brought them to their inn, which they entered through an upper window.

Back in their room, they swiftly gathered their goods. In the distance, they could hear the continuing uproar.

"By Crom, girl," said Conan, "when I found you gone I thought nothing of it. Then as it grew dark it came to me that you had embarked upon some mad scheme. Lucky for you I reached the pit when I did."

"I should be angry with you," she said, "but you saved my life so now I am in your debt." She stuffed the last of her few belongings into a saddlebag.

"You saved mine, so we are even. Anyway, it did me good to kill that Gunderman. I wish I could have killed the other, but under the circumstances it came out well. Come, let's away before the king's men have the city gate blocked."

They made their way to the stable and saddled their sleepy mounts. As fast as they could in the dimness, they rode for the gate. They found that they need not have worried. Men were fleeing through it in such numbers, mounted and afoot, that the royal forces had no chance of stemming the tide. In passing, Kalya snatched a cloak from a running man, to replace the one she had abandoned in the Traveler's Paradise. In minutes, the two were fleeing into the moonlit night.

Kuulvo and Axandrias rode behind their leader as the town of Croton dwindled in the distance behind them. In time, the tall Hyperborean noticed that Taharka rode doubled over the pommel of his saddle. Had he been wounded in the hurried flight, first from the inn, then from the town? He rode even with the Keshanian, took him by the shoulder and pulled him upright. To his amazement, he saw that his chief had been laughing as he rode, tears of merriment streaking his face.

"Saw you ever such a scene?" Taharka said when he had breath. "Chaos and confusion! It is the very stuff of life, my friend. Blood and madness make all else worth the trouble!" He flew off into laughter.

After thinking about it, Kuulvo found himself roaring with mirth as well. "Aye, Chieftain, you are right! I can see that I have fallen in with someone who sees the world the same way as I." The two continued to whoop with maniacal laughter.

Axandrias was glad to be alive, and he was just as happy to be rid of the two Gundermen, but now he felt that he was caught between two utter madmen. He sighed and shook his head as their steps led them toward the bloody fields of Ophir.

When all chance of pursuit was gone, they slowed their mounts to a walk. There was little point in riding through the night, so they picked a spot near a small stream to camp. There was abundant dead wood, and while Conan picketed the beasts and rubbed them down Kalya started a fire with flint and steel.

He returned to find her sitting in the firelight, her folded cloak beneath her. He smiled as he eyed her appreciatively. "You made a pretty sight there in the pit. I think the oil helped."

"You saw it all, then?" she said.

"I'd not have missed it," he answered. "While it was you and Axandrias, I'd not have interfered. When the Gundermen entered the pit, I knew it was time for me to take a hand."

"You saw when I showed him what used to be my eye?" she said, he hoarse voice sounding strangely wan.

"Warriors have many scars, and hold them to be signs of honor. Surely, for a mere child to survive such a thing is proof of a warrior's mettle."

"Thank you for saying it." She leaned back upon her hands, and her still-oiled body gleamed golden in the firelight. Her expression was distant. "My mother was a widow, very lonely and very wealthy. We lived in a fine house in Tarantia. One day a handsome young man came to call. Axandrias. He was of a decent family and claimed to be a friend of my dead father. My mother was as trusting as she was lonely, and soon the snake was visiting every day. I detested him, but my mother would hear nothing evil about the man."

She took a deep, shuddering breath and continued. "One day, I came home from a neighbor's home to find two of our servants lying dead in their blood on the floor of our atrium. I ran to my mother's room and found Axandrias there, with two other men. My mother was tied to a chair, naked, and they were torturing her, screaming at her to reveal where her wealth was hidden.

"Before I could run, Axandrias snatched me up and

held me before her. He took a glowing dagger from a brazier and held it to my eye, screaming that he would blind me if she did not speak. So great was her horror that she lost control of her voice. That did not please Axandrias, and he pressed the hot iron into my eye."

Conan said nothing as she pressed on with the agonizing story.

"I lost consciousness, as you might imagine. I woke to terrible pain, but what I saw still in the chair was worse. I would not have believed that it was my mother had I not last seen her in that chair. I tried to cry out, but I no longer had a voice. It took me most of the day to crawl into the street and get help.

"Relatives grudgingly took me in, and saw that I had a decent education. Despite my single eye and my scarred throat, they hoped my family connections would assure a good marriage. They needn't have worried." She stroked the hilt of her sword. "I married the sword."

"That was a cold wedding," Conan said.

"But it suited me. When I felt I had trained long enough, I said farewell to kin and friends and I went hunting. I caught the other two within the year. They did not die swiftly, although they experienced nothing like the pain my mother felt in dying."

Conan took her hand and drew her to her feet. "We will both have our vengeance, you and I," he vowed. "But, just for tonight, let us forget about such things."

As she came into his arms she put a restraining hand against his chest. "A moment. Those for whom you seek revenge. Was one of them your woman?"

"Yes," he said, "but she is dead, now." He crushed her in his arms, and her mail was cold against him. But not for long.

Eight

Before them lay the grassy plains of Ophir. Not true steppeland like the vast stretches of grassland to the east, the Ophirian plain was gently rolling, with frequent ranges of low hills. The land was cut by many streams and small rivers.

"This is a great land," Conan said, "and we have lost their trail. How shall we find them in this place?" There was no discouragement in his voice. He would be content to range about this land for the rest of his life, until the last of his enemies were dead.

"We shall find them," Kalya vowed. "But it would waste time to go wandering aimlessly about, hoping to blunder into them. Rather, we shall let them come to us. Word of them shall, at any rate. Such men as these cannot abide in any place for long without gaining notoriety. This is my counsel: We must go to one of the war-torn provinces, where the scent of carrion is most likely to draw these vultures. There we select a town, one of good size where several roads meet. All the gossip of a district passes through a market where roads meet."

Conan nodded. "Aye, I take your meaning. If they are in the district, sooner or later we shall hear of a dark man of the south who leads a band of marauders. It is a good plan. Have you such a town in mind?"

"I have never been in Ophir. I think we need but follow this road. At each village we ask about promising locations. It should not take us long to find our place." They nudged their mounts and descended from the hills of Aquilonia to the plains of Ophir.

Their road, little more than a track at this point, took them to a border village. This area was too remote to interest the warring factions, but from the village a wider thoroughfare led to a market town on the edge of the fighting. Here there was as yet no true devastation, but signs of the war abounded. Crippled and wounded soldiers were to be met on the road or recovering in the town. In the nearby pastureland, sheep and cattle had been driven into remote dells in hope of being overlooked by foragers.

None thought it odd that the pair asked directions to the thick of the conflict. It was assumed that Conan was a mercenary seeking employment, and most thought the same of Kalya, for few knew her for a woman at first sight in her enveloping cloak, showing only her hard face with its lone eagle eye.

Between towns, wearying of preserved food, they hunted in the low hills near the road. Among Kalya's belongings was a short hunting bow. Between her archery and Conan's skill with spear and sling, they feasted often on fresh meat. In quiet times the local lords and their gamekeepers would have hunted down any such poachers, but the war had them fully occupied at present.

Conan told Kalya of Halga's family, and of Naefa, and of the slaughter in the small Cimmerian steading.

Beyond that, he was little inclined to speak of his past. It was sufficient. So thorough was Kalya's dedication to her revenge that she needed to know little more than the similarity of Conan's mission. Nothing else could have given them more in common.

At length, they reached the town of Leucta. It lay in level ground, at the juncture of three major roads, near where several minor routes joined these large arteries of commerce. The walls of the town were high and stout, topped with the banner of an important satrap. Though it lay in war-torn territory, only a large army would seek to take such a town.

"I think we have found our roost," said Kalya. "See how the wall glitters with spear-points and mail. Helmets gleam at every crenel. I'll wager this place now houses three times the garrison it supports in peacetime. Here we shall find news of the cutthroats." There was a note of sadness in her voice, for this meant that their long idyll on the road was over, and their bloody business must resume.

"Aye," Conan said, brooding. "But what shall we do while we wait for word? I know little of life in cities, and most of what little I have known involves fleeing from the lawkeepers or waking up on the musty straw of a dungeon."

"First," Kalya said, "we must stay out of trouble. We have enough gold left to pay our way yet a while, so there must be no thieving and above all no brawling. The place is crawling with soldiers, as we can see even at this distance. Keep your sword sheathed and a tight rein on your temper. Should we run low on gold, we shall see what offers itself."

There was a heavy guard at the gate, and archers on the wall above stood with arrows nocked to string, their eyes suspicious as they surveyed the travelers below. Conan and Kalya found themselves waiting among a motley band of traders and traveling entertainers as they awaited their turn to pass within.

To pass the time, some of the mountebanks began tumbling or juggling, keeping themselves and their neighbors entertained with their antics. Conan was especially taken with a man who juggled six daggers simultaneously, turning them into dazzling silver pinwheels but always contriving to catch them by the handles. The Cimmerian always admired surpassing skill, especially when it involved weapons.

"Are those weapons keen?" Conan asked when the man took a break.

A look of annoyance crossed the man's face. "See for yourself." He sent one of the daggers spinning toward Conan. The Cimmerian caught it easily as it whizzed by his face. The leather-wrapped handle gave a secure grip and he admired its perfect balance. He thumbed the edge and found it to be as keen as that of his own broad dirk.

The juggler's expression brightened at the adroit catch. "You seem to know weapons, my friend! Most men would have drawn back in fright at a dagger thrown so near their faces."

"Most men fear steel," Conan said. "I love steel as most men love their families." He tossed the weapon back and the man did not merely catch it, but sent it spinning upward, quickly followed by the others. The move had been so swift that Conan had missed the actual catch. It almost looked like magic, but Conan usually could feel the taint of true magic. He knew that he was seeing superlative skill.

As they reached the gate, a clerk looked them up and

down without favor. He sat behind a small folding desk with pots of ink, a rack of bronze-nibbed pens and sheets of Stygian papyrus ranged before him. He had the ink-stained fingers and air of self-importance common to petty officials. They gave him their names and he wrote them down.

"What is your business here?" the clerk asked.

"We are traveling through," Kalya said. "Perhaps we will seek employment."

"Mercenaries?" the man asked. "If so, we allow no such recruiting in our town."

"The times are unsettled," she answered. "Many caravans pass through your market. Some of them may be looking for guards."

"Two more vagabonds," he said, "in a town that has too many already. You understand that it is against our laws to contract unpaid debts? The penalty is flogging."

"We can pay our way," she said, hefting a clinking purse while Conan fumed at such insolence.

"Very well," said the scribe. "You must arrange for lodgings for yourselves and your animals. There will be no sleeping on the streets or in the public square. As soon as you have found a place that will take you in, you must report your location to the office of the city watch. Each day of your stay, you must confirm your location before noon, or the watch will search you out and throw you into the city dungeon if you cannot pay the fine. When you leave, report to me so that I may cross your names off my list. Is that understood?"

"Perfectly," she said through gritted teeth. They paid their toll and rode into the town.

"I have slain men ere now for using such a tone,"

Conan said. "If this is the way cities are run, I prefer the life of a barbarian."

She smiled at him, a rare occurence. "I have been in far worse places, where a stranger is issued a papyrus which must be signed each day by the authorities and surrendered upon demand to any official. If you are caught without it, they clap you into the dungeon. But, do not worry. The worst places are the small remote cities like this one. They are eager to prove how civilized they are, and so they insist upon these niggling little rules. The great cities like Tarantia are wide open and there you may do as you like, within reason."

"When this task is finished," he said, "I think I shall seek out such cities." Barbarian though he was, Conan found the marvels of civilization to be seductively enticing.

"Perhaps I shall as well," she said, without conviction. In truth, she had given little thought to a life after the destruction of Axandrias. She could scarcely remember a time when she had any other reason for living.

They found a stable for their horses and cramped accommodations for themselves; then they spent a long afternoon in the market and the taverns, inquiring after the Keshanian and his band. None had heard of such an outlaw.

"It is too early to be discouraged," Kalya said as they emerged from the fifth tavern. "If they have come this way, they could have reached the district only a few days ahead of us. It will take him time to gather a new band together, then to find a likely area to raid, then a little time longer to gain some notoriety. We must resign ourselves to staying here a while longer, perhaps for weeks."

"That is not a pleasant prospect," Conan said. "The amusements of this place must soon pall. I am not sure that I can occupy my time in naught but behaving myself."

"Then we shall have to find something livelier for you to do," she said.

That evening, they found a large, outdoor tavern adjoining the market square. The tavern proper was a small building with a cramped common room, but its courtyard was a spacious pavement, surrounded by a fence of ornamental iron. Small tables were scattered about, mostly occupied by soldiers of the garrison or travelers sojourning in the town. A large space in the center had been left open, and within it acrobats were performing.

"This looks a likely place to pick up gossip," Kalya said. "Let's see what is to be learned here." The two swaggered inside, attracting much attention. Much of this was due to Kalya's having thrown her cape behind her shoulders so that it hung down her back, much to the astonishment of many who, earlier in the day, had taken her for a man. Conan attracted attention as well, but the young barbarian was regarded with calculation rather than admiration. The host led them obsequiously to a table near the open center.

"Are those not the mountebanks with whom we waited outside the gate?" said Conan.

"So they are," she answered, admiring the art of the tumblers.

There were eight of them, four men and as many women. They bent their bodies into incredible contortions, leapt spinning to what seemed certain disaster, only to be caught by a partner and held in some unlikely state of balance, seeming to defy gravity. The eight piled atop one another, arranging themselves into various formations, many of them quite obscene, eliciting wild applause and raucous laughter.

The acrobats made a sweaty exit and were followed by fire-eaters and jugglers. These were followed by a spell of more sedate entertainment as a group of minstrels played upon instruments, singing of the latest news from near and far. Conan and Kalya listened closely to these songs, but none mentioned the men for whom they searched.

When the singers left to scattered applause, the knife-juggler Conan had spoken with took the center, accompanied by a young woman. She was a sinewy creature, her hair bound tightly back and wearing nothing but the briefest of loincloths and some jewelry. As attendants set up a wooden backboard the size of a door, the man juggled his knives with dazzling dexterity. When the board was secured, he sent the knives spinning high, and each came down to stick in the center of a table. There were shouts of appreciation at this, and the spectators tested the weapons to satisfy themselves that they were truly sharp.

Conan plucked out the blade that had stuck quivering in their table and tossed it back to the juggler, who gave him a nod of recognition. When he had retrieved his knives, the woman stood against the board while he threw the blades, outlining her in steel. This was not an uncommon act and drew only moderate applause. Retrieving his daggers once more, the man began to cast them directly at her. As each blade seemed about to skewer the woman, she dodged it, limber and swift as an eel. Spectators gasped as she avoided death by the narrowest of margins, for the juggler threw his weapons in rapid succession and she never dodged past the edge of the backboard.

"There must be some trick!" Kalya gasped. "You have two eyes, Conan. Tell me, is he faking his throws, with some mechanism to make the daggers spring from the board? I have heard of mountebanks using such a ruse."

"Nay," Conan said. "The knives are flying true. They are both marvelously skillful. When I was a boy in Cimmeria, we would amuse ourselves by casting blades at a target, but never have I seen anything like this. I would not wish to offend that man were he beyond easy reach of my sword."

"I must learn how she does it," Kalya insisted. "You spoke with the man today. Ask them to our table when their act is done."

Amid much cheering, the woman ceased her frantic gyrations and the juggler gathered the blades again. The applause died down as the onlookers realized that the act was not yet over. The woman stood against the backboard stiffly, legs together and arms tight against her sides. The juggler discarded all but five of his daggers; three in the right hand, two in the left. He paused dramatically, while all held breath, waiting to see what would transpire.

Simultaneously, both hands shot forward and the five blades spun toward the woman. Abruptly, her feet shot apart and her arms flew out to shoulder level. At the same instant there was a thud of steel meeting wood. The two knives cast by the man's left hand flanked her throat, close enough to indent the skin. Of the three right-hand knives, two had landed just beneath her armpits, the leather-wrapped handles pressed against the sides of her small breasts. The fifth knife had landed between her legs, so close that its upper edge touched the narrow strip of loincloth. They bowed as thunderous applause broke out.

Conan's keen eye had noted that the blades flew somewhat less swiftly on this last feat, but the skill and nerve required by both were appalling to contemplate. He signaled for both to join them at their table. The juggler nodded acceptance. By the time he had stowed his blades and supervised the removal of the backboard, the woman returned from the inn, now dressed in a brief, colorful gown.

"That was splendid!" Kalya said as the two took their seats. "How ever do you gain such skill?"

"It is simple," said the juggler. "You are born to the art. You spend many long years practicing, then, when your skill is adequate, you marry a trusting woman." He had a wide-mouthed, engagingly ugly face.

"She is more than trusting," Kalya said. "It takes more than trust to move like that! I account myself more than adequately swift and coordinated, but I could not move as you did on my best day. Did you gain the favor of some god to be so gifted?"

The woman laughed musically. "No, it was ordinary hard work that developed my skill. Like my husband, I was born to my art. My family have been acrobats, dancers, and tumblers for generations. From birth, my parents put me through exercises to make my joints supple. Before I could walk, I learned tumbling. By the age of seven I was performing with the family troupe. We were touring Zamora when Vulpio's family of jugglers joined us."

The servers brought their dinner, whereupon Vulpio took up the tale. "I learned early that my specialty was to be knife-throwing. It is only an amusing stunt with-

out a live target, especially a pretty one. Ryula was
reaching marriageable years about the time we joined the
troupe. Unlike her sisters, she was not terrified of
blades.''

''Yours was a spectacular finale to the show,'' Kalya
said.

''Oh, ours was not the last act,'' said Ryula. ''There
is yet one to follow, after people have had a chance to
eat and drink. It is worth watching.'' As they ate,
Conan noted that the two mountebanks only sipped at
their wine and they ate most abstemiously. Besides
bread, thin-pared cheese and vegetables they ate only a
few strips of grilled fish. It was clear that their liveli-
hoods, even their very lives, depended upon a clear
head and perfect physical condition. Conan decided
that such a life would not suit him. He liked to overin-
dulge from time to time.

As the platters were cleared, a man dressed in extrav-
agant garb jumped into the center of the cleared area and
spun a loud rattle.

''Honored guests!'' he cried. ''This night, we have
for your entertainment the most wondrous mage ever to
grace this city or any other with his marvelous feats.
Prepare your eyes for dazzling sights never before seen
outside the mysterious monasteries of Vendhya and far
Khitai. I present to you, the great Hurappa!''

There was mild applause. This was a cosmopolitan
audience, most of them widely-traveled and skeptical. It
would take more than a fulsome introduction to impress
them. They wanted deeds, not words.

''Watch this,'' whispered Vulpio. ''He joined us only
a short time ago. I assure you you have seen nothing
like it.''

The man who stalked onto the performing-floor did

not look like the typical stage conjuror. He did not wear a voluminous robe spangled with mystical symbols, nor did he wear outlandish headgear. He did not have false eyebrows or a beard dyed some absurd color. He carried no paraphernalia, not even a wand of hazelwood.

Hurappa was very tall and lean. His robe was sleeveless, exposing long, wire-muscled arms. It draped from shoulders to ankles and was somber black and without ornament of any kind. His head was completely hairless, with little more flesh to it than a bleached skull, and of the same hue. The mouth had no visible lips. His eyes, black as burned-out stars, stared out from darkened pits.

"Set!" whispered someone near Conan's table. "The royal executioner's a merry sight compared to this specter!"

"Good evening, my friends," said Hurappa. His voice belonged to something that might dwell in a barrow-tomb. "I crave your indulgence for a fleeting while. Please give me your attention, and I will attempt to divert you with a few examples of my negligible skill. Do but observe." He gestured with one hand and a roar of consternation went up from the crowd. The entire tavern was surrounded with towering flames, as if the city were ablaze. Benches went over backward as people leapt to their feet in near-panic. The bustle ceased abruptly as the flames faded out, leaving behind neither heat nor smoke.

"Just an illusion, my friends," intoned the mage. "Illusion is my art. Remember that all you see is just an idle illusion, a mere entertainment to while away a summer's evening. No harm can come to you from the exercise of my poor craft." This last statement rang false even to Conan's unsophisticated ears.

As the spectators watched enthralled, Hurappa caused huge flowers to bloom among the tables, so real that one could smell their perfume, yet when a hand went forth to pluck one, it winked out of existence. In a corner of the courtyard a small, winged sphinx of Stygia sat, a decoration placed there by some long-dead owner. At the magician's command, the stone creature stood and came down from its pedestal. Its body was that of a lion, its evil-faced head that of some ancient Stygian priest-king. At a word from Hurappa it spread great bat-wings and soared off into the night. At a woman's exclamation, the audience turned back to see the pedestal, where sat the little sphinx as it had for many years.

Illusion followed illusion. Snow began to fall, and a sheathing of ice covered every surface. Great icicles hung from nearby eaves and people shivered in the midst of the balmy evening. The snow and ice disappeared, replaced by a swarming jungle alive with bright birds and insects. The jungle faded as the stars above began to rearrange themselves and dance to unheard music. The stars dimmed as the sun rose above the horizon, so realistically that some thought it was truly dawn, until someone called out that it was rising to the north.

Then the sun set and the night became once more as it had been before the man had worked his magic. "I thank you for your kind indulgence," he said. "And now, I hope to amuse you with one final illusion, and I caution you to remember that it is *only* an illusion." For the first time, the man closed his eyes and began to mumble a low chant.

Expecting some crowning marvel, Conan was startled when a small mirror formed before his eyes. Round and no more than a handsbreadth in width, it quickly ex-

panded until it was as high as a standing man. He was
reflected in it faithfully, then the image faded and was
replaced by another. It was that of a tall, well-built man
whose black hair and short beard had gone iron-gray.
He sat at a desk of precious wood, reading from a
scroll. Conan could not see his face, but his clothes
were magnificent and his forehead was circled by a
narrow band of gold. On a stand next to the man were a
splendid formal robe and crown. He turned as if he had
heard something, a puzzled look on his face. Conan
drew a breath of astonishment. It looked like the face of
his father, but where would a Cimmerian blacksmith get
the trappings of a king? Then he realized that he was
looking at his own face, aged by thirty years or more.

Then the king and his chamber disappeared and he
was staring into a vast gulf of space where stars in their
death-throes cast blazing tentacles of cold fire into un-
thinkable reaches of aether. Conan felt he was plunging
through those mind-destroying vastnesses to some far
destination. Then he was in another room, this one far
more magnificent than the one he had seen before.

The chamber was ablaze with barbaric splendor.
Golden panels covered the walls, embossed in lascivi-
ous scenes. One wall was set with shelves from floor to
ceiling, and each shelf was lined with preserved human
heads, many of these wearing crowns. Coffers heaped
with jewels stood everywhere. In the center of this
savage magnificence stood a throne on a high dais. Men
in fine robes bowed on their faces to the man who sat
on the throne, beautiful, naked slaves chained at his
feet. He wore golden robes and laughed as he quaffed
wine from a goblet of carved ruby. His lined face was
dark, surrounded by graying hair. It was a face Conan
had glimpsed but once, in a crowded inn at Croton.

Then he saw only his own reflection in a mirror, and the mirror shrank to nothingness.

Conan blinked. There was a great noise in his ears, and only after a moment did he recognize it as applause. People at the tables were cheering and clapping frantically. The illusionist had disappeared. Kalya was looking at him strangely. He shook his head. What had just happened?

Vulpio and Ryula rose and made their goodbyes, promising to join them again on another night. Conan brooded as he and Kalya walked back to their lodging. He bolted their door securely as she lit their single lamp. As she stripped off cloak and armor, he said, "What did you see in the mirror?"

She turned, her body pale in the lamplight. "Mirror? Of what mirror do you speak?"

"Why, the wizard's last illusion. Did you not see a great mirror before you, and strange sights therein?"

"I saw no mirror," she said. "I saw the great dragon, like everyone else. He chanted for a minute, then the great scaly beast rose above the wall as though it stood outside the city. It looked to be more than a hundred paces high, and when it spread its wings, it blotted out much of the sky. People screamed when its fiery breath seared the air above the town, then it flew off like the sphinx. It puzzled me when the illusion vanished and I saw you sitting there staring straight at me, but as if you saw something far away."

She sat beside him and his great arm went around her shoulders. "Let me tell you what I saw," he said. As best he could, he related his vision of the mirror. When he finished, she pondered for a few minutes.

"This is a mystery," she said. "Clearly, the evil emperor on his golden throne is Taharka, grown old and great. As for the other, perhaps it is a prophecy. It may mean that you shall live long and become a king.''

He lay down and drew her down beside him. "I hope not. That was not a happy king I saw. His face wore the cares of a multitude.''

The following days proved unproductive. They saw much of the traveling entertainers, but Conan was reluctant to seek out the magician to ask about his vision of the mirror. He feared that it portended no good. When at length he made some cautious enquiries, he found that the illusionist had disappeared after the night Conan had seen him. This had caused the head of the troupe no end of trouble, as the man had failed to cross his name from the clerk's list upon his leavetaking.

To keep busy, Conan hunted in the hills nearby, selling his game to the innkeepers. His semi-respectable poaching kept him in reasonable repute with the authorities. Kalya gave lessons in the use of the blade to young bloods of the town who wanted to polish their swordsmanship.

One evening, as the season grew late, they were in a wide stableyard near the lodgings of the mountebank troupe. Kalya was learning some evasive moves from Ryula while Conan and Vulpio threw daggers at a post. Ruddy light from the setting sun shattered off the blades as they spun through the air to thunk solidly into the post.

"You learn faster than any man I have ever taught," Vulpio said as they pulled the daggers from the wood. Conan needed a firm pull to free his, for he had a tendency to fling the blade with excessive force.

"I have a feel for bladed weapons," said the Cimmerian. "But I could never match your skill."

"I have no art to practice save juggling the knives,"

Vulpio said with a shrug. "You are a warrior, and must be master of many weapons. You cannot spend many years practicing just one."

When the light grew too dim to practice by, they rejoined the women. Kalya was blotting sweat from her body with a rag. Ryula looked as cool and elegant as ever. A man came toward them whom Conan recognized as Gorbal, the head of the troupe.

"At last!" Gorbal cried, flinging his arms wide in a theatrical gesture. "At last, we can leave this town, where people grow weary of our performances and now fling more melon rinds than coins!"

"That is good news," said Vulpio. "We should have been far to the south by this time."

"Aye," said Gorbal. "Tomorrow a great caravan leaves this place to take the great southern road. Finally there are enough merchants and travelers going in that direction. A small caravan would fall easy prey to the raiders."

"Raiders?" Conan said. "Are there many such to the south?"

"Aye," said Gorbal. "Did I not hear that you were a caravan guard, young Conan? You should seek Hazdral, who is to be the chief of the train. He should pay well for a good sword. I'll wager he would hire the warrior-woman as well." He shook his head. "Especially with this new band roving about."

"There is a new band?" Kalya said, her voice carefully casual.

"So it seems. Word reached town today of a powerful band raging to the south. Its leader, so they say, is a great brown fellow, with the airs of a king and the heart of a viper. His lieutenant is a fierce Hyperborean, and that one is as cruel as his master, so it is said."

A slow smile spread across Conan's face. "Kalya, let us go and find this man Hazdral."

"By all means," she said. "I, too, grow weary of this town."

"We shall feel safer with you along," said Vulpio. "Here, if you are going to protect us you might as well have a decent weapon on you." He tossed Conan a sheathed knife, one of his finely balanced throwing daggers.

Conan tucked the weapon beneath his belt in the small of his back. "Thank you, my friend. And now, we must bargain for our wages. Fear nothing as long as we defend you."

Happy for the first time in weeks, the two went in search of the caravan master.

Nine

Axandrias had found the perfect lair almost by accident. From the moment they had crossed the Ophirian border, they had attracted vicious, hard-riding rogues as a lodestone attracts a blacksmith's iron filings. Rascals with cropped ears, branded foreheads and tattooed faces came singly and in small groups when they heard that a chief was assembling a band for some large-scale raiding. Within a short span of days, Taharka had a pack as large as that with which he had entered Cimmeria. All they needed was a secure base of operations.

Axandrias had gone scouting, anxious to regain favor with his chief and eaten with jealousy that Kuulvo stood so high in Taharka's esteem. With a pair of silent Shemites he rode for half a day from the spot where the band had camped. In the open, they needed to post a large guard, with may outlying sentries to give warning of approaching forces. Such discipline did not please the bandits, who were a lazy, improvident, and unruly breed.

At noon the three riders had reined their horses and

dismounted to break out their rations and unstopper their wineskins.

"Listen," said one of the Shemites, cupping a hand to his ear, "I hear running water. There is a stream nearby."

"I hear it, too," said Axandrias. "But where is it? I see nothing. Let's find it before we eat." They rode along the flank of a hill, but saw no water.

"Now the sound is behind us," said the other Shemite.

"This is strange," mused the Aquilonian. "Let's try upslope." They rode up the hillside until they came to a narrow cleft that was invisible from below. They urged their mounts into the cleft and gazed at the unexpected view that opened before them. Inside the hill was a huge hollow, its floor level and grassy. At the far end was the gaping mouth of a great cavern, from which issued the stream they had heard. It flowed across the hollow and plunged into a sinkhole at its rim. Apparently it plunged far underground, for it did not emerge outside the hill.

Axandrias dismounted and drank from the stream. Its water was pure and sweet. They rode to the cavern and dismounted to explore. At some time in the past men had used this place as a stronghold, for a crude wall of rough stones had been heaped across the entrance, high as a man's head and with only a narrow slot wide enough to admit one man at a time. Beyond the wall was a huge chamber, illuminated by shafts of sunlight coming through holes in the hillside above.

"This is perfect!" Axandrias said. "The chief must see this."

The next day, Taharka had surveyed the hollow and the cave, and had pronounced himself to be delighted. "This place will serve us well, my friend. There is confinement and grazing for our animals. The cave will shelter us and we have fresh water. A single sentry in yonder notch can give us ample warning of the approach of any dangerous force. You have done well, my friend, very well indeed.''

Axandrias smiled and preened himself with satisfaction. ''There is yet more, my chief, but the others must not see. Come with me into the cave.''

The two entered the great chamber. Bearing a torch, the Aquilonian led his leader far into the bowels of the place. ''I discovered this after I sent the Shemites back to fetch you,'' he said.

They went into a side-tunnel that ended in a heap of brushwood. Axandrias tugged at the brush and it swung back, revealing a low passage. The brush had been tied with withies into a sort of door. They ducked into the passage and a short walk brought them to an opening in the hillside.

''Tether a couple of horses here, master,'' said Axandrias, ''and keep a few sacks of loot in the passage. Then, should the worst happen, it is always possible to make a new start.''

Taharka laughed richly and clapped him on the shoulder. ''Ah, you are a valuable man, my friend. I have always known it. Let this be our secret. It would never do to let these rogues think that I might abandon them. Besides, should the worst happen, it would get uncomfortably crowded in this passage if everyone knew about it.''

Once firmly established in their new abode, they commenced organized raiding. The full force of the band was seldom needed, so Taharka usually divided them into three parts to raid separately and thus cover more territory. He took one band and the other two would be led by Kuulvo and Axandrias. He continually rotated the personnel of each band, so that the men should not develop loyalty to one of his lieutenants.

The chief established one firm rule: They were not to raid any place closer than a half-day's ride from their roost. The longer their hideout remained secret, the longer they could maintain their operations. Should they become too great a pest in the district, even the squabbling satraps of Ophir might put aside their quarrels long enough to stamp out the rogues.

For weeks the bands rode out of the hollow hill, and rode back with their loot. Nothing was safe from their depradations. From humble farmsteads to rich caravans, all became prey for the loot-hungry scavengers. Never did they come back empty-handed. Even when a lengthy expedition turned up no treasure, on their ride back they would take some unfortunate herdsman's livestock for the sustenance of the band. So this night brought only beef or mutton; tomorrow's raid might net them riches.

The raiding was remarkably easy. The powers in Ophir were so preoccupied with their civil war that they had no time nor manpower to spare for the protection of their own people. It was a simple matter for Taharka to place a few men in nearby towns that housed garrisons. He would receive word when a garrison rode out to engage an enemy, and one of his bands would raid the district thus left unprotected.

Soon the cave was heaped with their loot. Many caravans passed through Ophir, and even in small towns there were houses belonging to wealthy merchants that could be entered and despoiled. Also numerous were the country estates of rich nobles. Such men always had the local overlords bribed to leave their estates in peace, but this meant nothing to the bandits.

Chests of jewels and gold coin were heaped against the walls of the cavern. Bolts of dyed silk from the east, pound for pound worth more than gold, were stacked in a profusion of riotous color. The dank, smoky air of the cavern was relieved by the rich aromas of spices and incense, along with those of even more exotic drugs and the gums of medicinal plants.

The grassy floor of the hollow had been divided into a series of pens. Closest to the entrance were the horses of the raiders. In the area of best grazing were penned the finest of the livestock they had taken: magnificent warhorses, fine racing steeds, animals trained for hunting or for the swift passage of royal messengers. Human livestock was kept in another pen, with subdivisions for the more valuable. The largest pen held those destined to be simple laborers in the quarries and building projects of Stygia. Another held skilled artisans destined for the manufactories, workshops, and plantations of the south and east. There was an enclosure for educated boys who were in demand as house slaves in cultivated households.

Separated from the others and under watchful guard was a pen for the beautiful young women, girls, and boys who always commanded the highest prices. A roof of tent-cloth had been erected over this pen to protect its inhabitants from the beauty-destroying effects of the elements.

Late one afternoon, Taharka sat at his ease amid his takings. Chests, cushions, and silken cloth had been piled and arranged to make him a rude but splendid throne. He drank rare vintage from a golden cup while his men caroused before him. A great fire-pit had been dug by prisoners in the floor of the cavern, and now fat cattle from a noble's prize herd were turning on spits.

Beside the pit stood a huge silver basin from a raided temple. A slave-cook had concocted a sauce from the precious spices, and now women captives were dipping brooms into it to baste the huge carcasses.

All the men were now dressed in mismatched finery, jeweled weapons, and splendid armor. Like their chief, they drank fine wines from cups of precious metal or crystal. Serving them were women who were comely but not so beautiful as to class them among the prize livestock who were to be kept unsullied for sale.

Taharka rose to his feet, somewhat unsteadily, and called for silence. Immediately, the hubbub quieted. Axandrias smiled cynically as he sipped from a chalice of silver set with amethysts. He knew what was coming, and he had heard this speech in many variations in the past, spoken to other bands, now dead or scattered.

"My friends," he called, gesturing grandly with his golden cup, "is there any among you who is dissatisfied with my leadership and the life I have given you? If so, you have but to ask of me and I shall give you all you wish!" There was a great roar of denial from the men. "You are content then?" This time the roar was affirmative. "Excellent! For my part, I cannot imagine a better life for a man." Importantly, he strode toward the fire and pretended to sniff the air.

"It grows close in here," he proclaimed. Stooping to a chest he withdrew a great handful of a crystallized aromatic gum. He cast the gum on the coals and immediately the cavern was filled with a fragrant smoke. "There, that is better. A fortune in incense, destined for the great temple of Mitra in Numantia. Now it perfumes our air and sweetens the savor of our meat. Is this not fitting, my men?" A roar of acclamation was his answer. "Thus we shall always live!" Taharka proclaimed in his ringing voice.

"We shall eat our fill of the finest meats flavored with the most precious of spices. We shall drink the vintages of nobles. Our raiment shall be silk and velvet, with ornaments of gold, jewels, amber from the north, pearls from the east, coral from the southern seas! Our steeds shall be taken from the herds of kings. The choicest of slaves shall be ours to fulfill our every desire!" The men now cheered with unrestrained fury, whipped to ecstatic visions of loot by his words. Scant weeks before, they had been semi-starving vultures, hiding in the hills and cutting throats for a few copper coins. Now they saw themselves living a lifetime of luxury and debauch.

"Wherefore," Taharka shouted when the roar subsided, "let us now feast to our great content, and tomorrow ride out to make ourselves richer yet!"

With a savage shout, men fell upon the carcasses, slicing off cooked flesh with their daggers and stuffing the dripping meat into mouths more accustomed to the stale bread and foul water of the dungeons and prison work-gangs. The lazier among them lounged upon piles of silk and bade the serving women fetch their food upon chargers of massy silver.

Taharka surveyed the scene with satisfaction, marveling as always at how easily men were to be bought. He saw the tall, sardonic figure of Kuulvo striding toward him through the jostling crowd of gorging bandits.

"My chieftain," said the Hyperborean, "I think you should come with me. There is something I wish to show you." He paid little attention to the feasting. Like Taharka, Kuulvo's tastes in food, wine, and women were fairly moderate. He took his greatest delight in chaos and bloodshed. Taharka knew him for a serious man, so what he had to show must be important.

"Of course, my valued lieutenant. It is a fine evening for a stroll, and in any case I was planning an inspection of the slave-pens. Lead on."

The two walked out of the cave, and the men cheered them as they passed, only sour-faced Axandrias holding his silence. As hard as he tried, the Aquilonian could not drive the memory of the one-eyed woman from his mind. How had this phantom from his past come back to life to haunt him? Bad enough that she had returned from the dead, but she had publicly humiliated him! In the presence of his chief, he had been bested and very nearly slain by a mere woman. And who was that hulking Cimmerian who accompanied her?

After their escape from Croton, he had related to Taharka the incident which had earned him the woman's enmity. "I was much younger then, master," he had explained. "I lacked prudence and judgment. Now I would never be so clumsy as to leave a living witness to such a deed."

Taharka had tendered his usual false sympathy. "Young men always make mistakes, my friend. I made many in my youth, but we all learn from those youthful follies, do we not. And, for my part, I think it very petty of the girl to take the matter so personally."

Since the fight in the pit, Axandrias had grown more gaunt and his face had aged. He drank far more than had been his wont, and he ate little. Thought of the woman gnawed at his guts and ruined his appetite. What hellish working had turned the dead child into a fierce demon of vengeance with her ruined face, splendid body, and glittering sword that was a blood-seeking serpent in his memory.

Axandrias brooded into his cup, then he drained it and bawled for more wine.

Outside, Taharka strolled leisurely through the sprawling encampment. He stopped by the pen holding the beautiful captives and the guards stepped aside as he entered. He ran a hand over choice specimens of flesh here and there, testing for softness, firmness, texture, or resiliency depending upon what he was fondling at the moment. He poked a finger into a belly to test for a pleasing springiness, then opened a mouth to assure it was full of sound teeth. The smell in the pen was disagreeable, but that was one of the burdens of the slaver's trade, and the livestock would be washed before sale.

A glance sufficed to assure him of the condition of the other slaves. He spent more time on the fine horses. He considered himself a connoisseur of horseflesh, and he had picked out several for his personal string. Already, the swiftest had been penned near the back entrance discovered by Axandrias. The bolt-hole debouched to the rear slope of the hill, and since his men were not explorers by nature, it was unlikely that they would ever discover his insurance.

"The slave-pens grow overcrowded," Taharka announced. "Soon it shall be time to send a coffle south to the slave markets of Stygia."

"Soon a number of steps must be taken," Kuulvo said. "It is of that I wished to speak. Come but a few steps farther."

He ascended the sloping, narrow road that led through the notch. The two men passed through the gap and out onto the forward slope of the hill. The sentry on duty bowed as they passed. This prospect commanded a view of the rolling plain below that was miles in extent.

"It is a fine view," said Taharka. "Now, what did you wish to show me?" Casually, he let his hand rest upon his sword-hilt. He never let lapse his suspicion of treachery.

"Look," said Kuulvo, pointing to the slope below, then the landscape beyond. "When first we came here, there was no path leading to this place, only grass. See how it had changed." His arm swept outward, indicating the wide, bare roadway that now ascended the slope. On the plain below, this road split into three smaller but still apparent tracks, indicating the three routes favored by the bands when they went raiding.

"These trails grow wider and plainer with each passing day," said the Hyperborean. "There is no escaping it, with so many men and horses riding out each day. It is only a matter of time before some satrap's forces search this district. The moment their scouts cuts one of these trails, our time is short."

Taharka stroked his beard. "I see what you mean. Yet, this is such a fine roost, I hate to leave it."

"It is a good place," Kuulvo pointed out, "only so long as it is secret. True, it cannot be seen from below, but the road shall be followed. Hear my counsel: Let us leave this place, and soon. We have looted the district well, in any case. It is still rich, but there is no sense in picking its bones clean. Let us ride to the eastern end of the country, where we are still unknown, and find another lair. In six months or a year's time, we may return here. The grass will have grown high and all sign of our presence shall be gone. What is more, the district must be recovered and ripe for plucking again."

"This is excellent advice," Taharka said. "I have already remarked on the crowding of the slave-pens.

Let us raid a bit more to make up a full coffle, and in a few days time you may take it south. With you, take one-third of the men. When you rejoin us, we shall remove to a more secure district.''

''I counsel that we move immediately, Chief,'' said Kuulvo. ''I will take the slaves south, but I advise that you and Axandrias take the others and go at the same time. We can arrange a place to meet when I return.''

Taharka clapped him on the shoulder with a laugh. ''It is good to be prudent, but you grow too cautious, my friend. Life loses its zest when one worries too much. Come, let us return to the feasting. Thus far, we have not encountered a single force belonging to any local lord. In three or four days you may leave with the slaves. There are plenty of untouched places for us to raid while you are gone, and we shall still be well away before the hounds of authority catch our scent.''

''As you say, Chieftain,'' said Kuulvo with a shrug.

As had Axandrias before him, the Hyperborean had noted Taharka's tendency to play too close to the edge, leaving little or no margin for safety. It was as if there was something in the chieftain's mind that prevented him from grasping the reality of the storm raised by his depradations wherever he went. It mattered little in any case, he thought. Soon he would be away with his band of men and his caravan of slaves. If upon his return, Taharka and the others had been destroyed, what of that? There were always more wars, more men, more rich districts to loot. To an outlaw, only his own continued existence had any meaning.

''Tomorrow,'' said the chieftain as they made their way back to the cavern, ''I want you to ride out to the north. One of the scouts rode in this afternoon, with word of a great caravan said to be coming down the great road from Leucta. Naturally, it is moving slowly, for many are on foot. Should you set your men in ambush near that road tomorrow, you will intercept the caravan, most likely upon the day after.''

"Is it heavily guarded?" asked Kuulvo.

"Unlikely," answered Taharka. "There will be a few guards, but caravan leaders are always niggardly in such expenditures. Instead, they will have gathered a great rabble, and trust in mere numbers to discourage us. As if any number of sheep would trouble a wolf.''

"Easy pickings then," said Kuulvo, grinning.

"Yes, but a demanding task of cunning and leadership. I shall raid to the west and be back here tomorrow night. I plan to send Axandrias to the south to raid for cattle. That should be easy enough for him.''

Kuulvo arched a sardonic eyebrow. "You no longer have confidence in the pretty fellow?''

Taharka sighed deeply. "Alas, he is not the man he was when I recruited him. Then he was swift, wily, and even moderately brave. Best of all, he was amusing. Now something eats at him. I am sure it is something to do with that one-eyed wench.''

"It was a hard blow to one who fancies himself a fighting man," said the Hyperborean, "to be gulled and then bested by a wench. If he confined himself to thinking with his head, instead of with his—''

The conversation was interrupted when men came boiling out of the cavern mouth, cheering and jabbering. In their midst were two men, snarling at one another vociferously. Once in the open, the two sprang apart and drew steel. The other outlaws spread in a wide circle around them.

"What is this?" roared Taharka, bursting through the circle, followed closely by Kuulvo. He saw that one of the brawling men was a Corinthian named Parva. The other, to his amazement, was none other than Axandrias. "Explain yourselves!" demanded the chief.

"This dog questions my authority!" shouted Axandrias, pointing a finger at Parva.

"I said you were a cowardly lickspittle who curries favor with the chief while shunning your share of the work and danger!" said the other. "And I say it again! Meet me blade to blade if you are half the man you boast of being!"

This was most unusual, Taharka thought. Perhaps his lieutenant was regaining a bit of his manhood, not that there had been all that much to him to begin with. "You all know the custom of our brotherhood," he announced. "I will play no favorites. An accusation has been made by one and denied by another. They must fight it out and one must die! How will you fight?"

Parva held up his curved blade. "You see my weapon!"

Axandrias hefted his own straight, narrow sword. "Here is mine, dog! Come and swallow a bit of its length." The two rushed together and a wild cheer greeted the first clash of steel. The conflict pleased Taharka. If Axandrias were truly unfit, better for him to die now.

The two men wasted no time in circling or feeling each other out. This seemed odd to Taharka, for Axandrias fancied himself a wily swordsman who relied more on skill and clever tricks than upon strength and fury. Instead, they attacked simultaneously, their blades licking out and ringing together without pause. Each man cut and blocked, thrust and parried, in a masterly display of speed harnessed to cunning.

Axandrias began to drive the Corinthian back toward

the slave pens, and Parva gave ground expertly, shuffling the soles of his Poitainian boots so as not to bring a foot down upon a stone. Before he was backed against the rail fence, the man rallied and pressed a furious attack, cutting at the Aquilonian's head, drawing the parry and simultaneously kicking high. His boot caught his opponent's forearm, sending the narrow blade spinning into a pen where it skewered a slave. The unfortunate man's cry of anguish was lost in the cheer that acclaimed the masterly maneuver, bloodthirstily anticipating the kill.

With a snarl of rage, Axandrias unsheathed his dagger, a broad Zingaran blade, a foot in length, slightly curved and with two razor edges. Not waiting to anticipate his opponent's next move, he rushed forward to close quarters. Parva was taken off guard by the move, and jumped back a step, bringing his blade in close to defend with a cut to the Aquilonian's forearm.

The blow was weak and ill-timed, and Axandrias swept it aside with his dagger. With his left hand he grasped Parva's wrist and, combining his grip with the leverage of his blade, he thrust the hand against a fence post.

With a grunt of pain, Parva dropped his sword. The dagger slashed out for his throat, but the man jerked back with the strength of desperation, pulling Axandrias with him. The dagger missed by half a finger's breadth. The momentum of the pull combined with the powerful slash sent Axandrias tumbling in a half-circle.

Instead of trying to stop, he rolled forward, coming up in a spin that landed him on his feet, facing his enemy. Parva saw that, should he stoop for his sword, he would be a dead man before he straightened. With a feral grin, he drew his own dagger, a lean dirk of Khauran.

"So," crooned the Corinthian, "you are not quite the weakling you pretend to be? You have surprised me, pretty man, but you will need more than this trickery to draw ten more breaths."

Axandrias reached forth a hand and crooked the fingers toward himself, as if beckoning the Corinthian to join him. "Come and let us finish our dance. The men grow bored. They have seen naught but the guts of cattle all day. It is time they saw those of a swine!"

Snarling, the two rushed together once more. Parva came in low, as if he were about to gut Axandrias. As the Aquilonian crouched to guard his vitals, Parva straightened and brought his blade shearing up from the side, cutting in toward his enemy's neck.

With wonderful speed and timing, Axandrias brought his left hand up, slapping Parva's knife-hand upward and aside so that it missed his neck by inches. As he beat the attack aside, he stepped in, his curved blade swooping in low.

The blade went into Parva low in the belly. There was abrupt silence from the onlookers as, for an instant, the two men stood pressed together, still as statues. Parva's hand continued past Axandrias's head and stopped. The limp fingers dropped the dirk. Axandrias twisted his knife to bring the convex edge up. He ripped upward, the blade carving through flesh and viscera, until the edge was stopped by the breastbone. He twisted the blade again, and thrust inward and upward, then he twisted it in a full circle, slicing through heart and lungs.

Bracing his left palm against Parva's chest, Axandrias pushed himself away from the man, who was now little

more than a standing corpse. For an instant, Parva
stood, his eyeballs rolling up in their sockets to expose
the whites. Then blood and entrails burst forth as if
some ghastly explosion had occurred within the body.
The corpse tottered and fell forward into the spreading
pool of blood and offal.

The men went wild, cheering the excellent fight and
spectacular evisceration. They crowded round Axandrias,
slapping his back, congratulating him on his victory. He
smiled, acknowledged their praise, and broke away to
stumble down to the stream. He knelt and thrust his
face into the water, drinking deep. With his thirst slaked,
he plunged his arm into the water. It was bloodied to
the elbow, and he washed hand and knife clean.

Taharka came to him as he sheathed the blade. "That
was excellent, my friend. I do not think you will
have trouble out of the men from now on."

Axandrias stood and nodded. His eyes were clear,
and he looked very weary. "Aye. It was beginning to
annoy me, all the sly digs when my back was turned.
When one of them insulted me to my face, I knew it
was time to put an end to it."

"Just as well," said Taharka. "Now, go and get
some rest. I have a leisurely raid for you to accomplish
tomorrow."

"I can accomplish any task you give me," he insisted.
"I am no less capable than that Hyperborean."

"I know that well," Taharka assured him. "You
shall have a more demanding assignment the next day.
Now, go rest. A mortal fight with a worthy opponent
takes it out of a man."

Axandrias nodded and turned to go. As he trudged
toward the cavern, the chieftain's gaze followed him.
The man would bear watching.

Axandrias stumbled back to his sleeping-place. It was a small alcove in the wall of the main cavern, handy to the escape tunnel. His usual woman came to join him, but he waved her away. By the light of a taper, he checked the little wooden box. There was yet a good store of the pills he had obtained from the priest.

When he had heard Parva insult him, voice raised so that he could not help but hear the man, Axandrias had come back here and had taken one of the balls of green gum. As soon as he had felt its effect, he had gone out and challenged the Corinthian. After all, the priest had said that anyone might do this much without great risk of harm. It was only after they had gone outside and steel had been drawn that he had decided to make doubly sure, and had muttered the spell. Surely, the gain was well worth the risk.

And it was only this once.

Ten

Conan rode to the top of a small hill and surveyed the caravan. Close behind him rode Kalya. She now carried a long lance, its butt planted in a socket at her stirrup. The Cimmerian had not been trained to use the lance from horseback, so he relied upon his sword.

The caravan stretched for nearly a half-mile. In front rode some guards in glittering armor. A smaller rear-guard shone as brightly. Between them straggled a long train of pack beasts, heavy-laden wagons, travelers on foot, even palanquins borne on the shoulders of slaves. The spectacle was bright and colorful, but Conan was in no mood to admire the sight.

"Crom curse them all for fools!" he said as Kalya rode up. "Look at them! Spread out like a broken-spined serpent! This mob is a gift to any pack of bandits who happen along. Together, only a powerful force could attack them with impunity. Like this—" he waved a hand in frustration, "even a small band could take them."

"You could try telling Burra," she said banteringly.

Burra was the chief of the guards. He was an arrogant lout whose judgment was as low as his intelligence. He considered Conan to be a subhuman outlander and made no secret of the fact. He had assigned the two to the tiny flanking guard because he wished to keep his social inferiors at a distance.

"I'll tell him," Conan said, "and I'll tell that fat fool Hazdral as well."

"You might as well tell the lizard on that rock for all the good it will do. Besides, would it not be best for us if the bandits *did* attack? Should we not present a tempting target, the slavers might keep their distance and rob us of a chance to come to grips with them."

"Aye," he said, "you are right. Still, it goes against my grain to court attack when I have promised these people my protection."

"We cannot protect them all. That is the duty of the whole guard force, and you have seen what a mockery that is. Besides, what are these sheep to us?" She thought a moment. "Well, Vulpio and Ryula are friends, but I would not give the others the sweat off my—"

"Ride with me," Conan said. "We'll have one more try at convincing these fools. If they refuse to listen, their blood is upon their own heads." He kicked in his heels, and, with a hopeless shake of her head, she followed.

When they drew close to fat Hazdral's overloaded horse, the caravan master was conferring with Burra. The two looked at the young Cimmerian and the one-eyed woman without favor.

"Why are you not at your post?" demanded the head guard. His fine Turanian armor gleamed in the sunlight. He was a squat, square-headed man with a shaven pate and long mustaches that drooped from his upper lip almost to his chest.

"Because I cannot do any good there or anywhere else on this caravan," Conan said. "Sprawled out as we are, a small force could strike us at any point and be away with their takings before the guards could make a difference."

"You are too fearful, young man," said Hazdral. "You do not know the ways of the caravan trade. I have been on the trails since I was a boy, and this is three times the size of any caravan I have ever led ere this. Bandits are a timid breed, else they would be warriors. They will not attack such numbers as we have here."

"If this were the Pictish Wilderness," said Conan, "we would have been cut to pieces long ago."

"This is not one of your cold northern forests, boy," sneered Burra. "These are civilized lands, and you know nothing of them. Hold your tongue and do not presume to advise more experienced men. Now, go back to your post!"

"You are a fool and you will die like one!" Conan snarled. He wheeled his mount and rode away, followed by Burra's screamed imprecations.

He rode back to the center of the train, where a line of huge, slow carts carried valuable wares. In their midst were smaller carts carrying the goods of the troupe of mountebanks. Most of the performers walked alongside the carts, many of them practicing their acts as they walked. The juggling, tumbling, and singing ceased as he rode among them.

"Stay close together," Conan said. "We are in great danger now. Keep your weapons close at hand. You are nearest the most tempting prey for bandits," he pointed as the great, lumbering carts rocked along, their wooden wheels screeching loudly, "and you'll have precious little protection from the guards should attack come." He wheeled and rode away, his horse's hooves raising a dust wake. Behind him alarmed muttering broke out.

Conan and Kalya were riding left flank this day. "We should keep to the high ground," Conan said to her. "They will strike from the flank when they come, and I want plenty of warning."

They rode a little way ahead and found a prominence higher than the surrounding hills. Below they saw the caravan, straggling along at a leisurely pace. the sun was lowering in the sky, nearing the crests of the hills beyond the caravan.

"You are wrong," Kalya said, standing in her stirrups. "They come from in front."

"What!" Conan peered down the road before the train. A band of armed men blocked the road. They waved weapons and shouted. The foreguard howled back. Seeing that they outnumbered the bandits, Burra called an order and the men charged. After a moment's hesitation, the outlaws turned and galloped off, with the guard noisily in pursuit.

"Should we join them?" Kalya asked.

"No," Conan said. "Look." He pointed to the west, where two tiny figures were spurring frantically toward the caravan. "The main force is coming from the flank, just as I said, and with the sun at their backs."

Even as he spoke, a mass of horsemen poured over the rim of the hills to the west, descending upon the caravan with great speed. Backlit by the setting sun, their numbers were difficult to judge.

"Come," Conan said, "let's see if there is anything

to be done. But this fight is lost already. There is no sense in our dying as well.''

Together, they rode down into the chaos below. The bandits were among the wagons, leaping from their horses upon the baled goods, cutting down the teamsters, opening the bales and chests. Two bandits saw the approaching riders and rode out to meet them.

A shemite tried to spear Conan but the Cimmerian grasped the lance behind the point and wrenched the weapon from the man's grasp. In the next instant, his sword crunched through helmet and skull to drop the man dead upon the grass. He turned to see Kalya plunging her spear into a form that writhed upon the ground.

He took in the confused scene with a sweeping glance, and saw that one outlaw was a little aside from the others, pointing and directing the raiders. This had to be the leader, and Conan urged his horse toward him. The man turned toward him, and he saw that the face between the cheek-plates of the helmet was pale. Not Taharka, then. Next came a shock of recognition. It was the Hyperborean! At least they had found the right band. Their gamble in coming with the caravan had paid off.

The tall man wheeled his mount to face Conan, the white horsetail plume of his helmet whipping violently with the motion. He drew a massive sword and spurred his horse forward. The two blades clashed together once, twice, then the two men were past one another and wheeling again. A rogue with a dagger in his fist leapt from the top of a wagon toward Conan, but the Cimmerian slashed out with his sword, nearly halving the man in midair. Then the Hyperborean crashed into him, the other horse driving his own back, pinning

Conan's leg against the wood of a wagon. With a strangled cry of rage and hate, he made a wild back-hand cut, catching the Hyperborean's helmet above the temple, sending the man reeling in his saddle.

The other horse backed away, and Conan slid to the ground. He rolled beneath the wagon to be away from the flailing, trampling hooves. The pain in his thigh was intense, but a quick check assured him that it was not broken and there was little bleeding from the lacerations.

He heard the blast of a horn, and then the pounding of retreating hooves. He crawled from beneath the wagon and saw the bandits riding off, bundles and a few human forms across their saddles. Limping and wincing against the pain, he trudged along the line of wagons amid the wailing of women and the groans of wounded or dying men.

"Kalya!" he called. "Where are you?" Then he saw her riding toward him, leading his horse.

"When I saw you fall I feared you were done for," she said, "but then I saw you roll beneath the wagon." She handed him the reins and he hoisted himself painfully into the saddle.

"It was not my finest moment as a warrior," he admitted ruefully, "but I still live. Took you any wounds?"

"None I feel at the moment. Do you see any?" She turned this way and that, and he scanned her scantily-clad body.

"I see none, and on you it would show plainly. How many did we lose?"

"Who cares?" she said. "Come, let's see if Ryula and Vulpio are still alive."

They jogged toward the smaller wagons and carts. There was much lamentation, as Conan had expected.

The best-looking women in the caravan had been among the entertainers. They found Vulpio bending over a dead bandit, retrieving one of his daggers from the man's throat. He looked up with anguish on his face as they rode up.

"They have taken Ryula!" he said frantically. "One of them rode off with her thrown across his saddle like a sack of meal. I had already thrown my last dagger."

'How did that slippery eel allow herself to be taken?" Kalya asked.

"A spear-butt struck her from behind as she was helping a fallen friend," he said. He saw another bandit trying to rise from the ground and cast a dagger, spiking him through the eye. "She was still dazed when the rogue snatched her. We must ride after them."

"My very thought," said Conan. "We have every intention of chasing the rogues. Find a good horse and we'll be after them."

They saw a group of horsemen riding toward them and recognized Hazdral and Burra in the fore. "What is the situation here?" asked the caravan master.

"They have taken off some women," Conan said. "We are riding after them."

"You shall do no such thing," said Hazdral. "We have better things to do than rescue a few mountebank sluts. I am having enough trouble out of the merchants whose goods were taken. Join the other guards."

"I am riding after them," Conan barked, "and so is Kalya. As for the guards," he surveyed Burra and the rest with open contempt, "I do not see a bloodied weapon in the lot."

Burra nudged his horse next to Conan's. "So," he said, "you are too good to ride with us, savage? I have had enough of your insolence!" He began to draw his sword, and had it halfway out before Conan moved. In a single, sweeping motion of his arm, Conan drew his sword and slashed the man's head from his shoulders. It struck the ground a few seconds before the long mustaches came fluttering after.

"There," Conan said to Hazdral, "I have earned my pay. Your caravan is much safer now. However, you may keep your gold, fat man." He glared at the other guards. "Does anyone else wish to hinder me?" They all seemed to be looking somewhere else. "Very well."

There were many horses riderless, and soon they had rounded up several. Besides Conan, Kalya, and Vulpio, four acrobats asked to be included in the pursuit. Their women had been taken and they wanted them back. When all were armed and some provisions had been gathered, they began to ride.

With Conan in the lead, they rode for no more than an hour before having to stop. "It is too dark to follow their trail further this night," he said.

"But," Vulpio protested, "they will not stop! They will be many hours ahead of us by the time the sun rises."

"That is true," Conan said, imperturbably, "but if we ride on now, we might well lose the trail entirely. Better to keep their tracks before us and continue early than to spend all day tomorrow trying to find it again."

"He is right," insisted Kalya. "We make camp here." The other men muttered and cursed, but they obeyed. While the horses were hobbled, Kalya came to Conan.

"That was the Hyperborean that unhorsed you, wasn't it?" she asked.

"Aye. He'll not do it again. It means we will find them soon, Taharka and Axandrias." When he saw the eager gleam in her eye, he added, "We may also find a hundred more men with them. This may take some planning.''

Taharka came from the cavern to inspect the loot being unceremoniously tumbled from the saddles of the returned raiders. Bags of goods and semiconscious captives were dropped alike to lie on the grass in a mixture of bright materials, glittering metals, and white flesh.

"A good haul," the chief commented as Kuulvo dismounted beside him. "You met with resistance?" He had noted the stained bandage wrapped around his lieutenant's head.

"Very little," said Kuulvo. "But what we did meet was more formidable than most. It was that Cimmerian youth from Croton. By Ymir, he made my ears ring with that blow! Had my helm not been a good one—"

"The Cimmerian?" Taharka said. "Who is this man? And why does he dog our every step?"

Axandrias had heard these words as he stooped to examine a groaning woman. "Was the one-eyed woman with him?" The haunted look returned to his eyes.

"I saw her not," said the Hyperborean with a shrug that made his plate-and-mail armor rustle.

"I did," said an evil-faced man in a Stygian helmet of blued steel. "A near-naked wench with an eyepatch was among them. She slew three with a lance."

"Clever with the lance as well as with the sword," remarked Taharka. "This is a woman of many accomplishments. I suppose it might be mere chance. The two are skilled with weapons; they hired on to a caravan as guards and chanced into our territory. Recall that it was we who attacked the caravan, not they that came to us."

"No!" said Axandrias. "Those two are demons, and

they have been sent by some vengeful god to destroy us!''

"You become overwrought, my friend," said Taharka sternly. "Cease this unthinking prattle lest you upset the men.''

Axandrias grew calmer and bowed his head. "I am sorry, my chief. These two jackals so prey upon my thoughts that I forget myself.''

"There is no need to worry," said the chief. "They are only two, and we are many. Should they cause us too much annoyance, we shall do away with them. Now, on to more important things.'' He examined the captives appreciatively. "Who are these?''

"Acrobats, tumblers, and singers," said Kuulvo. "It seems a great gaggle of entertainers were traveling with the train. We picked some of the more comely ones.''

"Excellent. Women with such rare physical skills will fetch a handsome price in the brothels of the south. The House of Ultimate Delight in Khorshemish is always interested in purchasing women whose suppleness of limb and joint are outstanding.''

"When shall I take them south?" asked Kuulvo.

"My own raid of yesterday netted a good many captives," said Taharka. "With these, the crowding has become intolerable. Pick your men this evening, gather all the chains and shackles you can find, and start south at first light. Tonight, we will arrange a place to meet upon your return.''

That night, after the customary carousal, Taharka sat brooding upon his throne. It was not characteristic of him to brood, for he was a creature of the moment, for whom past and future had little meaning. From his surroundings he took what he wanted, and other humans were mere objects to be used at his pleasure.

Riches and luxury were pleasant, so he acquired them without the consent of former owners. The world to him was a dead thing unless it was filled with excitement, so he raised as much chaos and confusion as he could, wherever he was. If people troubled him, threatened him, or merely became inconvenient, he slew them without compunction. He was equally willing to betray those who trusted him.

In all these activities he was sustained by his intelligence, his abilities to plan and organize, and above all by his outstanding qualities of leadership, his capacity to charm other men and gain their confidence. Always, he had found these qualities of his sufficient to master his world, which was filled with lesser men.

Now something had changed in his world. Someone had taken a personal interest in tracking him down. The one-eyed woman, undoubtedly, wished to exterminate Axandrias. The Cimmerian youth, however, was different. Somehow, Taharka was certain, the boy was after him. It had to be something involving his raid into Cimmeria. Such lust for vengeance was something beyond the Keshanian's comprehension, but he knew it to be a powerful force in the lives of other men. What had he done to so obsess this man that he had already tracked Taharka halfway across the world, had slain the Bossonians and the Gundermen, and seemed quite ready to spend the rest of his life and cross the rest of the world to slay him. This, from a man belonging to a nation whose inhabitants were notorious for their reluctance to leave home!

It was a puzzle, and Taharka had no love for puzzles. He was happy in his capacity to manipulate his world and its inhabitants. This upsetting episode was a violation of the correct order of things.

With these depressing thoughts in his mind, he raised a silver cup to drink. The cup stopped halfway to his lips when he saw an unnatural color reflect from it. The flash had been green, and he turned the cup in his hand, noting that there was no green stone set in its smooth metal.

He looked around the cavern to see whence had come this unwonted gleam. The place rang with the snores of sleeping bandits. The fire-pit glowed a sullen red, its coals cooling after the nightly feast. Here and there were small torches, or tapers that men had set to illuminate their sleeping-places. He craned his neck to look behind him, and he saw the source of the green light far to the rear of the cavern.

His scalp prickled as he saw that a tiny side-cavern now glowed with a mysterious green light. It was a light he had seen before in his travels, most recently in a certain temple in the town of Croton. Slowly, he rose and descended from his throne.

He walked to a snoring guardsman and shook his shoulder. The man did not waken. Impatiently, he kicked the outlaw in the ribs, with the same lack of effect. Snarling a curse on all drunkards, he sought to rouse others. All continued their snoring unabated, and he knew that this was no natural slumber.

He debated whether to escape through his bolt-hole, then reminded himself that he had dealt with this situation before. There was as yet no need to panic. He took his sheathed sword from the dais and belted it to his waist. Slowly, with caution, he made his way to the rear of the cavern.

The side-cave was one he had not noticed before, but he had never made an extensive exploration of the cave system. Its roof was high enough for him to stand as he walked. He had gone no more than a score of paces when he saw the source of the light.

In a depression in the cave floor burned a green fire, from which no heat emanated. Behind the fire sat a man who wore a sleeveless black robe. He was cadaverous and had black, burning eyes.

"Greeting, Taharka of Keshan," said the seated man.

"And to you, priest," said the bandit, hand lightly upon hilt. "What brings you to my modest home?"

"Your destiny, as well you know. And you may forget any ideas of violence you may nurture. The priest of the temple in Karutonia, which you know as Croton, was careless. He had been for too long in a place far from the centers of Power, where the great events that influence the cosmos have their origins. I am far too powerful to suffer harm from your puny weapons."

"Ah, yes, the priest," said Taharka, sensing no advantage to be had from pretended innocence. "Since I had no desire for further doings with your sect, I slew him at first opportunity."

"You did not slay him," the seated man said. "He reported your deed within hours of its occurrence."

This was disturbing. "I slew him not? Yet I sought to make a most thorough job of it. I am not unskilled in that particular task." He was offended at the imputation that he lacked professional skill.

The man's narrow mouth crooked in a lipless smile. "We are not easy to slay. I might even say impossible to slay, save that certain gods have the ability to kill us."

"What would you have of me?" the chief asked, feeling impotent in the face of such power. He suspected that the wizard or priest or whatever he was lied mightily, but there was no question that the man had great puissance.

"Sit," ordered the man, pointing to a spot across the fire from him. Taharka complied. "Think back some few years, to a certain temple in Kutchmes. You recall the event, do you not?"

"Aye, so I do," said Taharka grudgingly. "I had taken some five or six well-born girls on a raid into Zamboula." He smiled at the memory. "Pretty things they were, none more than fourteen years of age and this was their first excursion from their homes. I was told that a certain temple of the town, dedicated to an obscure god, would give a good price for them."

"Yes," said the man seated across from him, "Certain ceremonies require such creatures. What occurred after you had sold your wares?"

The bandit chief's face grew distant, his voice haunted. "One of the priests bade me come with him to the inner part of the temple, where he had something to show me. On a whim, I followed. Far and far back did he lead me, until I was certain that I was the victim of some illusion, for the temple I had seen from outside was far too small to have such a spacious interior. And there was something strange about the pillars, wrought in the form of serpent-headed men, for their scaly heads seemed to follow me as I passed.

"By the pit of the great flame, which burned green and heatless even as this one before me, he bade me gaze therein, and hold forth my hand amid the flames. Under some strange compulsion I did not comprehend, I did as he instructed. He explained somewhat of the secrets of your sect, and that I was born at a certain place, under a specific conjunction of the stars and other powers, and thus was destined for a crucial part in the history of my time."

"And was this destiny not attractive? Did he not reveal to you some of the delights of your destiny?"

Taharka laughed bitterly. "Oh, aye, that he did. He showed me riding in triumph through crushed cities, beheading with my own sword defeated kings. I saw myself amid luxuries undreamed of, with nobles prostrating themselves before me, thousands of the fairest slaves to do my bidding, a whole world at my feet for my amusement."

"True, true," said the man. "We now approach a time when mighty adventurers, be they but bold enough, may seize the thrones of the world in their bloody hands. Certain of them, through their ruthlessness, may go on to rule empires. There are some, a very few, so surpassingly without compunction in their pursuit of absolute power that it is in their power to conquer and rule the whole world of men! Did he not reveal all this unto you?"

"Aye, that he did," Taharka hissed, "and he showed me as well what lay at the end of my reign! He showed me the unspeakable god that your sect would conjure from the blood of the slaughter wrought by me in my climb to the throne of the world. He made plain to me how that god would devour my substance and that I would reign for ten thousand years or more as some sort of obscene hybrid!" He sat back and his expression grew to be as stone. "Nay, I thank you, priest, but I choose to remain a simple bandit, taking my ease and enjoying my modest pleasures, living day-to-day. The attractions of empery are pleasant, but the price of them is too high."

"He showed you too much," the man said. "It is not

good to reveal too much of the truth. Very well, there are others. We had hoped that you would be the one, for your capacity for evil is greater than that of any other candidate. However, you are not the only prospect.''

Taharka was little satisfied with the man's words, but he was anxious to be rid of him. ''Tell me something, you that know so much. Who is this Cimmerian who has become as my shadow?''

''Cimmerian?'' said the black-robed figure, ''I know of no Cimmerian.'' There was a powerful, rushing noise and the flames leaped up to fill the room. Taharka's eyes were dazzled and he raised his arms before them as if to protect his face from true fire.

When he opened his eyes again, all he could see was a bewildering after-image. ''Priest?'' he called.

There was no answer. He groped before him, but his hand met nothing but the far wall of the cave. With a curse, he fumbled his way out into the main cavern. In time the blinking lights within his eyes faded and he could once again see the torches and tapers. He strode to a torch and seized it from its rough sconce made of mud.

For the better part of an hour, he searched the rear of the cavern, but he could find no sign of the cave wherein he had spoken with the mage. He slept ill that night, for his life had become entirely too complicated.

By noon of the second day, Conan was doubting the wisdom of leading this band of would-be rescuers. Whatever their other talents, the acrobats were not horsemen. Grim and purposeful though they were, the men quickly became saddle-sore, and so frequently did they fall from their mounts that only their skill in tumbling saved them from death or severe injury.

"We may have to leave them behind," said Kalya as she trotted her horse by the Cimmerian. "We waste time in this fashion."

He was inclined to agree with her. "I know they wish to bring their women back," he said, "and I wish we could take them with us, especially Vulpio, but I fear—what is that?" He extended an arm to indicate a plume of dust on the horizon. "Riders! Might it be the bandits heading back this way?"

She peered into the distance. "The direction is wrong, unless they made a wide circle. What shall we do?"

"We wait here," Conan said. "Rest the mounts as long as we can. When we know what they are, we'll know whether to flee or stay."

The mountebanks joined them and they waited, poised to make a run for it. They saw a large body of horsemen riding their way, and they relaxed somewhat when they saw the banners flying above them. Bandits would not bear such things. The leader of the cavalry force held up a hand as the horsemen neared Conan's little group and the troop slowed and halted in disciplined fashion. A few officers rode forward.

"We are the Eagle Squadron of the King of Ophir," said the man who wore the most splendid armor. "We search for a great mob of outlaws who have harried this district, taking slaves and loot. Have you seen such?"

Conan forebore to ask which claimant these men represented. "We are on their trail," Conan said. "They raided the caravan we were with and took some women captive. If you wish, I can guide you."

The officer looked surprised. "You can follow a trail in this trackless plain?"

"Easily," he assured the man. It seemed odd to Conan that people raised in this land could not follow the plain signs left by a sizable body of horsemen, but perhaps that was a part of the price of being civilized.

"Lead us to them," he said, "and your reward shall be generous."

"I will ride a little ahead," Conan said. "Do not let your men get ahead of me, lest they confuse the trail."

The officer gave the necessary orders, and Conan set out. The soldiers cast many puzzled or admiring looks toward Kalya, but they held their tongues.

Eleven

Axandrias looked up at the sentry's shout. The man was waving his spear vigorously, trying to attract attention. The Aquilonian left the horse he had been inspecting and vaulted over the fence. As he ran up the slope to the notch in the hillside, he exulted in the energy and strength he felt in himself.

He had awakened that morning with a ringing head, a sour stomach, and a general feeling that death was not an undesirable thing. He had drunk too deep the night before, as had recently become his habit. So, as an experiment, he had halved one of the pills with his dagger and swallowed it. He used no spell this time, so surely he could take no harm from it. In minutes he was fully recovered, feeling like a youth again. He had spent the morning at sword practice with a succession of men.

"Look, captain!" said the sentry as he arrived. "Horsemen riding this way! Many of them!"

"Mitra!" Axandrias gasped. He felt no fear, only a stirring of the blood. "Stay here while I summon the chief."

He ran back down into the hollow, then across it to the mouth of the cave. "Master! Come out here. We are about to have visitors, and I'll wager they wear royal colors!"

Taharka strode out, buckling his armor. "How many?" he asked brusquely.

"It is too soon to tell, but they raised a great cloud of dust. It is an ill time for them to show up, with a third of our strength gone."

"Perhaps they will not find us," Taharka said. "You yourself only found this place by chance." He said this only to forestall panic, for he knew that anyone with eyes could find the lair as it was now. "I go to the sentry post to have a look. Call the men to arms and assign some of them to guard the heights surrounding us, lest they place archers above us and pick us off like rabbits. When you have finished with that," he continued in a low voice, "see to our bolt-hole and our horses. Place fresh water and provisions there, should a sudden urge for southern climes come upon us betimes."

"Aye, Chief," said Axandrias, smiling.

The cavalry force slowed and stopped as they neared the base of the hill. For the last few miles even the dullest of the soldiers had been able to see the bare paths in the grass where the outlaw bands had converged upon their return to the lair. Now all could see the wider track that led up the hill and disappeared at the notch.

"Now this is a puzzle," said the Ophirian officer. "Truly, all the signs indicate that they rode up that hill, yet I see no one up there. Have they vanished into insubstantial air? Is this wizardry?"

"I think not," Conan said. "I'll wager that there is

more up there than we can see from here below. I was raised among mountains, and I know how deceptive they can be. Wait until nightfall, and I will scout it for you.''

The officer waved a hand dismissively. ''Hardly necessary. Either they are up there, in which case my squadron shall make easy work of them, or they are not, in which case I do not wish to waste more time.''

Conan shrugged. ''Do as you wish.'' He turned to Kalya and his little band of mountebanks. ''Come with me.'' They rode a little aside while the cavalrymen prepared for action.

''But they may kill Axandrias!'' Kalya protested hotly. ''I will not be cheated of my vengeance!''

''Nor will I,'' said Conan. ''But I think we need not fear. Whatever else we know of Taharka, we know he is no fool. Unless I miss my guess, those soldiers have an unpleasant surprise in store when they storm that hill. We shall keep well clear of them as they go. Do not expose yourselves needlessly.''

''How will we get Ryula and the other women out of that place alive?'' asked Vulpio.

''First we must see this lair,'' Conan said. ''Then we may start making plans. Until then, I fear the women must take their chances.''

There was a skirl from a shrill-voiced pipe and the soldiers began to ride forward. The advance began well, but as they rode up the slope it slowed. The natural declivity of the land leading to the notch caused the lead horses to crowd one another, jostling the riders together.

Abruptly, the notch and the immediate slope nearest it were alive with armed men. Arrows began to skewer the advancing soldiers and men with long spears thrust at the disorganized riders from all directions. The advance element began to fall back, throwing the following horsemen into confusion.

Conan, avoiding the beaten road and riding cautiously up the slope well to one side of the cavalry, could hear the officers screaming orders and trying to beat their men into some sort of order by liberal use of the flats of their swords. To the side of the notch he saw a high ridge leading from it like a castle wall above a gate. A number of men stood upon it, most of them plying bows. Fortunately for the soldiers below, these seemed to be indifferent archers except for a few Shemites, who practiced the craft from birth. Then he saw an imposing figure surveying the carnage with evident satisfaction.

"Taharka!" Conan growled, pointing at the man in the gilded armor.

Kalya hissed fiercely. "Where that great rogue is, can his yellowhaired dog be far away?" She spurred up the hillside, Conan close by her side.

Taharka turned and saw them, consternation writ large upon his countenance. He pointed down at them and shouted something to the archers. They turned and drew down upon the two.

Conan leaned far out and seized Kalya's bridle, jerking both their mounts to a halt as arrows thudded into the ground before them.

"Back!" he shouted. "We have no shields nor armor fit to stop those shafts."

With a squall of frustrated rage, Kalya complied. The others were nothing loath to turn back. The mountebanks did not lack courage, but battle was not their special skill. As they rode down, they saw the soldiers also retreating sullenly toward the base of the hill.

"You were right, foreigner," said the commander as

the Cimmerian rode up to him. "I should have let you scout this accursed place ere committing my men to an attack. There must be a huge crater or some such beyond that notch, to hold so many men. And their horses too, I'll warrant." The man fumed darkly for a minute, then, "Will you scout the place for us tonight? I will pay much gold for the service."

Conan was about to refuse payment when Kalya broke in. "How much?"

"Fifty gold royals?" the man hazarded.

"One hundred," said Conan, learning fast, "and I'll bring you back a prisoner to question."

"Done," said the officer. "What will you need? Weapons? Armor? You need but name what you will."

"I have all I need," Conan told him. "I will go there after midnight, when most of them will be asleep."

"As you will." The commander turned away from him and began issuing orders to his sub-officers, deploying his forces to prevent an escape by the bandits. Conan rode a distance from the soldiers and dismounted.

Kalya rode up to him. "Take me with you!" she demanded.

"No," he said. "You are skilled with the blade, but you have never been trained to enter an enemy camp unseen. This is something I learned in boyhood. Besides, I go there only for information. If you were to go, and should you see Axandrias, you would attack him and have the whole camp in an uproar before a man could draw breath. We would never come down alive. Now, leave me in peace. I need some rest before this mission." With that, he lay down upon the grass and was instantly asleep, hand on hilt. Fuming, Kalya stalked away from him.

Late that evening, the commander of the squadron sat

at a small fire, conferring with his sub-officers. There was a collective gasp as a ghostly figure came in among them.

"Mitra! What is this?" said an officer whose beard was dyed blue.

"It is only your scout," said Conan.

Weapons were resheathed when they understood who the bizarre figure was. The Cimmerian wore only a loincloth and weapon-belt. He had discarded even his sandals. His sword was slung across his back and all his metal had been muffled in strips of dark cloth to prevent both shine and noise. From brow to toes, he was streaked with soot.

"You look like some goblin from those Pictish forests you speak of," said the officer. "However, since you propose a reconnaissance rather than a parade, I suppose your attire is fitting. Bring me the plan of their camp, and a prisoner, and you shall have the gold you asked."

Wordlessly, Conan nodded and strode out into the gloom beyond the circle of firelight. He moved silently, so that none of the Ophirian soldiers noticed his passing. A short trot brought him to the base of the steep hill. He walked along it for a space, testing its nature and possibilities. He would avoid the notch, which was the one place sure to be guarded.

Instead, he chose a slope three hundred paces to the left of the notch, and so steep that he needed to use his hands to ascend it. Slowly, silently, he crept up the side of the hill, pulling himself along by grasping rock outcroppings and clumps of long grass, his soot-streaked body blending with the hillside so perfectly that a watcher twenty paces away could not have noticed him.

He gained the top of the ridge and found himself

gazing over its lip into a huge hollow dotted with scattered fires. Turning his head slowly, he scanned the ridge to both sides. To his right, toward the notch, he saw nothing. To his left, thirty paces away, a man sat hunched over his knees, snoring softly. The Cimmerian considered eliminating the man, but decided that he was no immediate threat and might be useful on the way back.

Like a lizard, Conan slid over the ridgeline and down the reverse slope to the hollow below. When he was well below the ridge, he stood and continued in a low crouch.

As he had anticipated, most of the men were asleep near the small fires, their weapons close to hand. There was little to fear from a night attack by a civilized army. Men unaccusomed to such warfare more often killed friends than enemies.

Here and there, men huddled by fires and conversed in low voices. Conan did not understand all the languages, but the tones were not those of high-spirited men. That was to be expected. The day's attack had been repelled easily, but they were penned here and had little chance of breaking out, while the Ophirians could send for reinforcements.

Conan crossed the hollow from one side to the other. He found pens for horses and for cattle and sheep, but where were the slaves? There were several empty pens, and he could tell from the lingering smell that these had held human cattle within recent days. Might the slaves have been moved into the cavern he saw at one end of the hollow? His bare feet made no sound as he traversed the hollow to the rock-walled entrance of the cave.

Stepping near the narrow opening, he could hear a

faint muttering of voices. He went to one end of the wall, beneath the overhang of rock. With the ease of a man climbing a stair, he pulled himself to the top of the wall and lay there on his belly. There were men in here as well, and the remains of a large fire cast enough light to prevent his approaching any closer.

Such voices as he could understand were discussing the prospects for the morrow, some seeming to favor a mass breakout, with each man betaking himself to a different direction, bearing as much loot as he fancied he could run with. Nowhere could Conan see any captives.

"Enough of this unmanly despair!" The voice rang out from the rear of the cavern with power and authority. Conan had never heard the voice before, but he knew whose it must be. He saw a tall, powerful figure stride into the dim firelight. The dark man still wore his gaudy armor, and he glittered with jewels and gold chains. The others fell into shamefaced silence.

"Are we women, that we see defeat in the presence of a handful of soft city guardsmen?" Beside the southerner was a smaller man who wore a silken vest. His hair was yellow and Conan knew it to be Axandrias. But the man had changed. His cheeks were sunken, and his eyes peered as from deep wells, darting nervously and malevolently like those of a predatory beast surrounded by enemies and looking for a chance to kill or escape.

"Did you not repel them easily this day?" demanded the man in a booming voice. "Did you not see the valiant Axandrias, standing in the gap, where he smote down three riders with as many blows? What have we to fear from this contemptible horde of parade-ground soldiers?'' There was a brief, half-hearted cheer from the bandits.

"We will drink their blood!'' said Axandrias. "Let none speak of defeat. Any such traitor shall answer to me. Does any here wish to counsel flight?''

Not a man would meet his eyes or raise a voice. It seemed to Conan that this ferocious specter little resembled the sleek, nimble man he had seen in the pit with Kalya. This was not the mystery that most occupied his mind, though. Where was the Hyperborean?

"At first light tomorrow,'' boomed Taharka, "we attack them! In a single great blow we shall scatter them as chaff is scattered before the wind!''

Conan pushed himself back off the wall. He had seen and heard enough. It would have been pleasant to cross the cavern and slay both men, but there was only one way out that he could see, and his chances of emerging alive from such a feat were vanishingly small. The battle on the morrow would afford him a better opportunity.

As he left the hollow, he collected the sleeping guard he had passed on his way in. A rap from Conan's dagger hilt deepened the man's slumber, and the Cimmerian threw the guard across a shoulder, carrying him the rest of the way. By now he knew he had little to fear from the ill-disciplined bandits, whose only wakeful guards were probably those at the gap.

In the camp of the Ophirian force, the Cimmerian dumped the prisoner at the feet of the commander. While the man slowly groaned his way to consciousness, Conan reported on the plan and nature of the outlaw camp. As he did so, they were joined by Kalya and the mountebanks.

"An excellent report,'' pronounced the commander when Conan's recitation was ended. "Would you be interested in joining my squadron as a scout? The pay would be generous, and no one would expect you to stand parades.''

"Perhaps later," Conan said. "I have a mission I must complete before I can take service with anyone.''

"As you will. And now, I think this scoundrel is ready to talk to us. Is the questioner here?'' A man came forward bearing a small brazier of coals in which rested several glowing instruments.

"May I ask him a few things first?'' Conan asked.

"You have earned it. He is yours.''

The prisoner now sat, his face a study in blank, fatalistic resignation, and most dejected. It was clear that no torture would be necessary.

"Where are the slaves you took?'' the Cimmerian asked.

"Gone south,'' the man said. "Two days ago, or perhaps three.''

"Did the Hyperborean take them?''

"Yes, and perhaps twenty other men. I wish I were with them.''

"Your fate would be the same. For what market are they headed?''

"Khorshemish.''

Vulpio came forward. "How are the prisoners bound?''

"In lines of ten," said the man, "each fastened to a master chain by a neckring riveted in place.''

Vulpio cursed. "This is ill-luck!''

"How so?'' asked Conan.

"Ordinary shackles or leg irons, ropes and such, my woman would be out of these in the blink of an eye. Escaping from shackles and other bindings is one of our most common acts. But no one can get out of a riveted neckring without cutting it.''

"We'll catch up to them before they reach Khor-shemish," Conan assured him. "They must travel at the pace of the slowest prisoner, while we shall be mounted."

"There is still the matter of twenty men, plus the Hyperborean," Kalya pointed out.

"Perhaps we can extract them by stealth," Conan said. He turned to the commander. "I return him to you. I wish you joy of him."

"He shall surrender his secrets to me, never fear. Go and get some rest. You have earned it, young barbarian. Remember my offer."

Near their horses, Conan and Kalya sat wrapped in their cloaks. The Cimmerian related in detail his adventure in the bandit camp.

"So, they are both alive," she said when he was finished. "Perhaps, tomorrow, our vengeance will be accomplished. If that is so, do you still propose to follow the rest and free Ryula and the others? Truly, they are not our affair. The Hyperborean had no part in your woes or mine, and he may live forever as far as I am concerned."

"That is true," Conan said, "but, having taken this up, there is something within me that makes me want to see it through. I told them, albeit half in jest, that they had naught to fear while I guarded the caravan, yet Ryula was taken from under our noses. And Vulpio has been a friend."

She smiled, although it was too dark for him to see. "And I know well that you are loyal to your friends. Yes, I feel the same way. Even if I slay Axandrias tomorrow, I, too, will know no rest until we have finished this matter. Now, let us sleep. First light is but three hours' time, and I would hate to sleep through the fighting.''

Morning light found them mounted and awaiting the attack. The commander, knowing what to expect, had arrayed his forces cunningly. Instead of a long, thin line, he had placed his men in three successive lines to absorb the force of a spearhead of charging men and he had placed his archers on the flanks to pour their shafts into the bandits, weakening them before they could smash into his horsemen.

They waited and the sun rose higher. Something had happened to the daybreak attack. When at last the bandits came, it was not in a single, concerted attack, but in small groups, each breaking for whatever escape it might find. Some risked the precipitous slopes in hope of avoiding the troops below, and a few broke away from the small groups to seek an individual escape.

Once he was convinced that this was not a ruse to distract him from a powerful attack, the Ophirian commander detached demi-squads to round up and deal with the fleeing outlaws. He caught sight of Conan and called out, ''How now, Cimmerian? What has become of your organized attack?''

''I know not,'' he answered, ''but I propose to find out!'' He urged his mount up the slope and gained the entry notch without encountering resistance. Most of the bandits seemed intent solely upon escape. As he rode through the notch a horseman blundered into him, swinging a sword wildly. Conan hewed him down and rode over his carcass and into the hollow.

Within, all was nearly deserted. He had seen no sign of Taharka or Axandrias. A few men were struggling to force their horses up the walls of the hollow in order to make an escape by some path other than the notch,

where the Ophirians awaited. After satisfying himself
that none of these were the men he sought, Conan rode
across the hollow and dismounted at the cavern entrance. Kalya was close behind him.

"When I go through," Conan ordered, "count two
breaths and come after. Come through too quickly, and
you may end up impaled upon my steel."

Sword in hand, he rushed through the narrow doorway. He swept his blade right and left, almost too
swiftly to see. Had any been waiting immediately within,
they would have been halved. The Cimmerian whirled
in a complete circle, whipping his blade through a
series of deadly arcs. Then he knew that no man waited
inside. There were times when a fighting man had no
leisure to survey the grounds and make measured
decisions.

An instant later, Kalya came through, crouched, her
sword extended. When she saw Conan sheathing his
blade she straightened and did the same. Her eyes
widened at the chests and bales of loot that lay scattered
about, overturned or torn open by the bandits as they
frantically tried to salvage a little in their precipitous
flight.

"Where are they?" she asked. "Could they have
made their escape with the others?"

Conan shook his head. "I think not. Axandrias might
have hidden himself in such a way, but I would have
seen Taharka. That man would have been as plain as a
lion among dogs."

The two explored the cave, not neglecting to appro-
priate some small, valuable items. Conan turned this
way and that, and soon they were joined by the Ophirian
commander and a few of his men.

"Well, we have most of them, and few of the others

will escape our net. Their heads will decorate the high road for many a mile." He looked about the cave. "Here's a task! I shall have Set's own work keeping my men's thieving hands off this treasure. What are you doing, young Cimmerian?"

"I feel a wind," he said.

"Then your senses are finer than mine," said the commander. "What of this mysterious zephyr?"

"It means there may be another way out of this place. My homeland is rich in caves. Come with me." He led them to the rear of the cavern and down a side-tunnel. There was a heap of brush at its end and he hauled it aside. Daylight came through and they stepped out onto grassy sward.

The commander pointed to some piles of dung on the ground. "Horses tethered here. Two beasts, I should say. It seems that our chieftains were prepared for such a fate as overtook them."

Conan cursed luridly for a few seconds, then broke into roaring laughter.

"What is wrong with you?" shouted Kalya, her face crimson and knotted with rage. "We had them, and they slipped through our fingers again!"

"What a rogue!" Conan said through his mirth. "Such a ringing speech, such brave words, and he was readying his escape all the time! He stirs his men to a pitch of courage and loyalty, then he abandons them when they need his leadership most! Was there ever such a scoundrel?"

"Assuredly," said the commander, "this man has the guile of a serpent and the morals of a courtier! Well, nothing to be done for it now. We must tally these goods and be on our way back to garrison. Let him be the King of Koth's problem. Two years ago, a plague came here from Koth. Perhaps this will even things.''

"Will you not set out to recover the slaves they took?" Conan said. "Most are your king's subjects."

The commander shrugged. "At another time, I would certainly do so. But now we are at war, and there are far greater problems than the woes of a few captives. My orders were to destroy the outlaw band and return to my lord's command immediately. I wish you good fortune, however."

Axandrias and Taharka rode through the night. Each had a number of bags of varying size hanging from his saddle. They had chosen the contents carefully, for maximum value with minumum weight and bulk. As the sun rose, it revealed that the Keshanian wore his customary look of complacent content, good-humored and optimistic. The Aquilonian was somewhat downcast, but he lost his gloom as the sun rose.

"Even now," said Taharka, "our late friends make their foray against the Ophirians. If they follow my plan carefully, it may be that the bulk of them shall escape."

"I think not," said Axandrias. "They are useless knaves and would not press home so bold an attack without good leadership."

"You seem not so sorry to be gone as you were last night." Taharka had nearly had to use force to persuade Axandrias to depart. The Aquilonian was still in the pugnacious mood that had gripped him in recent days. He actually had wished to remain behind and take part in the fighting.

"My blood was up," said Axandrias. "I was ready for a good fight. Upon consideration, it seemed but a poor way to throw my life away."

"Aye," said Taharka, "it can be a hard thing, to pass an opportunity for swordplay. When the warrior blood sings in the ears, it calls us to glorious butchery."

"Yes, so it seemed to me," Axandrias said. "But there shall be ample opportunity to exercise my sword-arm in future days."

"Oh, aye," Taharka said, "ample, indeed."

Inwardly, he laughed. It was clear that his lieutenant had been dipping into the drug supply. It was alarming how swiftly the demonic concoction was using the man up. Fierce, swift, and powerful he might be under the influence of the drug, but he had aged ten years in as many days. The once-glossy yellow hair hung thin and lank, the color of dull brass where once it had been golden. Flesh had fallen away from the sleek body, leaving it gaunt and wiry.

"What shall we do now, master?" Axandrias asked. "We have lost everything, all but his trifle we brought away with us."

"How so?" said Taharka. "We took the bounty of the land, at little cost to us. Were you planning to set up as a lord, or as a merchant? Had you planned to marry upon your gains and raise fat children? What have we lost? We lived as kings for a while. Soon we shall be in another land and do so again. All we lost back there were some men. What of them? I think I can safely prophesy that there shall be many more such men in the land to which we now go."

In spite of his sour mood, Axandrias could not but smile. "Aye, master, I daresay you have the right of it. What are men, or women, or gods, to the likes of you and me? Let us go forth and make another land our treasure chest!"

Taharka laughed loudly and leaned over to slap the

Aquilonian upon the shoulder. "There, that is the spirit! That is the Axandrias I recruited three years ago, and loved as a brother! What we have left behind is a trifle. The great days lie before us yet! Come, let us see what great things, what marvels await us!"

"Splendid, my chief," said Axandrias, aware that his master was quite mad and would one day play his game too close to the edge, sending them both tumbling into the abyss. "What shall we do next?"

"We shall catch up with Kuulvo and his slave-train. We shall rehearse a story of how the Ophirians descended upon us in overwhelming force and drove us forth. He has a goodly band of men, as many as we took into Cimmeria. With the price the slaves shall fetch, plus what we have here, there will be no difficulty in establishing ourselves in business once more."

"That sounds good, master," said Axandrias. "Shall we raid the countryside, as we did in Ophir?"

Taharka thought awhile. "No, we have done much of that, and I grow bored with it. Why make for oneself so splendid a life, if it lead only to boredom? And, in any case, the land is at peace and conditions would not be so favorable there. It is in my mind to travel yet further south, through Shem and to the border of Stygia."

"But, master," said Axandrias, "surely Stygia is a well-regulated land, where we might meet with severe opposition."

"But Shem is quite ill-organized," Taharka pointed out, "and the border is none other than the Styx itself. For some time now I have been turning over in my mind the possibilities of preying upon the commerce of that great waterway. It carries more traffic than any royal highway of the Hyborian lands."

"Raid river commerce?" said Axandrias, enthralled

despite his doubts. "Bandits upon the land are a commonplace. Pirates on the seas are known everywhere. Do you propose a sort of hybrid rogue, a river pirate?"

"It has been done in the past," Taharka said. "In my absence, it was never properly done."

Twelve

Kuulvo was bored. He was not unhappy to be out of the bandits' lair, which he considered to be little better than a trap designed to hold the band while organized forces moved against them. However, this was little better. There were few tasks more onerous than chivvying a coffle of slaves from one place to another, especially if the two places were separated by a considerable distance.

On such a journey, horsemen had to lounge about on their beasts as if in the seats of a city theater. Slaves were even slower than infantry. At least foot soldiers were trained to march. If the coffle included women, as this one did, the situation was even worse. Worst of all were children. The customary method of dealing with such hindrances was to brain the impediments against the nearest rock, but then the grieving mothers disturbed everyone's peace of mind with their wailing and keening. It was all a great bother, and, except for the great riches to be reaped from relatively little effort, the life of a common mercenary soldier seemed preferable.

The Hyperborean rode up and down the line of live-stock, applying his whip wherever necessary. There was one line of slaves that gave him less trouble than most of the others. Like the rest, they were chained together in a line of ten, but five of these were women. They carried themselves erect and did not seem to tire like the others. Upon reflection, it seemed to him that they were probably some of the women seized from the caravan. If they were traveling mountebanks, it was no wonder that they were better able to withstand the rigors of a long march than some others.

He took a kerchief from his sash and wiped the back of his neck. It would be a long ride to Khorshemish. He looked up at the hail of one of the outriders.

"Captain! Two riders come from the north."

Kuulvo reined in. "Two riders can scarcely be a threat," he said to those riding near him. Nevertheless, from long habit he loosened his sword in its sheath. A change of climate could cause a blade to bind in its sheath at the most embarrassing moments. He peered into the distance where the two approaching riders grew larger by the moment.

"The greater of the two is our chieftain, Taharka, unless I miss my guess," he said, "and who could the other be save Axandrias of Aquilonia?"

"Where are the rest of the men?" said a bandit who wore armor of iron splints, colorfully lacquered and laced.

"For that, we shall have to hear the story from their own lips," said Kuulvo, already sure that he knew the answer.

Taharka and Axandrias rode up with a flourish. "Good day, my men!" shouted the chieftain. "Have you had a pleasant journey thus far?"

"No worse than was to be expected," said Kuulvo. "I see that you have been traveling light, fast and alone. How does this come about?"

"Ah, that is a sad story," said Taharka, "a sad story, indeed. However, the life of an outlaw is a chancy one, full of unforseen events and happenings. A raiding-party was careless and was seen returning to our lair. Soon a great force of Ophirians, horse and foot, were camped at our doorstep. There was a mighty battle and we all fought heroically." He heaved a sigh. "Nonetheless, there could be but one outcome. All were slain or scattered. Only by a miracle were Axandrias and I spared to carve our way through the multitude and make good our escape."

There were cries of dismay from the bandits, and many alarmed looks were cast back the way the two riders had come. "Do the Ophirians pursue?" asked one.

"Nay, we lost them many leagues back. Is it not amazing that we have been thus preserved?"

"We rejoice that you have escaped from the jaws of death, Chief," said the Hyperborean dryly. He had noted Taharka's unmarred armor, his lack of the slightest wound. At least Axandrias looked as if he had been fighting. Kuulvo had his own suspicions of what had turned the Aquilonian into such a lion these last few days.

"Now, gather round me, my loyal men," shouted the Keshanian. "I have plans, great plans for us all. Hear me, while we drive our livestock to market."

The others listened respectfully while he outlined his dreams of bloodshed, glory and riches. Besides his voice and the moans of the slaves, there was no sound save the gentle clopping of hooves and the occasional crack of a whip.

"How shall we do this?" Kalya asked.

With Conan, she lay atop a low hill, gazing to the south. Far away, almost at the limit of vision, they could see the slave-train, antlike in the distance. They had left their horses and the other riders below the crest of the slope lest a slaver, glancing back, should see them silhouetted against the horizon.

"We wait for nightfall," he said. "Then we can get close. They seem to fear no pursuit, and that is good. Perhaps they will not mount a strong guard."

"There are at least twenty of them," she said, striving to count the faraway horsemen, "perhaps more. Can we come upon them in the night, do you think, and slay them all before they fully awake?"

"Little chance of that," said Conan. "Not with Taharka and the Hyperborean among their number. No, I have a surer way. It will take a few days, but there are many days left before they reach their destination."

"How shall we do it?"

"Not we," he said, "just me." He saw the mad gleam return to her eye and grinned. "Have no fear. I'll not kill Axandrias until you've had your chance at him."

"I will hold you to that," she vowed. "How will you destroy them by yourself?"

"Like a Pict," he said.

That night, she once again helped him streak his body with soot. The others sat dejectedly, knowing that their women were near, suffering the degradation of slavery, and they could do nothing about it.

The Cimmerian stood and prepared to go. Kalya held something up to him. "Your sword," she said.

"This is all I need," he said, transferring his dirk from the belt to his loincloth. It was a heavy weapon, ten inches long, thick-spined and broad of blade, but its single edge was sharp enough to part a floating hair. Without another word, he stole away into the darkness.

Hyras of Zamora was unhappy. With his companion, another Zamoran named Nargal, he had been detailed to stand watch all night at the northern edge of the encampment. He would much rather have been disporting himself among the women slaves.

"Why must we endure this duty?" he groused to his friend. "After all, our chief has told us that they were not pursued."

"Aye," said Nargal. "He fancies himself a great general and must have sentries and," he spat pointedly, "discipline." The man's pockmarked face twisted into an ugly scowl. "Had I wished to live this way, I would not have deserted from the army of Zamora."

"Sometimes," said Hyras, "the Shadizar barracks seems preferable to this windy wasteland."

"At least here we are not flogged," said Nargal. "But this guard duty is useless. Set take our chiefs. They are fast asleep now and I shall do the same." He leaned back against his saddle and shut his eyes.

With no one to talk too, Hyras found himself nodding off where he sat. After a few halfhearted attempts at wakefulness, he, too, nodded to sleep. Neither man had sensed the form that had glided, snakelike, within arm's reach of them.

Hyras woke with a start. The sun was yet below the eastern horizon, but its first rays were turning the sky pink. The stars were fast fading above and small birds were beginning their day. Hyras looked around guiltily, but it seemed as if their dereliction of duty had gone unremarked. Nargal still sat slumped back against his saddle, and as the light grew and the sky began to turn blue, he saw that his companion's head was still nodded forward as when he had gone to sleep, his pointed, blue-black beard resting against his crimson shirt.

Hyras yawned and scratched himself, wondering whether the man detailed to cook had prepared anything for breakfast. Then a thought occurred to him. Surely Nargal had been wearing a yellow shirt the day before. He had been inordinately proud of the garment, and had carefully killed its former owner by breaking his neck in order not to stain it.

He crept over to his friend and put his hand upon the man's shoulder to shake him awake. He jerked his hand back and gazed in horror at his palm, now wet and sticky. Nargal flopped back bonelessly, his head dropping back, eyes staring without sight toward the brightening sky. His throat was a single, gaping wound.

Hyras's eyes bulged, and he leapt to his feet with a strangled cry. He looked about wildly, but there was naught to be seen. Screaming, he ran to the camp. "To arms! Nargal has been slain! To arms!" As he reached the camp, amid shouts and confusion, Taharka grabbed him in a grip of iron.

"Who has slain Nargal?" demanded the chieftain.

"I do not know!" shouted Hyras, still in a state of nearly hysterical panic. "I must have closed my eyes for a moment, and when I opened them, he was dead! It is the work of demons!"

Taharka cast him away to sprawl upon the ground.

"Demons! Fool! Let us go see this work of demons."
Together with the other men, he strode out to the post
where he had placed the two men the previous night.
There was much exclamation and muttered speculation
when they viewed the corpse of Nargal.

"Truly, this must be demon's work," said a bandit
from Khoraja, a man famous among his fellows for his
many superstitions. He waved an arm, indicating the
nearly flat grassland surrounding the site. "See, there is
naught here save grass. How could any enemy be so
stealthy as to come here unseen and unheard? There is
not even a clump of brush to hide a foe. And what
natural creature could slay a man so near to another
without waking him?"

Kuulvo snorted. "What demon needs a blade to slay
a man? I have seen many a throat-cutting, and I recognize the method here. It looks to me as if Hyras has
nursed a grudge against Nargal and, when the man
slept, took the opportunity to kill him. What was it,
Hyras? A woman? Some inequity in the division of
loot?"

"I swear it is not so!" the bandit shouted. "He was
my friend! We deserted from the Zamoran army together and roamed side-by-side from many years!"

"I think you lie," said Taharka. "A fair duel between two men is one thing, but I will not have my men
murdering one another in their sleep." He nodded to
Axandrias and the Aquilonian whipped forth his blade
and skewered Hyras through the heart before the amazed
Zamoran could blink.

Taharka surveyed the two corpses with satisfaction.
"This one has been justly punished for murder, and
Nargal deserved death for sleeping on duty. Now that

this has been settled, let us go and have our breakfast. We have a long march today.''

They went back to the camp, where the slaves sat or lay, dull-eyed. The men began to roll up their blankets, then a frightened cry split the morning air.

''It is Pushta!'' said a Nemedian, his voice trembling. ''I thought he still lay here asleep. Yet he is dead, just like Nargal!''

The other men gathered around the new corpse. ''Two murders in the night?'' Taharka said. ''This is alarming.'' Despite his outward calm, his mind was seething. How could this happen?

''He lay next to me all night!'' said the Nemedian. ''I never heard a thing!''

''Nor did I,'' said an Ophirian, his voice full of superstitious dread. ''And I slept on the other side of him!''

''Perhaps we were too hasty in executing Hyras,'' said Axandrias.

''If your friends are dead,'' boomed Taharka, ''it is because you louts sleep too deep when you should be alert! I marvel that a single one of us is alive, with the way you louts drink yourselves into a stupor every night. Some night, these slaves will simply strangle you all with their chains and I will be rid of you! Now, break camp and mount. I want to be away from this accursed place.''

As they rode away, Taharka brooded on the strange events of the night. Had this aught to do with the priests and their ancient, horrid gods? Were they herding him toward some purpose of their own?

That night, the men stayed wakeful. In low voices they chattered nervously while with wide eyes they peered into the gloom beyond the circle of firelight.

Yet, for all their attempts at alertness, some nodded off to sleep. When morning came, there were two more corpses, their throats slashed from ear to ear.

This time the uproar was even greater than the day before. Some were for saddling and riding away immediately, abandoning their slaves and anything else that might slow their flight. Taharka had to summarily execute two men to bring the others back into line.

"We cannot stand much more of this, Chief," said Kuulvo as they rode south that day.

"What can it be?" Taharka said, growing dangerously close to panic himself. "What evil force can come into a guarded camp in the darkness and slay men with total silence? It is not natural."

"Natural or unnatural," said Axandrias, "another night like the last two, and they will be killing each other in their unreasoning fear."

"Aye," said Kuulvo, "he is right. I counsel that, from now on, the three of us camp a little apart from the others. They are no protection for us now, and are more likely to slay us than not. If one of us stays awake at all times, we might be safer."

"It is better than nothing," Taharka said. "How many more days until we reach Khorshemish?"

"If we drive the slaves hard," Kuulvo said, "we should reach there on the evening of the third day after this one. By tomorrow night we should be in more settled land, where there are farms and villages."

"One more night in the wilderness, then," said Taharka. "If we gain a good-sized village tomorrow, we shall fort up there for the night. A livestock pen with a stout mud wall may be a secure place for ourselves and our unwilling charges."

"What good are mud walls if our enemy is supernatural?'' said Axandrias. His eyes were deep-shadowed now, and his gums were drawing away from his teeth at an alarming rate, making them look twice their former length. Streaks of white now showed in his hair. Since the killings began he had been taking the drugs almost constantly.

"Even you, my friend?" said Taharka. "I had thought you of all men the least likely to fall prey to superstitious fears."

"I do not truly think this is demonic work," said the Aquilonian sullenly. "Yet it hardly seems like the work of mortal men."

Taharka did not wish to reveal his own fears concerning the priest who had come to him in the cavern. Yet, surely, this was a strange way for that accursed order of wizards to harass him.

That night, something new was added to the terror they had been enduring for what seemed an endless time. The surviving bandits built a large fire and stayed close within the circle of its light. All remained quiet, so that, by the hour before dawn, the sleeplessness of recent days began to make itself felt. Men began to drowse. They were jerked from their half-sleep by a shriek. A Nemedian was staring down at the feathered shaft of an arrow, six inches of which protruded from his chest.

Instantly, the others were on their feet, swords out and spears at the ready. Their eyes were wide and terror-filled as they peered into the surrounding gloom.

"Which way was he facing when he was struck?" demanded Kuulvo. A dozen opinions were offered, none with authority.

There was an impact as of a riding-quirt striking a saddle. A man staggered from the circle, the bloody

point of an arrow thrusting from his chest. They turned
to face the way the arrow had come from, and there was
another sound, this time a grunt of pain. An Ophirian
bandit fell to his knees, then flopped forward onto his
face. There was a dagger-hilt standing just below his
left shoulder-blade.

"We are all doomed!" screamed a hook-nosed
Shemite. The man ran, mad with panic, into the surrounding darkness. His shouts ended in a hideous, blood-
gurgling scream.

Taharka snatched up a whip and strode among the
chained prisoners. "On your feet, dogs! Stand up!" He
turned to his few remaining men. "Come here among
these cattle! We'll have a rampart of flesh if we cannot
have one of stone."

Hurriedly, the men darted among the slaves, hauling
on the chains to form the prisoners into a surrounding
wall. The slaves were bewildered, but they stood obedi-
ently, their downcast faces showing little. There was
one exception. One of the women, a wiry, black-haired
beauty, elbowed the women nearest her and she nodded
toward the man who lay with the dagger in his back.
With their faces turned so that the slavers could not see,
the five women smiled.

"The sky lightens," said Kuulvo. "Now we will be
able to see what has been causing us such grief." But
when the sun rose it revealed nothing but gently-rolling
grassland.

"There are eleven left," Conan said. "Tonight, we
will strike them one last time."

"I am happy that you let us go along last night,"
Kalya said. "Letting you have all the sport was beginning to wear me down."

"Aye," said Vulpio as his short-legged bay ambled along beside their mounts, "it did my heart good to plant a blade in the back of one of those swine. And to see with my own eyes that my Ryula is still well."

"By tomorrow's dawn," Conan said, "the two of you shall be reunited. When we go in among them," he instructed the mountebank, "I want you to stay near me. Do not try to cross swords with the bandits; that is not your art. When I point at a man, put a dagger into him, and do it swiftly, before he has a chance to dodge."

"They shall never see my blades, I promise. In the eye or the throat, every time."

"Kalya, do not try to fight Taharka, he is mine. If he comes for you, run. I counsel that we take care of the others before we engage Taharka, Axandrias, or the Hyperborean. Once busied with those men, we shall have precious little attention to spare for anyone else."

"All I care about is Axandrias," she said. "You may have the rest, but I cannot promise to run."

He glowered at her. "You are a difficult woman."

She returned his glower with a smile, "If I were not, what good would I be to you?"

The village was ancient, its mud-brick houses built atop the ruins of earlier structures. There was an old stone temple, its main structure fallen to pieces, its walls scavenged for stone to build shepherd's pens. In one corner of the village was a large pen for livestock. The lower five feet of its wall had been built of stone in more prosperous times, and over the years another five feet of mud brick had been added.

Taharka struck a bargain with the village headman

and the sheep were moved out of the pen to make way for his slaves. When the chained wretches had been moved in and set to cleaning the place somewhat, the Keshanian surveyed his new domain with wrinkled nose.

"What a stink! Sheep are worse than slaves for smell. At least a mere stench will not kill us, which will be a welcome change. Kuulvo, I charge you to see to it that none of the men go to a tavern and get drunk."

"I'll see to it," said the Hyperborean, "but we have more to concern us than drunkenness. Desertion is a greater likelihood."

"Then we must keep them all here for the night. Axandrias, go you and arrange for a good meal to be prepared. Take along a few of our slaves to bear it back. That should raise the men's spirits somewhat. But bring only enough wine to wash down the meal, and make sure it is heavily watered."

"You do not think we are safe here, Chief?" asked the Aquilonian.

"Until I know exactly what dogs our steps," the Keshanian said, "I shall assume that we are still in danger. Do you likewise. Kuulvo, stay near the gate and let no man leave."

"Aye, lord," said the Hyperborean, setting out to do his master's bidding.

Taharka took out a comb of fine ivory and ran it through his scented beard. After the previous night's doings, he was fairly assured that it was no supernatural agency that made his life a living hell. Arrows and thrown daggers were decidedly earthly instruments. But who? Could it be the one-eyed wench and the Cimmerian? He was reluctant to accept that. How could two mad youngsters wreak so much devastation? And why did they track him with the tenacity of avenging demons?

Taharka had heard tales, ancient legends of kings and heroes who had sinned so mightily that the gods took notice and assigned certain horrid creatures to haunt the offenders night and day, wherever they tried to flee, until madness or self-inflicted death overtook them. But that was mere idle myth. In any case, he could not see what he had done to incur such enmity.

No, he thought, it was far more likely that this had something to do with the black-robed priests and their hellish plans. The sweat sprang out anew upon his scalp when he thought of them. At all costs, whatever and whoever he had to sacrifice to do it, he had to avoid those priests.

As he made his way to the village's sole tavern, Axandrias was in no such quandary. He was now certain that it was Kalya who stalked him, teasingly slaying his companions as she closed in upon him. She had become a permanent nightmare to him, appearing in his dreams and in his waking thoughts. Sometimes she appeared as the child he had known, sometimes as the one-eyed fury he had seen in the pit at Croton. There were nights when he woke screaming with the stench of burned flesh thick in his nostrils.

At the tavern he gave orders for an elaborate meal to be prepared, but the savory smells that came from the kitchen gave him no pleasure. Taharka had not ordered *him* to refrain from drinking wine, so he ordered a cup. When it arrived, he fund that the taste repelled him. For the last few days he had had to force himself to eat enough to sustain life. Nothing seemed to have importance any longer save blood and battle and the woman who should have been dead long ago.

As the shadows lengthened and the light dimmed, Taharka drew Kuulvo and Axandrias aside. "My friends," he said, "as you know, I am a prudent man. Therefore I have taken certain precautions. If you will follow me." He led them outside the walled pen. Behind them, the sounds of men feasting filled the enclosure.

Conan, Kalya, and their followers skirted the sleeping village in the darkness of late night. In the distance, a dog barked, perhaps sensing their presence. A shrill squeal signaled that some rodent had just made the acquaintance of an owl. Otherwise, all was silence.

They gained the wall of the livestock pen without being detected. Conan signaled to the mountebanks and one of them stood with his back against the wall, hands cupped before him with fingers laced. Another placed a foot in the laced hands and stepped lightly to his friend's shoulders and stood there likewise, fingers laced before him. They had planned this move carefully, but there had been no way for them to practice it in the fields outside the city. The other two acrobats went up the human ladder of hands with magical swiftness. These were followed by Vulpio.

Conan took a deep breath and raced toward the lower man, stepping into the hands, springing up as swiftly as he could. His far greater weight buckled their knees, but he managed to scramble atop the wall without incident. Sprawled on his belly, he reached down a long arm and pulled Kalya up. As she scraped over the wall, her armor grated harshly against the hard-baked mud of the wall.

"What is that?" shouted one of the men below. "More fuel on the fire!"

Snarling a curse, Conan sprang to the ground, ripping out his sword. There was no time now to pull up the other two acrobats. Kalya landed beside him, her eye bright, searching for Axandrias. He heard Vulpio step behind him and he advanced toward the fire, now flaring brightly with an armload of fresh brushwood. All would depend upon surprise now.

"They are only men!" said someone wonderingly.

An evil-faced Argossian charged Conan with a two-handed, curved sword upraised. Conan's first blow knocked the descending sword aside, his second slashed the man across the face, and his third carved him down through the shoulder.

As he pulled his blade loose he saw two men closing in on him from right and left. He pointed to the one on the left and turned to engage the other. The man, in Ophirian garb, thrust at Conan's belly with a viciously barbed lance. Conan grabbed the lance behind its head and yanked it toward himself, pulling the man straight onto the point of his sword. He released the lance and took a two-handed grip to wrench the weapon free of the man's ribs. He saw that the other was down with a dagger in his eye. Kalya was sweeping her blade across the throat of a Corinthian.

Another Ophirian came for Conan, but an arrow shot by one of the men atop the wall skewered him. Then three more charged in and he had hot and busy work for several seconds. Barely seeing a sword coming from his right, Conan twisted aside to avoid it, sweeping his own blade in a backhand blow that took the sword-hand off at the wrist. He ducked a club-blow, but it glanced from his crown even as he gutted the wielder with a horizontal slash. Stars burst before his eyes, but he kept his feet and turned awkwardly to face the third man, who braced himself to swing a double-bladed ax. A dagger appeared in the ax-wielder's throat, and he toppled backward, sending up a tall spray of blood as he thudded onto his back.

Another man staggered by, trying to reach back far enough to grasp the arrow that protruded from his back. Another thudded in a few inches from the first, and the man toppled face down into the fire.

Conan made a quick count of the bodies. "There are three more! Where are they?" With Kalya, he prowled all over the enclosure while the acrobats embraced their women and the other slaves clamored to be released.

"They aren't here!" cried Kalya. "Does some god protect them? Are they always to get away from us?"

Conan ran to where Vulpio and Ryula were noisily reuniting. "Ryula!" he shouted. "Where are the other three! The dark man, and the Aquilonian and the Hyperborean?"

"They left the enclosure this evening," she said. "They told the others that they would keep watch outside the gate."

Conan ran to the gate, only to find that it had been barred from without. He sprang as high as he could, and just managed to catch the top of the wall with his fingertips. His great muscles coiled beneath his skin and he hauled himself to the crest of the wall. From the top he could see nothing, but in the far distance there was a sound of galloping hooves.

Cursing luridly, he dropped to the other side and unbarred the gate. Villagers were peering from their windows and doorways, drawn by this unwonted activity. He went back to where the others were gathered by the former prisoners.

"It looks as if we leave you here," Conan said. "They have slipped our grasp yet again. Ryula, did they say where they planned to go after they sold you?"

"They spoke much of—" she paused to kiss her
husband yet again, "—going south to the Stygian
border—" another kiss, "—and setting up as pirates on
the Styx." She was weeping and laughing simultaneously, and her words were difficult to understand.

"This must be a form of knavery they have not tried
yet," said Kalya. "It is only to be expected that they
wish to plumb every depth."

"We shall try to pick up their trail when it grows
light enough," Conan said. "Vulpio, you have been a
stout friend, and although you are not a warrior, I was
glad to have your daggers backing me this night. Here,"
he withdrew some gold coins from his pouch, "take
these. The village blacksmith will have a long day's
work tomorrow to get all these neckrings off. This will
pay for it and buy you some food to feed you all on
your way back home."

"We do not know how to thank you," said Ryula.

He shrugged. "I am here because there are some men
I must kill." He turned and walked away. Kalya walked
with him, wiping her blade.

"There were only four or five of them," said Kuulvo.
"We should have slain them and we'd have been done
with this business." The three rode south, their bags of
loot making a comfortable weight across their saddles.

"I agree, it is tiresome," Taharka said. "But there
were others on the wall. We know not how many and
some of them had bows. The advantage was with them,
and it would have been inadvisable to fight them under
such conditions. If they should ever find us again, we
will set the conditions."

"At least we know who they are now," said the
Hyperborean. "Not spirits, but mortals."

Axandrias's deep-sunk eyes were haunted, a look they never lost now. "Those two," he croaked, "the woman and the Cimmerian. I am not so sure that they are mortal."

Thirteen

"That is a river?" Conan's jaw had dropped in wonderment at the sight before them. The Styx lay in a broad, muddy band nearly a mile wide. Villages lined its shores so thickly that there was scarcely any division between them. Broad, fertile fields stretched back from the banks, and over everything lay a glittering network of irrigation canals.

In the distance, they could see the towers and domes of great temples, and along both banks of the river there ran broad, paved highways crowded with traffic, mounted, wheeled, and on foot. Most impressive of all, though, was the river itself. Its size alone was staggering, and it was alive with boats, rafts, barges, and even craft large enough to be considered true ships.

Most of the boats bore triangular sails on slanting yards. some moved by means of long sweep-oars, and others were sculled by men standing in the sterns, working their long oars like the tails of fish. Small boats were worked close to shore by means of poles, and even lighter craft were paddled.

"Look!" said Kalya, pointing. Around a bend in the river came a huge craft. It had two ship-sized hulls, connected by a broad deck. Hundreds of oars protruded from both sides of each hull, dipping rhythmically into the water, flashing in the sunlight, dipping again. Two high masts bore slanting yards, their purple sails furled. From the foremast hung a huge scarlet banner, worked with the semblance of a cobra in gold thread. The hulls were painted in brilliant colors, with blue and green predominating. Gilding brightened the stem and sternposts, worked into the shape of the heads of cobras, vultures, jackals, and lions. In the center of the connecting deck was a wooden tower plated with polished bronze, and it glittered with weapons and armor. Tower and deck bore numerous catapults and other engines of war.

"What is it?" Conan asked. He had never imagined such a thing. It was like a floating fortress. Across the water there came to them the deep booming of a great drum, in time with the rising and falling of the oars.

"It is a Stygian barge of war!" she said. "I have seen pictures of them, but they gave but a vague idea. It is said that the priest-kings have hundreds of them."

"Hundreds!" Conan said. "Surely there cannot be that much wealth in all the world!" He was dazzled by all that lay before him. Surely it was for this that he had left the cold, misty hills of Cimmeria.

"It is true," she said, "that the wealth of other nations is a paltry thing compared to the gold of the priest-kings of Stygia. That is what I have always heard, but I never truly believed it until now. Look there!" She pointed to a far smaller barge setting out from shore. Every inch of it appeared to be gilded, even the blades of the oars, worked by black slaves matched for size and color. At its stem was the sculptured head of a lioness; the sternpost bore the broad-horned head of a cow. "It must be the barge of a princess or noble lady."

"How can you tell?" At this distance, he could not make out the gender of the personage who sat enthroned amidships.

"I have read that the cow-goddess and the lioness-goddess are the protectors of women."

Conan had been standing in his stirrups since they had reached the high bluff overlooking the river from the northern shore. Now he sat back again. "This is marvelous, and I could spend years exploring it all," he said, "but it does not bode well for our mission. How shall we find them in so populous a country? There must be more people living within sight of us here than I have seen in all my life! And there are many dark people here. To the north, it was easy to ask after Taharka."

"We shall do it somehow," she said. "Surely we have not come so far to lose them."

They had ridden across Koth and Shem, losing the trail of the bandits frequently, having to ask at every village and farm they came to until they found someone who had seen the three pass. It had been days since they last had reliable word of their prey, and now they were at the river.

"Could they have crossed?" Conan asked.

"Possibly. But I think not. The Stygian side would be more dangerous for them. It is an unthinkably ancient land, and the whole nation is more powerfully controlled than an Aquilonian city. There they would be strangers and would be always under the eye of authority. It is my belief that they will commence their operations from the northern shore, or perhaps from some island in the river.''

"And in time, you think, they shall make themselves known to us?''

She laughed hoarsely. "Can you imagine that great rogue Taharka being anyplace for more than a few days without causing an uproar? Come, let us find a town with much traffic from both banks of the river. Soon we shall hear stories of death and destruction, and we shall know that we have found them.''

The town was called Pashtun. It was on neither shore of the Styx, but rather was on a large island just north of the center of the great stream. For the convenience of both nations, it was claimed by neither Stygia nor Shem and served both as a riverport and clearing-house for goods traveling or crossing the river. It was near a confluence where smaller but still navigable tributaries joined the great river, and was a natural place for merchants and travelers to gather, for agents of the various nearby kings to intrigue and trade secrets.

In the center of the island was a high rock outcropping, and here several inns had been built. Conan and Kalya had installed themselves at one of these. Prices were high on the island, but they were willing to pay well for so favorable a position. As the sun lowered on the evening of their third day on the island, the two sat on the roof-terrace of their inn, gazing southward to the Stygian shore. In the distance were huge pyramids, and Conan still found it difficult to believe that these were the work of human hands and not natural features of the landscape. He had been told that they were the tombs of priest-kings, and were many centuries old.

"Why do they do all this?" Conan asked, waving

toward the far shore. Immediately opposite them was the towering facade of a temple. Tiny, white-robed figures endlessly filed from one entrance to another, swinging censers and rattling sistrums and beating drums, unheard in the distance. "They perform these ceremonies day and night, and for what reason?"

"It is their tradition," Kalya said. "They believe that their devotion to the gods has made them so rich and powerful. The priest-kings keep their power by telling the common people so, at any rate."

Conan shifted uncomfortably. "What good is it to be rich if you must spend your life chanting and making dull music for gods that never say anything or appear to their worshippers?"

She smiled. "You are a true barbarian, Conan, and you do not understand the ways of civilized men."

"For which I would be thankful, except that we never thank Crom for anything." He took a sip of cool, spiced wine. It had tasted alien at first, but he was growing fond of it. It had a tart flavor, and bits of fruit pulp floated in it.

"What kind of god is your Crom?" she asked.

"He is remote and terrible. He cares little for us, nor we for him. He lives in a cave on a high mountain in Cimmeria. When we are born he gives us a warrior's spirit, and the power to endure hardship and slay our enemies. We think that sufficient gift from a god. The rest of his time we believe he occupies with his feud with Ymir of the Nordheimers."

"He is a god to match your cold northlands," she said. "The southern gods are more exotic. The Stygians have hundreds of them. I spoke with a scholar this morning, and he went on for hours, telling me of the properties of the various gods. There are gods for every type of weather, for every bird, beast, fish, and reptile, for every day of the week, and for every organ of the human body. Greatest of all is Set, the Old Serpent, but he is served only by a college of priests, and the others try not to think about him, so terrible is he.''

Conan remembered that the priest of the strange temple in Croton had mentioned Set, saying that he was an infant compared to the gods of that temple. Suddenly he was depressed at all this talk of gods and their submissive worshippers.

A man came up the stair to the rooftop terrace and stood looking for a vacant table. He wore the garb of a merchant from Khemi, the port-city at the mouth of the Styx, where the great river met the Western Ocean. Seeing all the tables occupied, he walked to the one occupied by Conan and Kalya, which yet had vacant seats.

"May I join you?" he asked. At their gesture he seated himself.

"I see you are from Khemi," said Kalya. They were quickly learning the ways of the river. "How goes the river trade?"

"It prospers mightily," he said, waving a hand toward the broad stretch of water. "As you can see, Father Styx provides for us all. Look there." He pointed to an immense train of connected barges, their heaped cargo covered by canvas held down by a hempen net. "Grain destined for Messantia, to relieve a famine in southern Argos. And over there"—he indicated a flotilla of small fishing boats setting out from the northern shore, their nets draped from long booms, torches set at bow and stern—"the night fishermen who replace the day fishermen. During the day, they fish deep. With the onset of evening, great swarms of insects descend upon the river to feed. Fish come to the surface to feed on the insects, and fishermen go out to catch the fish that men may feed upon them. It has a certain beauty, not so?''

''Indeed,'' she said. ''Yet is the river always so benevolent?''

''I percieve that you are foreigners from the north,'' said the merchant, accepting a cup from Kalya's hand. ''Is this your first visit to the great river?''

''We are but newly arrived,'' Conan said.

''Well, then,'' the man grew expansive, ''know that, while Father Styx is bountiful, he is also whimsical and may capriciously send dangers along with riches. The southern reaches of the river are alive with crocodiles and the great hippopotamus. The hippo is comical in appearance, but can be an irritable and dangerous beast. There are river adders whose venom is surpassingly deadly, and since all serpents are sacred in Stygia, one may not kill them.''

He leaned back, warming to his subject. ''The river is tranquil now, but storms of great destructiveness are frequent, and they appear without warning when two gods have a dispute. The water is shallow, so great waves build up quickly, and boats overturn easily, because river craft have shallow draft. Many drown every year.''

''Are there robbers on the river?'' Kalya asked, toying with her goblet.

''Rarely, but occasionally they appear. They never last for long, for when they become a nuisance the nearest satrap sends a war-barge or a force of cavalry to clean the nest out. Such action must soon be taken in Khopshef Province, which I have just passed through. It is to the west of this place, a district of no large cities.

Outbreaks of river piracy have been frequent there over the years.''

"What has happened in Khopshef Province?" Conan asked. He tried not to betray his eagerness, but he squeezed his cup so hard that it began to crumple in his fist.

"For some weeks now," said the merchant, "boats have been found drifting in the river, stripped of their cargoes and their occupants gone. Usually, holes have been knocked in the bottoms, but vessels rarely stay submerged in the river, for the currents usually bring them up again. Likewise, bodies and parts of bodies have appeared on shore. Always they are eviscerated, to keep them from bloating with gas and thus coming to the surface, but always a few will surface, albeit in pieces. This is Father Styx's way of telling his children that evil haunts his course and something must be done about it.''

"What sort of vessels have been thus attacked?" Kalya asked.

"They have been small merchant vessels, the sort that carry light cargoes and passengers. Mostly they are craft of the better sort.''

"Thus the cargoes are more valuable," said Kalya, "and the passengers richer?''

"Just so," said the merchant. "As it happens, now is the season for wealthy Stygians to go on pilgrimage to some of the more famed temples of the land. Travel by boat is more comfortable than by road. Often, they carry much wealth with them.''

They spoke long into the evening with the riverman. He was a repository of information about the river, its people and its ways. For his part, he was delighted to find someone who knew nothing of his specialty, and who wanted to hear all about it. They plied him with spiced wine, and he regaled them with tales of the river. When the evening was over, Conan and Kalya retired to their expensive room to make plans.

The next morning found them at the downriver wharfs, inquiring about passage to the west. They had sold their mounts and saddles when they removed to the island. There were so many borders and checkpoints on the great road that they had decided to travel by river whenever possible.

Great numbers of craft were tied up at the wharfs. Some were dirty or smelled of fish. Some looked too old and rickety to trust. They found one preparing to cast off, its deck heaped with bales of silk and there was a smell of herbs and spices coming from the hold. It appeared to be sound, and the few passengers visible wore costly clothing.

"Where are you bound?" Conan called to a man who stood in the waist, giving orders to a work gang.

"For Khemi," he said.

"Have you room for two more passengers?" the Cimmerian asked.

"All my cabins are taken," the man said, "but if you are willing to board this minute and accept deck passage, I have room."

The two jumped aboard. "I hear you will be sailing through dangerous waters," said Conan. "We are handy with our weapons."

The boatman shrugged. His turban was of scarlet silk and a gold ring winked in his left ear. "Then your lives will be safer. The price of passage is the same. It is set by law, twenty silver shekels of Shem, or two golden cobras of Stygia for passage from Pashtun to Khemi."

"But we are not going—" Conan began, stopping abruptly when Kalya nudged him in the ribs.

"Done," said Kalya. She handed over the money and the boatman waved to the bare deck.

"Pick a spot for your blankets. When the sun is high, we erect an awning for shade. I am Boat Captain Amyr, and my word is law aboard the *Pride of Luxur*." He turned from them and began to bawl at a gang of roustabouts who idled ashore. They bestirred themselves and began to carry small casks down the gangplank.

"Why did you pay full fare?" Conan grumbled. "We are not going all the way to Khemi."

"Because it would make him suspicious if we were to say we were going only as far as the pirate waters."

They spread blankets on the deck and watched with interest as the *Pride of Luxur* cast off. The grandly named boat was a flat-bottomed barge perhaps twenty-five paces long and ten paces wide. It was not new, but its wood was brightly painted and all aboard appeared to be well maintained. They soon found that most of the deck passengers were the servants of those who had rented the tiny cabins.

"Never have I seen so many unarmed men," said Conan as the two stood by the stempost, surveying the broad sweep of water and its traffic.

"This is a well-regulated land," she said. "You have seen how the shore crawls with soldiers and king's men. The rulers are rich and powerful, the land is peaceful, and the people rely on the governments to protect them. They have police and courts and other civilized customs."

"Such a thing breeds weakness," Conan said. "Men should rely on their own swords."

"I'll not argue with that," she said. "I can see that

our man Taharka has found a fine hunting-ground, although his days are numbered once the local authorities come looking for him.''

"Once," Conan said, "on the Pictish coast, I heard some sailors telling of the pirates that raid upon the Western Ocean. The Vanir are great raiders, and their longships descend upon coastal villages for loot and rapine. They spoke of Zingaran pirates and others that have lean fighting-ships. They sail out from islands and bays to attack merchant shipping. Taharka must have taken a boat and armed it and crewed it with cutthroats. The man never seems to have difficulty in finding such rogues as he needs.''

She stood staring into the distance for a while. "I think there may be another way,'' she said at length. "A raiding-boat would need a base and would be likely to attract attention. We have seen how densely the banks are populated, and how heavy is the river traffic. It would be difficult to attack a boat on the river without being seen.''

"They could operate from a small island,'' Conan said. "There are many such. They could fall upon their prey at night, while they are tied up at islands or near the shore. Some craft even travel the river at night.''

"Possible, but consider: We had no trouble in gaining passage on this boat. It must be so on many others. If we were river-robbers, would it not be easy to idle about the docks until we found a likely victim, then book passage? As we neared our lair, might we not kill the crew and passengers, probably in their sleep? Then our confederates could come out from shore in small boats to take off the loot, while we went on to dispose of the bodies and the craft well away from our lair.

Then we would simply row ashore and find another victim to take us back in the other direction.''

"It makes sense," Conan said. "Such a gang would be difficult to detêct, even with many patrols searching for them.'' He grinned at her. ''You have the mind of an outlaw.''

She nodded solemnly. "I would have been a good one. I have dedicated my life to catching a rogue, so I have had to become a rogue myself.''

The downriver passage was tranquil. When the wind was astern, the broad sail would be set to supplement the power of the current. Conan learned that an upriver passage was far more strenuous, with oars being necessary most of the way.

The barge made frequent stops on both sides of the river, dropping some passengers and taking on others. Some nights it was moored at a river port, others it was simply tied up in the shallows. Conan and Kalya asked anyone they met from downriver if the depradations in Khopshef persisted. Word had it that new signs of robbery and slaughter were found almost every day. There was as yet no great uproar. With so heavy a traffic, the occasional disappearance of a small craft seemed incidental and unthreatening. This last fact depressed Conan.

"With so many craft on the water," he said, "how shall we find them?''

"We may have to spend a long time at it," she said. ''Taking various craft through the district. It would be most convenient if we were on one of the craft to be victimized.''

"Our money would not hold out long at that rate; it would be eaten up by passage fares," Conan protested.

"You could learn to row," she said.

"I am a swordsman," he protested, "not a drudge to sweat over an oar!"

"I jested," she assured him. "Anyway, it strikes me that their loot is not all silver and gold. If they are taking bulkier goods, they need some place to dispose of it. Somewhere in that district there must be a merchant who takes deliveries late at night. It is there that we may find our lead to the pirates."

"How do we find such a man?" Conan asked.

"Leave it to me. You may be a great warrior in the northern wastelands, but I know the ways of civilized thieves."

"What month is it?" Conan asked as they carried their belongings ashore. The boat captain had been surprised when they wanted to terminate their passage less than halfway to Khemi, but since they did not try to haggle the balance of their money back from him, he was content. He now could take aboard two more travelers and their fares.

"This is the second week after the first full moon of the year. The Month of Famine, by Aquilonian counting. Why do you ask?"

Conan looked around them, at the palm trees, the heavy-laden fruit orchards, the peasants toiling in the grain fields, planting the year's second crop. "In the north, this would be the bitterest time of winter, yet here it is spring. Or perhaps summer. It is difficult to say, here where there are no seasons."

He hoisted a bag to his brawny shoulder as they walked into the small town named Nakhmet. Despite the Stygian name, it was on the Shem bank of the river. Such names were not uncommon, for the great nation of the south had frequently included much of the northern bank within its empire.

"True," she said, "this land is like something from a dream. Here there is no winter nor summer, but men divide the year by the rise and fall of the river. One crop is harvested while another is being planted, and trees in one field bear ripe fruit while those in the next field are in full bloom. It seems unnatural, somehow."

"And it is hot," Conan said, "but I like it for all that. Over on the other side, in Stygia, the land is too priest-ridden for my taste. The people are too tame and fatalistic. But here, I like this land."

"It is pleasant," she said, absently, "but I fear that Taharka is at home here. The south is his element, and it might give him some advantage. In other places, he was an interloper, but here he is almost like a native. The land of Keshan is on the Styx, south of Stygia."

The thought of lands even more remote than Stygia stirred Conan's spirit. "I have spoken with travelers about those lands. Punt, and Zembabwei, rich in gold and ivory, and Kush and Darfar, where all the people have skins black as ebony. They say that, farther south, there are huge black kingdoms of which men here know not even the names. Someday, I will visit them all."

"You have the spirit of a wanderer," she said. "I, too, have traveled far, but only because my vengeance called me to."

Conan did not ask her what she would do after she had slain Axandrias. He already knew that the half-mad young woman had no thought whatever beyond that consummation. She grew wroth any time he raised the subject.

The town boasted a large temple to one of the Shemite gods. They already knew that the people of this land were not especially religious, but having a large temple was a matter of civic pride. Always the temples were being renovated or expanded. Many towers they had passed on their travels were encased in scaffolding, as the townsmen sought to raise theirs a few feet higher than those of the neighboring towns.

They found a sprawling inn next to such a temple. The house of worship was dedicated to an ugly little brute of a god named Baal-Sepa. The innkeeper was a greasy, unctuous man with a beard dressed in the fashion of the land: trimmed square and arranged in geometrically-precise rows of tight ringlets. It shone with pomade and its perfume was powerful enough to be smelled from several paces away. He doffed his cylindrical hat at their approach and bowed almost to his green slippers.

"Greeting, friends. How may I be of service? Have you visited our temple yet? It contains more statues of Baal-Sepa than any other in Shem. It also has finer marble reliefs than any other. Its minaret is five feet higher—"

"An imposing structure, I am sure," Kalya said. "We will be sure to examine it closely at leisure. What we need now is a room and a meal."

"We are famished," Conan said, more to forestall the keeper's effusiveness than to hurry dinner. They had reached the common room and it looked promising.

"You shall have my very best room," the innkeeper promised. "Here, seat yourselves, take your ease. I shall send a servant to see to your every whim." Puffing and sweating, he ran off to greet another newcomer.

"Now," Conan said as they sat, "this is more like it." The occupants of the other tables were mostly men, many of them exceedingly disreputable in appearance.

Three roads that cut southward through Shem met here. Many of the men had the look of caravaners and the smell of camels. "All that well-regulated law and order was about to drive me mad."

"Aye, these people appear to be more our sort," said Kalya. "This should be a fine place to pick up word of our slaver-bandit-pirates."

After their meal, the innkeeper showed them to his "best room" which was identical to his others. It was small and cramped, but they had tolerated far worse accommodations in their long trail of blood. At least it had a large window to admit fresh air, and it seemed to be vermin-free.

"This will serve," said Conan. "Tell me, my host, suppose one were to have a few items for sale, items of value that one did not wish to be seen by the authorities. Where would one find a safe buyer for these things?"

With a smile of complicity, the innkeeper stuck his head out through the doorway and looked down the hall in both directions. He pulled his head back in and spoke in a low voice. "Should you have some items of small bulk, and should you not wish to go through the tedious formalities of licensing, excise, duties and so forth, well, I might be interested. May I see them?"

"Actually," said Kalya, "we do not have these things with us. You must understand that discretion is of importance. And they are not truly small in bulk. Whoever buys them must have the resources to dispose of a large quantity of merchandise." She dropped her cloak to the floor casually, and the innkeeper's eyes bulged.

"Ahem! Ah, yes, I see. I am afraid that I cannot handle goods of any bulk, but there is a merchant in the next town to the west, Ashabal. His name is Ra-Harakhte.

He is Stygian by birth, as his name reveals. He is known for a liberal attitude toward commerce.''

"How far is this town?" Conan asked.

"It is but a short morning's walk along the river road. Should you be able to reach an accommodation with Ra-Harakhte, I only ask that you mention my name to him."

"We shall not fail to do so," said Kalya.

"Sleep well, my friends," he said, bowing his way through the door.

"I had not expected to find a promising lead so soon," said Conan, hanging his sword-belt on a peg.

Kalya sat on the bed, which was little more than a thin mattress over rope netting, crossing her feet over her thighs. Her mail and other accoutrements now lay in a small heap on the floor. "We may have yet a long search ahead of us. This may be merely one fence among many in this district. Still, it is a good start. And Taharka and the others may feel safe. They have not seen us in many long weeks. I'll wager they think they have lost us."

"They have," said Conan. "But we'll correct that." He sat next to her, then fell back upon the mattress in a sprawl of long limbs. "I would not have believed how tiring a long river voyage could be."

"How tired are you?" she asked, and the look in her eye was for a change not bloodthirsty.

"Not *that* tired," he said, drawing her down beside him.

Late the next morning, still bearing their bags of belongings, they stood before a long, rambling warehouse by the river wharfs in the town of Ashabal. Outside the doorway of the warehouse sat an enormous black man wearing only some cheap ornaments, a white loincloth, and white turban. He sat on a low stool, and leaning against the wall next to him was a short club studded with iron spikes. As they made their way toward the door, the black man stood and eyed them with belligerent suspicion.

"We seek a man named Ra-Harakhte," said Conan. "Is this his place of business?"

"He is my master," said the black man haughtily. "What is your business with him?"

"Our business we will discuss when we meet him," said Kalya.

"My master is a great and wealthy merchant," the man sneered. "What have ragged foreigners like the two of you to do with him?"

Casually, Conan smashed the man across the jaw with his fist. The man crashed into the wall, slid slowly down it until he reached his knees and collapsed across the doorway, a thin trickle of blood running from his mouth to the dusty ground.

They stepped over the mountainous carcass and entered the coolness of the interior. A man with a thin, sinister face was stacking some bales in a corner. He wore colorful robes and a turban of black silk. The jeweled handle of a curved dagger protruded from his sash.

"I always told that fat knave that his manner was entirely too arrogant. I knew that this would happen someday."

"Are you Ra-Harakhte?" Conan asked.

"The very same. And you?" Obviously, the man did not stand on effusive ceremony, unlike most southerners they had encountered.

"Conan of Cimmeria and Kalya of Aquilonia," he said.

"You are far from home. How may I be of service?"

The two looked around the warehouse, noting the great assortment of costly goods. "We seek employment," Kalya said, examining the weave of a fine silk hanging.

"I am not hiring," said the merchant. "Why do you come to me?"

"The employment we seek," Conan said, "is the kind in which the dangers and the rewards are likewise high. We are both experts with our weapons and we have no liking for the authorities. We were told that you have dealings with people who might have positions to offer." It was a gamble, he knew, but there was no point in wasting time.

"Then you have been told lies," the merchant said. "I am a law-abiding man and a loyal subject of the king."

"Then we will not trouble you further," Kalya said.

"Do not be too hasty to leave our fair town," said Ra-Harakhte. "Stay and admire our great temple to Ashar, God of Winds. It has the widest dome in all of Shem. Pray to the god for guidance. It may be that, should you sit at an outdoor table at the Inn of Four Winds this evening, men might contact you with employment to offer. The god is known to be generous."

"I have always placed my trust in divine guidance," said Kalya. "Let us go and see this wondrous structure, Conan."

They went back out into the daylight and picked up their belongings. "Perhaps it will be soon now," Conan said.

That evening they dawdled over untasted wine at an outdoor table while dusk fell over the town. The last rays of the setting sun gleamed from the gilded spires of the Temple of Ashar. They had indeed toured the temple. Kalya even went so far as to make a contribution, tossing coins into a great brazen bowl by the entrance, and had lit a stick of incense before the golden image of the god, a tall, thin deity whose cheeks were twin spheres constantly expelling winds.

When Conan chided this sudden access of piety, she shrugged and said, "It does no harm to stay in the good favor of the local gods."

Now she placed a hand on his knee. "Who might this be?" Two men were approaching. One was a Stygian, tall and well-made. The other was a brown man of the south. Conan stiffened, but he quickly saw that this brown man was not Taharka. His hair was a mass of tiny braids, and parallel scars had been cut on cheeks, brow, and chin. The two came to their table and seated themselves without invitation.

"We have been told that you two fancy yourselves outlaws," said the Stygian bluntly.

"It is no fancy," said Conan. "We have lived by our swords for some time now."

"Circumstances forced us to flee the northern lands," said Kalya. "This land is damnably peaceful. We heard that certain people of our sort have been prospering in this area. We would like to join such people."

The brown man grinned, showing teeth filed to points. "Who ever heard of a wench cutting throats upon the great river?"

"On the other hand," said the Stygian, "who would suspect such a one?"

"You'll not regret taking us on," said Conan. "We know how to fight, and we do not desert our companions."

"I am of a mind to give you a chance," said the

Stygian. "We can always use stout fighters who are not particular how they earn their keep, and we have heard of how you flattened that fat guard of Ra-Harakhte's with a single blow." The man laughed richly, exposing two teeth that appeared, to Conan's amazement, to be made of gold. "He did not waken for two hours, and the worthless lout will be eating gruel for weeks to come."

"Who is your chief?" said Conan.

The Stygian leaned close over the table and spoke in a low voice. "Our chief is a man of Keshan, named Taharka."

Conan kept his face expressionless, as did Kalya, but her nails dug convulsively into his knee. "Does he know his business?" Conan asked.

"He does, indeed!" said the brown man. "Great is the speculation about our deeds, but no man yet knows who we are, or where our base is. The Keshanian is too clever for that, and we his men live well."

"This is too public a place," said the Stygian. "Come down to our boat. It is tied at the southernmost wharf. There we may drink and talk without fear that our voices will grow too loud."

They accompanied the two men to the waterfront and boarded the boat, which turned out to be made of bundled reeds. It rode high in the water and rocked violently when they stepped aboard. Conan realized that, should the pirates have lured them here to attack them, even he might have difficulty. He was not used to this sort of footing, while they doubtless had years of experience with river craft.

"You are landsmen, eh?" chuckled the dark man. "You will have to learn the ways of the river if you would run with this pack of hyenas."

"Come," said the Stygian, "let us have a drink." He opened a hamper of woven straw and pulled forth a wineskin. They passed it around and when everyone had drunk the Stygian began to outline their technique.

"There are many small bands of us, you see," said the Stygian, gesturing gracefully with his hands as he spoke. "We favor little groups of four to six. Such small numbers attract no attention. We carefully observe the river craft, what sort of cargo it carries, what the passengers are like, and so forth. When we have spotted a likely boat, we board it as passengers. Always we board separately, or two at a time at the very most. Sometimes, some of us will hurry down to the next river port on foot so that we do not come aboard in the same town, and that further allays any suspicion."

The wineskin made another round. "What if it looks like you will need more men for a particular boat? Some I have seen bear many men, although they are not often armed."

"Then we merely stay aboard. Soon we come to another port where more of our brotherhood wait. We have sundry signals whereby we may know one another. If we sign that we need more men, they come aboard our craft."

"This sounds a good plan," Kalya said. She took another pull at the wineskin. "How do you deal with the crew and passengers when the time is right?"

"The best way is to kill them in their sleep," said the Stygian, simply. "When we reach the prearranged area, we wait until they are tied up in shallows or moored to some island."

"You must understand," said the dark man, "that we can leave no witnesses. Our chief insists upon it. Kill them, gut them, and over the side with them, with a weight to take them to the bottom." He favored them with his needle-toothed grin again as he gestured graphically with his right hand.

"Where is this place?" Conan asked.

"It changes from week to week. At some time I will be contacted by a messenger, and he will give me a new location. We do our slaying as near to that spot as we may, then, when we signal, small boats come out from shore to take off our loot."

"And if the opportunity for an easy kill does not come near the prearranged spot?"

"On occasion, it may be necessary to attack and slay in daylight," the Stygian said. "Or at night when they are still wakeful. That is why it would be handy to have two skilled swordsmen like yourselves among our number. If we all wore swords, we would instantly be suspected. But two such outlanders as yourselves . . ." He shrugged. "Everyone knows that northerners are savages and always drape themselves with weapons, so who will notice?"

He warmed to the subject. "For instance, on any given boat, there are rarely more than three or four men who might be expected to give us a stout fight. These may have daggers, or a club thonged to a belt. Rivermen are often tough brawlers, you see, although skilled swordsmen are rare. In such a case, at my instruction you would station yourselves next to such men. At my signal, you would draw steel and cut them down unawares."

"Once such men are taken care of," said the darker man, "the passengers are rarely a problem. Most kneel and plead for mercy. You may cut their throats like sheep."

"Unmanly behavior," muttered Conan. The two river

pirates thought he was speaking of the passengers, so they smiled and nodded in agreement.

"Yes, this sounds like a good plan," said Kalya. "We are tired of the law-abiding life." She turned to the Cimmerian. "What say you, Conan?" She feigned a slight drunkenness.

"Oh, aye," Conan said. "This sounds enjoyable. People who will not fight to keep what is theirs have no business owning anything at all, by Crom!"

"Not even their lives," Kalya agreed. Then, striving to sound casual, "When do we meet this great chieftain of yours?"

"Perhaps soon," said the Stygian. "He usually oversees the looting of a victim." He raised the wineskin in mocking salute. "Welcome to our brotherhood!"

Fourteen

Taharka sat upon the verandah of his villa and surveyed the tranquil scene before him. The river flowed past in a broad stream, its busy traffic passing by under his gaze, and he knew that he could have it all. It is almost, he thought, as if birds and beasts delivered themselves to me ready-cooked, with knives stuck through them for the carving.

It gave him a feeling of satisfaction to know that, unlike those who floated by, he knew the reality of the world, that beneath this peaceful surface lay blood and slaughter. A slave proffered a salver of sweetmeats and he selected one, popped it into his mouth, and bit down with strong, white teeth.

He had found the old villa, long abandoned, on a small island near the Stygian bank of the river. It shared the island with some other ruins, old temples for the most part. In Stygia, it was all but impossible to walk for more than a few minutes without encountering ruins, so ancient was the civilization of that land. It was a fine location, so he had appropriated the villa and had it refurbished by his men and his slaves. Now it was a comfortable residence and, should any passing craft take note that it was now occupied, it would be assumed that some merchant or noble had decided to establish himself there. Thus far, no official had come to investigate.

Looking down, the Keshanian descried a tall man coming up the long steps from the river. The lower steps were nearly black, because they were submerged by high water for part of the year. The rest gleamed white and smooth with age. It was Kuulvo, still wearing his Hyperborean clothing and armor, despite the warmth of the climate. It seemed to be a rule that barbarians would not accommodate themselves to local conditions.

"How goes it, my friend?" Taharka asked, gesturing toward a pile of cushions.

They Hyperborean seated himself with a grunt and pulled off his helmet. "Well, master. Six rich boats taken this week and the goods already disposed of. It is hard to believe that we can operate thus in the center of civilization. In other lands, it is the chaos of war and lawlessness that is most favorable to the outlaw's trade."

"Other lands, other methods," said Taharka. "Here, it is of utmost importance that we take no slaves and hold no prisoners for ransom. The material wealth of this land makes it unnecessary. The volume of traffic makes the loss of a few boats all but negligible. The great distances they travel ensures that it must be a long time before they are missed."

Kuulvo selected a piece of fruit and bit into it. "It is most convenient," he said. "North of here, a few slave raids bring down the king's men. One missing caravan can set a whole province in an uproar."

"Is this not better?" Taharka said. "Is this place and situation not made for the likes of you and me?"

"Aye," Kuulvo said, hesitantly. "But, then, there are things I do not like about it. It is too easy, too peaceful. Killing these bleating sheep is like working in an abattoir. There is no urgency, no fear, no hard riding with pursuit just behind your horse's hooves. It is almost like working for a living, and the work gets dull."

Taharka sighed. "I know, my friend. You are right. I miss the violence, too. However, things should liven up soon. This unnatural tranquility cannot last much longer. Sooner or later the forces of this land must come against us, and they are formidable indeed."

"Powerful but slow," Kuulvo said. "We'll be away and out of their grasp before they can close their fingers." He accepted a goblet of chilled wine from a beautiful naked girl whose features were those of the nomads of the southwestern desert. "I still wonder, though, about the Cimmerian, and about the one-eyed woman. Those two have given us more grief than all the king's men between here and Aquilonia."

Taharka shifted uncomfortably in his chair, a cloud now come between him and the beautiful morning. "We lost them long ago," he said. "Far away in northern Koth. They will never find us. Perhaps they are dead now."

He sipped his wine moodily. He glanced up the slope behind the villa and saw the huge ruin that topped the island. He had meant to send someone to explore that place. There might be something worth scavenging in the temple, perhaps some forgotten tomb full of grave-goods.

"They are not dead." The voice came from the

doorway leading into the villa, and the man who stood there might himself have come from a tomb. "The one-eyed demon woman is still on my trail. One who has died once will not die again."

Axandrias was little more than a skeleton with muscles like rope stretched over the prominent bones. His head was truly skull-like, its thin white hair plastered against the mottled skin like a fungus. The bloodless lips pulled back spasmodically, revealing long yellow teeth. His eyes were so hideous that even his hardened companions could not bear their gaze for long.

"Peace, Axandrias, my friend," said Taharka. "Even if they yet live, even should they find us and come here, what need have men such as we to fear them? One man, however warrior-like, and a woman with one eye and the voice of a raven? It is childish of us to fear such scum." For once, his voice lacked conviction, even the false kind he was so skilled in conveying.

"They will be here," said Axandrias in his sepulchral voice, "and soon." Still staring, he turned and wandered back into the villa.

"My chief," Kuulvo said, "that man is quite mad. Why do you not slay him and be done with it? It would be a mercy."

"To be truthful with you, my friend," said Taharka confidentially, "I confess that I am not certain that I *could* kill him. As his body has degenerated, he has grown more dangerous. He never sleeps now, so it is impossible to catch him unawares. He looks a cadaver, yet he is twice as strong and swift as he was when he fought in the pit at Croton."

He placed chin upon palm and brooded. "Yesterday, he walked by my side when we came upon a slave man and woman embracing in a corridor. For some reason this sight annoyed our Aquilonian friend. He drew his knife and killed them both so quickly that I scarcely saw the move. He nearly halved both bodies with a mere knife! It took all afternoon to clean the corridor." He sat back and drank deep. "No, my friend, I should have slain him as soon as he began taking those accursed balls of gum and scarab juice and the gods know what else! Worse yet, he has become a great bore! He used to be amusing. Now he thinks of nothing but the one-eyed wench. I almost wish she would appear so the two could fight it out. Then we could slay the winner while he or she was exulting."

"It is a great bother, master," said Kuulvo.

Taharka leaned toward his subordinate. "I do not suppose you would like to try to slay him now? All his share of the loot would be yours."

"I think not, Chief," said the Hyperborean. "I try to confine myself to killing natural human beings. But surely this drug must kill him within a few days. It is difficult to believe that he breathes now."

"It is to be hoped," said Taharka sullenly.

Kuulvo rose to his feet. "Well, I must be off. Word has come that two boats may fall into our hands this night. This will be enjoyable, but we do not wish to overdo it. Even the inert authorities of this land must bestir themselves sometime."

"Do not concern yourself about it," said Taharka, standing and stretching. "We'll not be here much longer. A few weeks, a month or two, and we shall try something else lest we grow bored."

"That would suit me well," said Kuulvo. "What is in your mind to try next?"

"We might take ship to the mouth of the Styx and thence to one of the more lively ports. Messantia, perhaps, or the Baracha Isles. This river piracy has been pleasant but dull. I have heard that piracy upon the great waters is most exciting.''

Kuulvo grinned. ''That sounds good. Real battle with blood and fear! Real fighting men instead of butchers and sheep. Aye, that is something to look forward to.''

Taharka watched the Hyperborean descend the steps to the tiny wharf where his lean, knifelike cutter was moored. It was a good life, but the man of Keshan would be glad to be away. There was something about this land that oppressed his spirits. Something about this island, in particular. Without knowing why, he once again looked up at the huge, ruined temple. Yes, he would be glad to be away from here. Perhaps sooner than he had planned.

The boat was larger than the one on which Conan and Kalya had traveled previously, and it was somewhat more luxurious. The cabins were larger, more luxuriously appointed, and more numerous. The Cimmerian had learned that most of the cabin passengers were wealthy pilgrims from a city many weeks' travel to the east. They were going to worship at the great temples of Khemi, and expected the round trip to take nearly a year. In short, they were ideal prey for the pirates. The cargo space was taken up largely with the sumptuous clothing and belongings of the travelers.

''We are getting close,'' Kalya said. The two of them squatted on the foredeck of the craft, amid a litter of coiled rope, mud-stained anchors, and noisy livestock cages where future meals squawked and grunted in blissful ignorance of their fate.

''It must be soon,'' Conan said. He sat crosslegged with his great sword across his lap, stroking its edge with a small whetstone. The blade gleamed brightly in the sun. His skin had always been weathered, but the blazing sun of the southern latitudes had burned him so dark that few would guess that he came of a fair-skinned race.

The two had come aboard three days before, booking deck passage. The Stygian and the dark southerner had boarded earlier, hiring on as crewmen and cargo handlers. They had insured that two such jobs would be open by cutting the throats of two drunken crewmen the night before.

The Cimmerian and his companion were left much to themselves. Both were of outlandish appearance, especially since Kalya had abandoned her cloak in the oppressive heat. This suited their purposes well. Thus far, neither of the other two had said a word to them nor made the slightest sign of recognition.

They glanced up as a pair of bare feet passed between them. It was the Stygian. He ignored them as he pretended to search for something amid a pile of tangled rope. "Tonight," he said in a low voice, "after we have tied up. They will be sleeping. Two boats will approach us from the north. As soon as we see them, we kill. Conan, stand you by the captain. Woman, kill the mate. We will take care of the crewmen." With no further word, he walked away.

"Tonight," Kalya breathed. "Tonight. This time, we cannot let them get away."

"They'll not escape us this time," Conan vowed, sighting along one razor-keen edge. He turned the blade over and looked down the other edge. Fancying that he saw a place less sharp than the rest, he began to stroke it with his whetstone.

When night began to fall, they were between towns.

Along this stretch of river, the villages were not so frequent as in other areas. On the south bank, the southern desert came almost to the water's edge, while the north bank extended into land that was for the most part pasture. Villages here were often several miles apart.

The passengers ate their dinner as the crew tied up the boat a few yards from the northern shore. "Behold," said a man in the robes of a priest of the minor god Bes, "the evils of war!" He pointed portentously toward the barren southern bank. "Once that was a rich province, with fertile soil, many people and fat cattle. Yet a priest-king of ancient times once ruled there, and he grew envious of his neighbors and made war upon them. In their lust for conquest they contented themselves with loot and neglected their duty to the land. Their irrigation canals silted up and became useless, their levees cracked, letting in the wrath of Father Styx; their fertile fields became mere pasture! When the priest-king finally died, their looted luxury was as naught, for the land was ruined." The travelers heard these words in respectful silence.

"It sounds to me," said Conan loudly, "as if they had a fine time while that fellow was king! Fighting your neighbors is better than following the rear end of a buffalo all day and paying taxes to support a horde of priestly parasites." He gnawed the last scraps of meat from a rib-bone and tossed it into the river.

"You are a barbarian and would think thus!" said the priest. It was likely that this was the first time in his life that his words had been challenged. "You northerners live like animals, butchering and eating one another, like the black savages of the far south. The purpose of a civilized man is to serve his king, worship his gods and honor their minions, the priests!''

"Then Crom preserve me from civilization,'' said Conan. "Such a life would leech the manhood from the strongest.'' Not a few smiled at the priest's discomfiture.

"Do you think,'' Kalya said as the Cimmerian resumed his seat, "that Taharka will be in one of the boats this night?''

"I doubt it,'' said Conan. "But you can be sure that someone in one of those boats will know where he may be found, and with him, Axandrias. We must save some alive for questioning.''

The boat was silent but for snores when something nudged Conan. It was the Stygian, holding finger to lips for silence. He squatted by Conan. "The boats are coming. Take your positions.''

Conan and Kalya stood, stretching. "Where is your brown friend?'' Conan asked, not bothering to lower his voice.

"Quiet!'' hissed the Stygian. "Do you want to rouse them untimely? He is just below us on the main deck, why do you ask?''

."What is the signal to bring the other boats in?'' Conan asked as Kalya descended to the lower deck.

"A lantern raised and lowered three times,'' said the pirate. "What is wrong with you?''

"Nothing,'' said Conan. He drew his sword and cut the man down without another word. A blow of the pommel crushed the Stygian's larynx, stifling any outcry he might make. The Cimmerian jumped to the main deck at the sound of a strangled cry. He found Kalya standing over the inert form of the southerner, wiping her long blade.

He strode across the main deck, where servants and

crewmen still snored. A few stirred, wondering what the noise had been. At the stern, by the large steering oar, the captain of the vessel peered past the coals of the cooking-fire which still smoldered in its earth-filled box.

"Who is that?" he asked in a low voice, solicitous of his wealthy passengers. "I thought I heard a cry forward."

Conan picked up the lantern that stood by the captain's foot. "Nothing to bother yourself about," he said. He leaned over the rail and raised the lantern, then lowered it almost to the water, raised it again, then a third time.

"What are you doing?" said the captain sharply. "Are you drunk? Mad?"

"None of those things," said the Cimmerian. "We are about to be boarded by pirates. If you would live, I suggest that you keep quiet and stay out of my way."

"Pirates!" said the captain, incredulous. "You are truly mad! You are—" he shut his mouth as a dark, evil face thrust over the bulwark.

"Are they all dead?" asked the newcomer.

"All dead," said Conan. "Come aboard."

The captain's eyes grew round as a half-dozen men swarmed over the rails. Another small boat approached farther toward the bow.

"Set!" one of the men swore. "These are not dead, they sleep!" On deck, sleepers were waking and an outcry commenced.

With a cry so bloodcurdling that all froze for an instant, Conan waded among the first of the pirates to board. A man stared at him wide-eyed as he hewed off the pirate's dagger-arm, then lopped the head from another. He saw Kalya's blade pass through a man from back to front, then there were more faces appearing at the rail as the second boat-crew arrived.

With a whoop, Conan leapt for the rail and split a turbanned skull as it protruded above the wood. His blade went through the chest of another as Kalya engaged a man who seemed to understand how to use a sword. A man scrambled over the rail and fell flat on his face, and Conan's descending foot snapped his neck before he could stand.

Then Conan saw a familiar form spring over the rail.

"So!" bellowed a voice, "have we found at last a crew that will fight?" The accent was thick and unmistakably Hyperborean.

The huge man stood balanced easily on the balls of his feet, a long broadsword in his hand. A pair of panicked crewmen tried to dash past him and he swatted at them with his blade, scarcely looking at the two, like a man brushing at pesky insects. The men fell howling, blood gushing from mortal wounds.

The Hyperborean's gray eyes widened to each side of his helmet's nosepiece as he saw Kalya's bare back turned toward him. He stepped forward and prepared to hew her down while she was occupied with the man before her. Before his sword could begin its descent, it was batted aside by Conan's. The Hyperborean, quick as a cat, whirled to face this new threat, his sword at guard.

"Cimmerian!" he growled. "So you are not dead! I rejoice to know it. Now I can kill you."

The deck was a scene of utter chaos as crewmen and passengers ran about screaming, unable to comprehend what terrible fate had overwhelmed them. The deck was now slippery with blood and offal, so that many lost their footing and went sprawling amid the gore. Others

tripped over the fallen and some of the bolder souls
drew ornamental daggers they were not trained to use
and smote around themselves blindly. The few who
kept their heads jumped over the rail on the shore side
and waded toward the bank.

"We do not want you, Hyperborean hound," Conan
spat. "It is your master we seek, and his snake,
Axandrias. Where are they?" Conan glared feral hate at
the man. The Cimmerian's sword was above his head
and slanting back, its long grip in both hands. Each
man waited for the other to make the first move.

"You'll be in their presence soon," said Kuulvo. "I
shall bear your heads thither. What is your name, boy?"

"I am Conan of Cimmeria, a warrior."

"I am Kuulvo of Hyperboria, a warrior. Why do you
pursue my master?"

"He slew friends," Conan said, not relaxing his
guard for an instant, ignoring the chaos around him.

"My master is a great outlaw, but he does not understand northerners." Then Kuulvo attacked.

His first blow came at Conan's side, quick as thought.
The Cimmerian brought his own blade down in time to
deflect the cut. He slashed forth at Kuulvo's neck, but
the Hyperborean stepped back slightly and brought his
own sword up and across, catching the Cimmerian's
blade a finger's breadth from his throat. They continued
the exchange for the space of twenty heartbeats using
short, economical cuts suited to close-quarter fighting.
The two huge men maneuvered the heavy swords as
easily and as swiftly as boys fencing with wands.

A pirate stumbled by Conan and the Cimmerian
crushed his skull with a quick blow of his pommel,
shoving the corpse into Kuulvo to prevent the Hyperborean's taking advantage of the distraction. He raised his

sword for a stroke that might have split the Hyperborean from shoulder to waist, but the blade buried itself in the wooden yard over his head.

With a howl of triumph, Kuulvo rammed into Conan with his shoulder, sending the Cimmerian crashing to his back against the rail. Conan blinked stars from his eyes in time to see a heavy blade coming straight for his face, and he rolled aside just as the sword smashed through the thick rail. Kuulvo grunted with the effort of withdrawing his blade, and Conan's thick arm came up between his legs. With the force of his whole coiled body, the Cimmerian heaved up and out, and the Hyperborean went flying over the ruined rail to make a mighty splash in the water beyond.

As Conan prepared to follow his enemy, he called over his shoulder, "Remember, keep one alive!" He was answered by an inarticulate squall from Kalya.

He dived toward the spot where Kuulvo had splashed into the Styx. When he surfaced, he saw nothing. He swept his head from side to side, his black hair whipping out and shedding water. Then a muscular arm went around his throat from behind.

He drew his dagger and thrust backward, but an iron grip caught his wrist and he could only struggle to breathe. It was futile, for the other man was using his greatest strength against Conan's weakness. With his remaining free hand, Conan reached back and grasped the plume-knob of the Hyperborean's helmet. With a powerful wrench, he broke its chinstrap and hauled it off. Reaching back again, he grasped the man's hair. With this firm grip, he kicked up and back with both legs, hauling himself up and over the man behind him.

It was impossible for Kuulvo to maintain his grip and he was forced to let go, although not before he forced

Conan to release the dagger. For several seconds the two wrestled for advantage, the muddy river bottom giving them little purchase. Then both of the Hyperborean's arms went around Conan at the waist, pinning the Cimmerian's arms and enclosing him in a spine-breaking grip. Conan's mightiest efforts would not free his arms. The Hyperborean was the strongest man he had ever encountered.

Had Kuulvo kept his head down, he might have succeeded in snapping Conan's back, or causing him to pass out and be drowned at leisure, but he had to gloat. He raised his face and smiled at Conan in triumph. The instant Kuulvo's chin went up, Conan buried his teeth in the man's throat. He felt the crunch of cartilage as the larynx gave way, then the hot rush of blood into his mouth.

Kuulvo tried to cry out but could not. He released Conan's arms in a frantic effort to pull the terrible jaws away from his neck. Conan grasped both wrists and held them down as he forced the Hyperborean backward, until they both disappeared beneath the water.

A few minutes later, Kalya looked up to see Conan climbing over the rail, looking more exhausted than she had ever seen him. He looked for his sword, then saw it embedded in the yard overhead. He wrenched the weapon free and resheathed it. He ignored the wailing passengers and the boat's officers who were trying to calm their charges.

"You have one alive?" he asked.

She gestured at the man who lay with her dagger at his throat. "He says that he'll not talk to a woman. I am going to persuade him."

Conan squatted by the man, eyes blazing and blood still dripping from his mouth. With mud and river weed still in his hair, he looked like some demon conjured from the bottom of the Styx. He grasped the front of the man's vest and drew the terrified face within inches of his own.

"Listen to me, river rat! I just chewed the throat from your leader, and am about to do the same to you. Tell us where Taharka's lair is or prepare to suffer as no man has suffered before!"

Instantly the man became voluble and eager to please. He was generous and precise with locations, directions, and distances. At the end of his recitation, Conan turned the man over to the captain of their barge.

"He is yours," Conan said. "We go now to kill their master. Come, Kalya." As they climbed over the rail and into one of the pirate boats, he turned back and surveyed the passengers disgustedly. "You are the most spiritless sheep I have ever seen. You deserve every pirate and bandit that comes to prey on you." They gaped wide-eyed and open-mouthed as the two rowed off into the foggy night.

Fifteen

Taharka was disturbed. His uneasiness about the island upon which he resided had been increasing, and this very day he had heard from a local tradesman that the place had an evil name, that people had avoided it for centuries. The man said that the pleasant location had caused many to seek to build there over the years, the most recent being the wealthy man who had constructed the villa. All had fled after a brief stay. Some had committed suicide. The evil rumors centered on the ruined temple atop the island. In this land of hundreds of gods, no man now remembered to which god that temple was dedicated.

He was ready to abandon his river operations immediately and had already given orders to begin packing. It would mean abandoning much of his loot still waiting in scattered warehouses or stored with fences, but he had never let such considerations hold him back ere now. There would be more loot to be found on the high seas, more slaves, more conquest. Now he only awaited the return of his trusted lieutenant, Kuulvo. Where was the man? He should have been back before nightfall. He turned at a sound and frowned when he saw who it was.

"It is no use," Axandrias said. "We can try to flee, but they will find us."

For a moment Taharka did not understand who the Aquilonian meant. "Find us? You mean your erstwhile victim and her barbarian friend? Do you really think that is why we are leaving?" He was incensed at the man's single-minded obsession.

"They will find us!" Axandrias shouted. "She haunts my dreams, sleeping and waking! A thousand times I have blinded her and killed her and still she comes for me!"

Taharka shook his head. The man's mind was as shattered as his body, and he regretted not killing him long ago. "You are wrong, my friend. Now go and—"

"No, he is not wrong," said a voice behind him. Taharka spun, snatching his sword from his sheath, hearing the hiss of Axandrias's blade as the Aquilonian drew.

"You see!" said Axandrias, his face almost ecstatic in its concentrated terror. "She has come for me, my little one-eyed beloved. Come to me, little creature, let me finish what I began so long ago." His voice had turned to a grotesque crooning.

Kalya stepped down into the sunken room. Behind her loomed the giant shape of the Cimmerian. Taharka quickly swept the room with a glance, printing in his mind the exact location of all doors and windows, the candlesticks, the weapon-rack by the door, all the furniture. He wanted no hindrances at such a moment.

Kalya was shocked at Axandrias's appearance. When she had last seen him, he had been a handsome man, not greatly different from the one she remembered from childhood. That comely serpent had somehow transformed into a ghastly skeleton in a few months. In her shock, she almost fell to his first attack.

He was blindingly swift. He sprang across the distance separating them as if by magic, his blade licking out with the unnatural speed of a cobra's tongue. She parried, parried again as he drove her back. Giving ground too quickly, she turned her backpedaling retrogression into a sidewise scuttle, circling the creature while she strove to protect herself, looking for an opening in his bewildering attack. He looked frail, but his blows were as strong as any she had ever felt. *What is this?* she thought, but soon she had no time for thought, only for battle.

"Who are you, barbarian?" said Taharka, wonder in his voice. "Why have you pursued me across the world?" He held a heavy sword before him, and a glance at the way it moved told Conan how immensely strong the man's arm and wrist were.

"I am Conan of Cimmeria, a warrior. In Cimmeria I returned to the steading of friends to find them slaughtered by your band." Conan stood with his sword dangling from his right hand. He ignored the furious battle between Kalya and the strangely changed Axandrias. He had agreed that this would be her fight, and that he would not interfere.

"The householder was Halga. Into the doorpost of his house he had driven the spear with which he slew his woman and his daughter, so that you and your foul pack should not have them. In Cimmeria, that sign means 'avenge us'. I would have in any case. They were not of my clan, but I was under their roof, taking their hospitality. I can know no rest until they are avenged."

"You cannot be serious!" Taharka said, sure that Conan was hiding some other, more believable motive. "No one would give so much time and effort to avenge the deaths of a few nameless barbarians!"

"Your Hyperborean dog was right. You do not understand northerners. He was evil, but he was a man. And the people you slew were not nameless. Their names live in the songs of their kin, and they are written here." He tapped his wide chest, over the heart. "Their spirits cry out for your blood, and they shall have it!"

The two men swung at the same time and sparks were shed from the broad blades by that first, powerful exchange. Conan was amazed. If the Hyperborean had been strong, this man was even stronger. The blades met and rang in a kind of demented music, always seeking flesh, never finding it. They drove one another around the room, now attacking, now retreating, always trying not to collide with the other two combatants.

Kalya was fighting in an exalted state, almost ecstasy, as she felt her whole life culminating in this climactic battle. Axandrias was breathing like a bellows, his inhuman speed slackening a trifle. She thrust toward his chest and as his parry came across she circled her blade under it and ran him through the belly. Her sword was out in an instant, parrying his counterthrust. He continued his attack as if he felt nothing.

By now she was sure that he had taken the drug which had so improved the prowess of the fighting-slaves. Undoubtedly, it was also responsible for his physical deterioration and unnatural strength. That was just as well, to her taste. She wanted to go on stabbing and cutting him for as long as possible. Even as she had the thought, she cut him on the neck and his blood ran down sluggishly. His next thrust nicked her thigh just above the leather armor, but she ignored it and slashed his sword-arm.

As Axandrias drew back she went in for the final exchange. She knew that she had him now. His drug was quickly losing its potency. She wove a dazzling web of steel around him, and his arm slowed as he blocked each cut. Then she threw herself forward in a full lunge, a move so extreme that her swordmasters had insisted that it only be used in an emergency, for it left the swordsman stretched out, off balance and vulnerable to any blow.

She had timed it perfectly. As his blade came up to stop what he had thought would be another cut, she came straight for him, arm to full extension, her entire body flying behind her hilt. The point went through his left eye, through the thin shell of bone and through the brain and out the back of his skull to stop a foot behind his scalp.

As he toppled, the blade was wrenched from her grasp. Kalya stood above the inert body and stared down at it wonderingly. Her cry of triumph rang through the villa.

Taharka could not believe it, but this young man was stronger than he. Never had he met his match in strength. Always he had taken for granted his superiority in physical power over other men. Not only was he stronger, but this savage youth was quicker and more skillful. Taharka was not afflicted with excessive pride. He had to escape. He backed toward a chair over which had been draped a fine tapestry, loot from some nameless river craft. As he passed, he snatched the tapestry from the chair and cast it at the Cimmerian. Conan raised his arms and stepped back, and Taharka darted past him toward the door.

Conan tore the tapestry from him and saw that Taharka was at the door, snatching at something in a weapon-rack. The dark man whirled, a javelin in his right hand, raised high. The arm darted forward and the spear flew toward the Cimmerian's chest. There was no time to bat it aside with his sword. Without thought, instinctively, Conan ducked. He was about to bound after the fleeing Taharka when an agonized gasp stopped him. Horrified, knowing what he would see, he turned to look behind him.

The javelin's long, sharp point had entered just above Kalya's hip. It had torn through vitals and its point, stained with maroon blood, stood out a handsbreadth from her other flank. She tugged at the wooden shaft, but the result was only greater agony.

Conan caught her as she fell. "Kalya!" he cried, lowering her to the floor. "Has he taken you from me as well?"

She looked down at the ruin of her body, then at the corpse of Axandrias. She turned her face upward and smiled at him wanly. Her face had gone ghost-pale. "It is as well, Conan. There was nothing left to live for, now he is dead." Her face twisted as a new wave of pain swept over her. "But let me say this," she gasped. "From childhood, I devoted myself to hating a man. I am glad that I had a chance to love one before I died." She reached up weakly and stroked his dark face. "Now, my love, go and kill that animal for me." Her hand dropped and the body in his arms seemed to lose all its bones.

Gently, he wrapped her in a priceless hanging and

laid her body atop a table of precious wood. Then he took his sword and went to search for Taharka.

The Keshanian was frantic. There was no boat! The madwoman and her friend had cast away all his craft, and had set their own craft adrift as well. He saw the Cimmerian on the path behind him and he began to run in the only remaining direction: uphill. A few minute's flight brought him to the ruins of the great temple. A fog was gathering, diffusing the light of the moon and causing the ancient stones to glow eerily. There was a silver shimmer coating the granite and the decayed marble. Taharka thought it must be a trick of the light. It must be only that.

The entire upper part of the structure was a ruin, but there was a doorway from which a long stair led to the darkness below. Perhaps, he thought, if he were to lurk in the shadows, he might be able to ambush the youth. Sword in hand, he descended the stair into the gloom below.

Conan came upon the ruin a few minutes later. His keen ears had detected the footsteps of the Keshanian, and he had come to inspect the ruin. Although Kalya's death had numbed him, something about this place chilled his blood. His senses were in tumult, but he was doubly driven by vengeance now. He would not leave this island alive without Taharka's blood upon his sword.

There was something repellently familiar in the stone-work. He saw the doorway and the stair and, somehow, he knew that this was where Taharka had gone. Cautiously, sword held diagonally before him, he descended.

It was not truly lightless in the deep, cryptlike chamber he entered. His ears were alert for the slightest sound. He could not tell where the light was coming from, but it seemed to suffuse the place, just intense enough to see by. He had an impression of huge, vague forms sculpted on the walls of the long corridor before him. When he looked, they were unrecognizable, but when he looked straight ahead, the vast, inchoate masses seemed to coalesce into something alien and terrifying.

He shook his head as if to clear it. He had no time to ponder the decoration. He had come here to kill a man and he intended to accomplish his aim before he went back up the stair. The corridor was immensely long, with no visible side passages. It seemed to him that the island itself could not be this long, but he had no time for such mysteries.

A light seemed to be forming ahead of him. It was faint and greenish, and he had seen its like before. That was of no interest either. As long as the unnatural light revealed his enemy, he would be content. He became aware of a sound coming, it seemed, from the same source as the light. It was the sound of a distant sea, thundering upon some unimaginably distant shore. At last he came to the source of the light. It was a high, arched doorway. He passed through it and gazed in astonishment at the room he had entered.

It was so vast that the roof and walls were only dimly visible despite the glare of the great fire in its center. Before him stretched a twin row of columns carved in the likeness of serpent-headed men. He had seen their like before, in Croton, but these were ten times the height of those relatively puny columns.

The fire burned in a great pit in the center of the chamber, and he saw the figures of several men outlined against the flame. Beyond the fire pit, he could just descry a multitude of men, and the sound of the sea was the sound of their chanting. He walked toward the group near the fire. As he neared, he saw that they were

black-robed men with shaven heads. With little surprise, he saw that one was the priest of the temple in
Croton. Another was the conjurer who had sent him the
vision of the mirror. But he cared only about the man
who stood between these two.

Taharka of Keshan held his sword at the ready, and
on his face was a strange expression of terror mixed
with triumph.

A third priest stood on the small dais which surrounded the fire pit. "Now the candidates are gathered," he intoned.

Conan ignored the enigmatic statement. "I have come
to kill that man," he said pointing to Taharka with his
sword. "Do not interfere."

"Hold!" said the priest, extending a bony hand.
Conan was stopped as if he had struck a wall. His mind
seethed with anger. Was he never to have the pleasure
of killing this monster?

"This must be done according to ritual," said the
priest. "Only one of you can live. Many gods watch
this struggle. Its outcome will determine whether our
Ancient Ones are to come again, or the youthful gods
are to continue their reign. Neither of you is a master of
sorcery, so the issue is to be settled by combat."

"That is what I intended," Conan said. "Stand aside."
He struggled against the invisible wall, but to no avail.

"The candidate of the Ancient Ones is Taharka of
Keshan. If he prevails, the reign of true evil will return," the priest's attempts at impassivity were marred
by a tone of obscene glee. "If Conan of Cimmeria
should triumph, we must dwell in shadows for another
fifty generations!"

The magician from the mountebank troupe spoke for
the first time. "The two of you are, of course, only the

vessels of the will of the gods. Your struggle here is only the earthly reflection of the titanic struggle now sweeping the cosmos as the gods battle for supremacy. It is indeed ironic that their chosen men of destiny are not kings, emperors, or great mages, but a pair of primitive savages. It seems that the gods are not without a certain sense of humor.''

Conan cared nothing for any of this. He longed for one man's blood and these priests were restraining him with their unclean magic and their incomprehensible gibberish. He saw that Taharka, too, was held in some magical pinioning.

The chanting of the black-robed multitude on the other side of the flame ceased being the sound of the sea and became the drumming of thunder. "Let the battle commence!" said the "conjuror."

The invisible bonds fell away from Conan. He did not hesitate an instant but charged Taharka at full speed. The Keshanian was as impetuous, and the three priests on the dais were bowled over to fall in an undignified sprawl of priestly limbs as the two men fought with maniacal intensity.

"You slew my friends!" Conan cried. "You killed my woman! I will drink your blood, Taharka!"

His demented fury was matched by Taharka's grim coolness. He parried and blocked all the Cimmerian's precipitate attacks, waiting for an opening. "Your friends were nothing to me, boy," he said, grunting out the words with the strain of his efforts. "As for your one-eyed wench, that was an accident. If you had accepted the javelin in your body as a hero should, she would not have died." He thought he saw a chance and slashed out, but the animal quickness of the young barbarian was too formidable.

Conan drove him completely around the pit, and the heatless flames rose to the ceiling. It seemed to Conan that Taharka was even stronger than when the two had fought earlier. Or was he himself growing weaker? The Keshanian changed his tactics and began to attack furiously. Now it was Conan who was driven back.

"You feel it, boy?" Taharka said, his face ashine with sweat. "Their Ancient Ones are cheating. They lend me strength. They are dishonorable gods, boy. That must be why they want me for their candidate to be Emperor of the World. Do not envy my victory, though. My fate is to be terrible."

"Then why do you fight?" Conan asked. Sweat was making his grip insecure. His parries were becoming less sure. He was gasping for breath and his last words all but exhausted him. He resolved to speak no more, until this issue was decided.

"Because I will have many years of pleasure ere their gods take me," he gasped, "and because you are before me to be slain, and I love to kill!"

A swift, redoubled attack drove Conan off the edge of the dais. He fell backward, too exhausted to keep his balance, and he landed heavily. The sword left his sweat-slick grip and clanged away down the corridor. As he struggled to stand, Taharka raised his sword for a final effort. Conan's fall had separated them by ten paces and the Cimmerian knew he had perhaps two seconds to live.

"Farewell, boy," said Taharka, savoring his triumph. "You were the best of the many I have killed."

Conan's hand flashed to the back of his belt, then came up and forward with all the strength and speed he had left. Taharka's eyes crossed, as if he were trying to study the handle of the dagger that suddenly protruded from between his eyes. He took two halting steps backward, then he toppled into the fire pit. The flames gushed high for a moment, at their crest spreading across the ceiling, then, abruptly, they lowered and became little more than a green glow.

"How can this happen?" said the third priest. "All the signs said the return of the Ancient Ones was at hand!" He glared immeasurable hatred at the Cimmerian.

"This one," said the priest from Croton, "is one of the great imponderables; the mortals who roam through history setting at naught the works of gods and men alike."

"The work and planning of centuries," said the "conjuror," "defeated by a mountebank's trick." The bitterness in his words was vast.

Conan cared nothing for this. He was mightily relieved to be free of his blood debt, and now he could mourn for Kalya. "You said yourselves that this was just the reflection of a greater battle. I think Crom just planted a dagger between the eyes of your Ancient Ones." He found his sword and bent to pick it up. When he straightened, the priests were gone, the multitude had disappeared, and the green glow was fast fading. He resheathed the blade and walked wearily from the chamber.

Conan climbed dripping from the river and stood upon the north bank. He turned to look a last time at the island. Smoke still rose from the villa. He had returned to it to find a pack of slaves busily looting the place. He had driven them out and built a crude pyre of precious wood. He laid Kalya's body upon it, dressed in her armor with the weapons sheathed at her side. Her feet rested upon the corpse of Axandrias. He then fired the place, walked down to the river, and swam the mile of water to the north shore.

He pondered which direction to take. North, toward his homeland? East, toward the lands that had called him when first he set eyes upon the rolling plains of Ophir? West, to the great sea with its tall ships and mysterious islands? South, to the lush lands of jungle and savages that he and Kalya had spoken of so much during the long nights of travel down the river? He had no idea which way to go.

There was an old Cimmerian custom to take care of that decision. He drew his sword. He would cast it as high as he could. When it came down, so long as it did not land point first, he would take the direction of the blade. His arm went back, then the sword flew upward, spinning and twisting, its bright blade flashing in the glorious southern sunlight.

CONAN

☐ 54260-6	CONAN THE CHAMPION	$3.50
☐ 54261-4		Canada $4.50
☐ 54228-2	CONAN THE DEFENDER	$2.95
☐ 54229-0		Canada $3.50
☐ 54238-X	CONAN THE DESTROYER	$2.95
☐ 54239-8		Canada $3.50
☐ 54258-4	CONAN THE FEARLESS	$2.95
☐ 54259-2		Canada $3.95
☐ 54225-8	CONAN THE INVINCIBLE	$2.95
☐ 54226-6		Canada $3.50
☐ 54236-3	CONAN THE MAGNIFICENT	$2.95
☐ 54237-1		Canada $3.50
☐ 54256-8	CONAN THE RAIDER	(Trade) $6.95
☐ 54257-6		Canada $8.95
☐ 54250-9	CONAN THE RENEGADE	$2.95
☐ 54251-7		Canada $3.50
☐ 54242-8	CONAN THE TRIUMPHANT	$2.95
☐ 54243-6		Canada $3.50
☐ 54231-2	CONAN THE UNCONQUERED	$2.95
☐ 54232-0		Canada $3.50
☐ 54252-5	CONAN THE VALOROUS	$2.95
☐ 54253-3		Canada $3.95
☐ 54246-0	CONAN THE VICTORIOUS	$2.95
☐ 54247-9		Canada $3.50

Buy them at your local bookstore or use this handy coupon:
Clip and mail this page with your order.

Publishers Book and Audio Mailing Service
P.O. Box 120159, Staten Island, NY 10312-0004

Please send me the book(s) I have checked above. I am enclosing $_____
(please add $1.25 for the first book, and $.25 for each additional book to
cover postage and handling. Send check or money order only — no CODs.)

Name _____

Address _____

City _____ State/Zip _____

Please allow six weeks for delivery. Prices subject to change without notice.